ACE
ON THE
HILL

D1736352

J.C. Wesslen

Copyright

Table of Contents

Copyright	2
Table of Contents	3
Dedication	6
Author's Note	7
Prologue	8
Part One: Elementary	9
Chapter 1	10
Chapter 2	12
Chapter 3	14
Chapter 4	16
Chapter 5	18
Chapter 6	22
Chapter 7	23
Chapter 8	27
Chapter 9	29
Chapter 10	30
Chapter 11	32
Chapter 12	35
Chapter 13	37
Chapter 14	40
Chapter 15	42
Chapter 16	43
Chapter 17	46
Chapter 18	47
Chapter 19	50
Chapter 20	52
Chapter 21	55
Chapter 22	57
Chapter 23	59
Chapter 24	61
Part Two: Middle	63
Chapter 25	64
Chapter 26	67
Chapter 27	68
Chapter 28	70
Chapter 29	72

Chapter 30 75

Chapter 31 76

Chapter 32 78

Chapter 33 80

Chapter 34 83

Chapter 35 85

Chapter 36 86

Chapter 37 88

Chapter 38 90

Chapter 39 93

Chapter 40 95

Chapter 41 97

Chapter 42 98

Chapter 43 100

Chapter 44 103

Chapter 45 105

Chapter 46 106

Chapter 47 108

Chapter 48 109

Chapter 49 113

Chapter 50 114

Chapter 51 117

Chapter 52 119

Part Three: High 120

Chapter 53 121

Chapter 54 124

Chapter 55 127

Chapter 56 129

Chapter 57 130

Chapter 58 133

Chapter 59 136

Chapter 60 137

Chapter 61 139

Chapter 62 140

Chapter 63 144

Chapter 64 146

Chapter 65 150

Chapter 66 154

Chapter 67 157

Chapter 68 159

Chapter 69 160

Chapter 70 163

Chapter 71   167

Chapter 72   170

Chapter 73   173

Chapter 74   175

Chapter 75   177

Chapter 76   179

Chapter 77   181

Chapter 78   182

Chapter 79   184

Chapter 80   188

Chapter 81   190

Chapter 82   191

Chapter 83   193

Chapter 84   195

Chapter 85   196

Chapter 86   198

Chapter 87   203

Chapter 88   204

Chapter 89   205

Chapter 90   206

Chapter 91   207

Epilogue   208

Acknowledgments   209

Dedication

For Abi and Chase

Author's Note

What follows is partly true. The rest is what could have been.

Prologue

Hey "Ace" –

Look what I found my old dresser, tucked into a tattered paperback of *Ball Four*. I can't believe this turned up after all these years!

J.

On the move *again*? I hope you hate it there and come back ASAP. Nah, I'm kidding. I want the best for you.

It wasn't that long ago, but 1975 was the BEST year of my life. You showed up and not long after that, so did the Gold Dust Twins.

Not trying to be sappy, but you've been more of a brother than the two guys who share a last name (and bathroom) with me!

Gonna miss ya, Kid.

P.

P.S. Go Sox!

Part One: Elementary

1

Let's begin with the unflattering part. I was a brat from the start. Of course, all kids act out. Some kick, some thrash, and some ball up like little bugs. Me? I liked to *throw* things.

My Uncle Sam (yes, that was his name) once said I grazed his head with a strawberry before I could even speak. I tossed a milk carton out the window at a Michigan daycare because it wasn't my usual chocolate flavor. Not long after that, I stepped away from my fifth birthday party to hurl a half-dozen 45 records against the brick wall in my family's backyard. The reason? I'd learned one of my friends had already turned five. To the casual observer, my parents—Joel and Louise Zimmerman—had their hands full. But the observer also needed to take this into account: by the time I was ten, our family had lived in *five* different homes. When the news was broken, the reaction wasn't pretty. If I couldn't throw an object, I'd throw a fit.

My little sister, Justine, began to copy my frustration as soon as she could talk. Instead of being annoyed by this, I welcomed it. I finally had an ally—it was going to be two against two from that point on.

Eventually, Mom and Dad began to use synonyms for the dreaded "M" word, but trying to soften the blow only created more frustration.

"*Plant new roots?*" I asked. "Can you explain?"

"Yeah," Justine said, crossing her arms. "Can you *eggs*-plain?"

All of this leads me to a Pennsylvania evening in the winter of 1975. By this time, I was eleven and Justine was eight. Looking back, maybe we should've seen it coming. Coasters, coffee table books, and ashtrays—all part of the normal living room landscape—had been hidden away. It wasn't because of some post-holiday cleaning. It was a defense strategy.

Justine and I were playing Monopoly on the living room floor. Mom was curled up on a nearby sofa reading a paperback called *Atlas Shrugged* (I wondered why anyone would write a book about someone *shrugging*). Meanwhile, Dad was in his favorite chair flipping through the *Wall Street Journal* like he usually did after dinner. He suddenly cleared his throat and set the newspaper on the floor.

"Hey, gang, let's have a little discussion," he said with a pleasant tone.

Mom gestured for us to sit up on the sofa, so we did. She closed her book, vacated her spot, and went to stand beside Dad.

"Your Mom and I want to share something with you both," Dad said.

Mom placed a reassuring hand on his shoulder. Something felt off, too staged, and somehow I just knew—

"We're moving!" I blurted, hopping to my feet.

"No!" Justine echoed, rising beside me.

My parents turned to each other in disbelief.

"How could he possibly know?" Dad asked.

"I did not say a word," Mom replied.

I looked around for something to throw. *Dang*. Where was everything?

"Could he have seen you moving the ashtray?" Dad asked.

"How could he? He was at school," Mom insisted.

"I don't even know why you guys have ashtrays," Justine said. "Neither one of you smokes."

"All right, enough!" Dad bellowed. "I said 'discussion' not 'rebellion.' Now both of you sit your fannies down."

Whenever Dad used a substitute word for buttocks, like "fanny," "rear end," "rump," or the French one ("derriere"), we knew he was close to blowing his stack. Justine and I dropped onto the sofa, and that's when my folks hit us with the news: we were moving to Massachusetts. They might as well have said Belgium—it felt that foreign. I begged for another location.

"Yeah, anywhere but there," Justine added. I doubted she knew the difference between Boston and Brussels, but as always, I was thankful for the support.

"I once had a substitute teacher from Boston," I argued. "Mrs. McQueeny. She'd say things like, 'Let's go ovah the ansahz heeya.'"

"What did he just say?!" Justine asked, her face scrunched in a knot.

I threw up my hands. "See?! We're gonna flunk!"

2

It took Dad three tries to finally close our Skylark's overloaded trunk. He checked his watch, climbed in behind the wheel, and started the engine. As Justine and I glanced longingly at our house for the final time, Dad tooted the horn at the handful of well-wishers who had gathered to see us off. With one final exchange of waves, we were on our way.

"So does this mean no more hoagies?" Justine asked.

"Oh, on the contrary," Mom explained. "In Boston, they're called 'subs.'"

"Doesn't sound that good," Justine mumbled.

I smiled at my sister's defiance and reminisced about the things I was going to miss, like trips to Valley Forge, the Devon Horse Show, and the Philadelphia Mint. Pennsylvania was where I learned how to jump on a pogo stick, skateboard, and catch tadpoles. What would life be like without the voice of Harry Callas announcing Phillies games—or local TV personalities like Gene London and Wee Willie Webber?

Then again, when I told my so-called pals at school about our move, they shrugged and asked if I'd still root for Philly teams. Justine's friends, on the other hand, cried. A few of them even suggested they hide her in their homes like Anne Frank. Maybe I needed better friends? On that note, the real estate agent from Boston told my folks there were plenty of boys my age in the new neighborhood. One could hope I thought, letting out a weary sigh, followed by a yawn…

I shifted in my seat, trying to get comfortable, when I realized I had dozed off. I glanced at Justine. The top half of her body was horizontal beside me, strands of hair spilling over our invisible dividing line. I thought about nudging her, but her eyes were closed. Of course, there was a chance she was pretending like we sometimes did on our long drives. "Operation Fake Sleep" occasionally brought some juicy gossip to light, like which neighbors were supposedly having affairs, or what kind of presents we could expect for upcoming birthdays.

"You have a mad crush on Alex Patukian," I whispered, referring to a fourth-grade boy who lived down the street in our old neighborhood.

No reaction…my sis was in dreamland. In front, my parents were quiet. Dad worked his jaw as he drove, the way he did when something was on his mind. Mom nibbled on a chunk of peanut brittle in the passenger seat, a parting gift from our neighbor Dottie Henry. Maybe Mom and Dad were all talked out. They'd been up late the night before, chatting as they packed last-minute items. I sat at the top of the stairs so I could hear them better (yes—the Zimmerman children—future spies).

I couldn't make out everything, but Dad used words like "salary," "bonus," and "territory." He threw that last one around so often, I wondered if he was a sheriff. It would be cooler if he were. A gun and badge were more impressive than a briefcase and tie.

"You know, honey, once we settle in, I'd like to find a good church," Mom said.

"You say that every place we go," Dad said.

"Well, I mean it this time. The kids are old enough, they can sit through a sermon. Besides, they know nothing about religion."

"You're exaggerating," Dad said.

"Really? Are you forgetting when Jay looked at the 'good book' and asked 'Who's

'Holly Bibble?'"

"He doesn't need religion—he needs a reading tutor," Dad joked.

I was jolted out of my recollection when Dad jammed on the horn.

"*Masshole*," he cursed under his breath.

"What's a 'Masshole?'" Justine asked, stirring awake.

Mom gave Dad an annoyed look before turning to face Justine.

"They're like potholes, honey. But in Massachusetts, they can be very dangerous."

"It doesn't feel bumpy," Justine said.

"Well, that's because your father tries to avoid them," Mom said.

"Not easy," Dad grumbled.

I grinned because I understood the reference and had my answer. We were finally in Massachusetts. It wouldn't be long until we were in our new home.

3

"So, your name's Jay?" Paul asked. Since he was the tallest of the guys and spoke first, I assumed he was the ringleader. He also looked like a young George Harrison, but I didn't tell him that.

"Yeah," I said, glancing from one member of the motley trio to the next. As it turned out, the real estate agent was correct: there *were* boys my age in the neighborhood. However, as we stood in a semi-circle in the driveway of my new home, drinking cans of grape-flavored Fanta mom had provided, the conversation felt more like a cross-examination than a welcome.

"Is it 'Jay' like the bird? Or the initial 'J' as in J. Edgar Hoover?'" asked Kenny. He was the smallest of the three and had wavy brown hair and a wiry build.

"Yeah, spill the beans," Matt said, in jest. He was stocky, with curly black hair and mocha-colored skin. I was fairly sure the word people used for his coloring was *mulatto,* but I wasn't sure if it was respectful.

"All right," I sighed. "My first name is *'Jayson,'* but it has the letter 'y' before the 's.' But pretty much everyone calls me 'Jay,' J-A-Y, for short."

"Huh?" Matt said.

"J-A-Y," Kenny said to him. "Try to keep up, Matt."

"Think we got it," Paul said. "And you're from around Philly?"

"Yeah. And about a hundred other places," I said with an eye roll, but I was met with only blank stares.

"What the hell's a Phillie, anyway?" Matt asked.

"I honestly have no friggin' clue," I answered. My lips were dry, so I took a swig of my soda. Too much, too fast—I belched.

There were instant laughs, and I relaxed. Thank goodness for burping, a no-fail ice-breaker among males of any age.

Paul held up his hands. "Look, this sewing circle stuff isn't our thing. I live near a field. You got a mitt?"

As luck would have it, I had packed my Wilson baseball glove, one of my most cherished possessions. I ran back into the house to retrieve it and shouted to Mom that I was going to play ball.

"Don't get any bug bites!" she yelled.

"Got it!" I yelled back as if I had a choice.

Moments later we trampled through a footpath in the woods and ambled down into an opening near Paul's house. The "field" is what the guys called it, but they were far too kind. It was more like a rugged patch of dirt and weeds in the middle of some undeveloped land. The area was also used by Paul's brothers and their friends, the so-called "Big Kids," as a motorbike course. On closer look, you could see divots and tread marks from tires. The outfield had what Paul called a "berm," which was useful as a warning track. The guys had put down some old yellow frisbees as bases and a tattered rubber home plate. The saying "putting lipstick on a pig" came to mind, but it served the purpose.

Over the next hour or so we tossed the ball around, hit fungoes, and played "pickle" (in Pennsylvania we called it "Running Bases"). At one point I threw Kenny out trying to run from second to third. The loud 'pop' in Paul's glove had everyone raising their eyebrows.

We talked some more about sports. What else was there? The guys were Boston fanatics, and I picked up on their passion and terminology. The Red Sox were the "Sox," the Celtics were the "Celts" (or "C's"), and the Bruins were the "B's." If you rooted for these teams (I said I would) then you were expected to root against their rivals: the Yankees, Lakers, and Canadiens. When I asked about the Patriots, the guys laughed and said that hell would freeze over before they won a Super Bowl.

"Hey, I just realized you guys don't have accents," I said.

"Neither do you," Paul said.

Fair enough, I thought. Just then the afternoon quiet was interrupted by the sound of a motorbike revving to life. Then another. And another.

"The 'Big Kids,'" Kenny said with a frightful look.

Paul tapped my shoulder. "It's been real, Jay, but we should probably call it a day."

4

Our new house on Moss Hill Road was pretty nice to look at, I'll give you that. It was a two-story white colonial with black shutters and cool features like a drop-down laundry chute, a screened porch with a built-in grill, and a ton of other things (crown molding?!) that probably made my folks go bananas. None of that excited me, though. Despite the possibility of running into the "Big Kids," I was thrilled about hanging out with my new friends for the weekend. That Saturday morning, I was up even before my parents.

After wolfing down a bowl of Sugar Smacks and a banana, I grabbed a sheet of notebook paper and drew a baseball diamond on it. I don't know if I thought I was Leo Durocher, or what, but I wrote the names of the guys and the position I imagined they'd play *if* they were major leaguers: Paul Boucher (pronounced Boo-shay) was tall and rangy, so first baseman, for sure. Matt Monetti? Kinda squat, so catcher. Kenny DeSantos? Quick and agile…. *shortstop*.

As I considered my role in this All-Star line-up, there was a tap at the door. I tore off a strip of paper from the bottom of the page, scribbled "Playing outside," and tossed it on the countertop. Pocketing the rest of my scouting report, I hurried to the laundry room and opened the door. There they were—the Moss Hill Crew—decked out in jackets and hats displaying their allegiance to the hometown teams.

"You guys look very…*Boston*," I said. "I don't have—

"Here," Paul said. He handed me a wadded red beanie.

"Wow, thanks," I said. With all eyes on me, I unfolded it. Stitched on the front was the familiar logo of a Minuteman hovering over a football.

"Patriots?" I asked, unaware that I sounded more disappointed than surprised.

"Ya gotta start somewhere," Matt said, slapping me on the arm.

I stepped outside into the early daylight and slipped on the beanie. We huddled again in my driveway, but this time things were more relaxed. The first item on the agenda, according to Paul, was to get the lay of the land. Moss Hill was the main road in the neighborhood and our house sat on the crest of the hill. Having a steep slope on each side made it a terrific location for skateboarding, I'd imagine, but not so great for playing ball (five seconds in either direction or your ball was history—unless you were a world-class speedster like Bob Hayes). Anyhow, Kenny lived across the street from us to the left, and Matt lived across to the right, so they were next-door neighbors. All three of our homes made a triangle at the peak.

We followed Paul along the path, just as we did the day before. But instead of trekking down an embankment to the field, we hiked up an incline that took us deeper into the woods.

"There's nothing out here that can eat us, is there?" I asked.

"Just the occasional horsefly," Kenny said. "They get pretty big in these parts."

It may have been too early in the day (or the season) for horseflies, but I did get up close to nature on our jaunt. I almost stepped on a snake, which scared the daylights out of me, and minutes later a bird pooped on my shoulder.

"Maybe you've got that Philly vibe," Kenny joked.

We passed a dilapidated outhouse and a barn that was home to an old horse named "Star" (who was fed on weekdays, I learned, by Kenny's older sister). The guys also showed me the best trees for climbing and which berries were edible.

"This reminds me of Euell-Fuckin'-Gibbons," said Matt, finishing a mouthful of blueberries and wiping the juice on his pants.

"Who's Euell? And when did you see him fuckin' Gibbons?" Paul snickered.

Kenny read my expression and explained how author and nature lover Euell Gibbons was the star of a recent Grape Nuts commercial.

When we made it out of the wilderness and back to the "streets," my friends gave me the scoop on various neighbors—for example, those who had fancy cars and friendly dogs. An elderly couple, Mr. and Mrs. McKelvey, owned the only house in the neighborhood with a swimming pool, but they had never invited any of the neighbors to use it. Paul claimed that didn't stop the "Big Kids" from crashing the property and taking a dip when the couple wasn't on the premises.

By that point, I was dying of curiosity.

"Who the hell are these guys?" I asked.

"Two of them are my big brothers," Paul said. "Tony's a senior, he's quiet but don't let that fool you. He used to box. Then there's Chris, who's a sophomore. He's just flat out mean."

"Then there's Dallas Folkes," Kenny added. "Don't look at him the wrong way. I'd trust him as far as I could throw him."

"And last, but not least, Brett Larson," Matt added. "He's plain nuts."

"They're both freshmen," Paul said. "But they all could pass for college dudes. Not that I foresee higher education in their futures."

There were some chuckles, but then the guys turned serious again. They said if there was mischief in the neighborhood, they were the most likely culprits. And if I happened to run across them alone, well, *run*.

So that pretty much filled in the picture for me. I was glad I asked. Much to my relief, we didn't run across them that afternoon.

5

Sunday was Church Day for the DeSantos family (and most worshippers across America), so Paul suggested a noon start for part two of my neighborhood introduction. This suited me fine because I was exhausted, sunburned, and itchy from our wilderness marathon the day before (contrary to Mom's wishes, I *had* been bitten by bugs).

Since the guys had already met my parents (albeit briefly), the family tour began at Paul's, which was at the end of Indigo Circle. I called it a dead end, but Paul corrected me and said it was a *cul-de-sac*, which sounded funny coming out of his mouth (I didn't remember anyone saying "Look at the *escargot*" the previous day when we saw a snail). Anyhow, it was difficult to describe Paul's place, other than it had a "lived-in" look. The three-car garage was open, and you could see motorcycles, machinery, and all sorts of junk inside. Car parts and rags were strewn across the driveway, and an old Winnebago was parked in the woods on the side of the property.

Paul's father, Ed Boucher, was a barrel-chested mechanic who sported a thick brown beard with patches of gray. He had an extra-long pinky fingernail which, according to Paul, was by design because he was often tinkering and liked to use it as a screwdriver. Mrs. Boucher, Terri, was a tall woman with round glasses and a streak of white in her hair. As she served us leftover slices of bacon and glasses of Tang, she joked about having her hands full looking after three boys. "Or four," she quipped. "If you count Ed."

The next stop was Matt's house. Mrs. Monetti introduced herself as "Mary" and said it was perfectly acceptable if I wanted to call her by her first name. I told her that wasn't going to fly. I explained how at camp the previous summer my counselor, Duncan, said the same thing (not that I could call him "Mary" but that I could call him "Duncan"). Even though he was 17, he looked older, and when Dad heard me say something like "Thanks, Duncan," he hit the roof. He thought children who did that were being disrespectful (to this day, I'm still not comfortable being on a first-name basis with grown-ups).

"How about we go with Mrs. M.?" Mary Monetti suggested, glancing at Paul and Kenny. "That's what these rogues call me."

Paul and Kenny grinned sheepishly.

"Sounds like a deal, Mrs. M.," I said, trying it out.

She gave me a subtle wink, which fascinated me. I envied people who could do that on the sly. Whenever I tried it, half my face moved. Mrs. M., meanwhile, took out a bag of celery sticks and a container of cream cheese from her fridge. None of us were hungry but we didn't want to be rude and pass on the offer.

As she prepared the snacks, I got the scoop on the family history from both her and Matt. Mrs. M. was a widow and Matt was her only child. Her late husband, Dan, passed away several years earlier from pancreatic cancer. It sounded tragic and all that, but she didn't let his death keep her down. She went on to earn her nursing degree, and despite working long hours at a local hospital, she managed the single-parent thing with the help of family and friends.

After forcing down a few celery sticks, I went to the washroom to clean my hands. On the way out, I stopped in the hallway to look at a collection of framed photos on the wall. One of the larger ones caught my eye: Matt, at about seven years old, standing with his arm around a slender Caucasian man in front of a cottage.

"Matt's late dad," Paul said, joining me.

"Right," I said, still studying the photo.

"He was adopted …" added Kenny, who had appeared behind Paul.

"Yeah, my biological dad was a word that rhymes with 'bigger,'" Matt said, entering the hallway from another direction.

"Matthew!" Mrs. M. exclaimed from behind Kenny. Now everyone was in the hallway, and suddenly I felt bad for using the washroom.

"What? It's not racist if I'm one, *too*," he protested.

"You're not—just, enough with that," she said, returning to the kitchen.

After that little fiasco, we felt it was best to push on. Our next (and last) stop was the DeSantos home. Kenny's folks, Chip and Ilene, were well known for their devotion to the Lord as well as their short rope when it came to discipline. Kenny and his big sister, Kelly—the one who fed "Star"—had been grounded so often that the guys had nicknamed Mrs. DeSantos "Ilene the Coffee Bean" (never mind the fact that coffee beans were typically grounded, not the other way around).

As we ambled across Matt's driveway and onto the DeSantos property, the happy couple was tending to some flowers along their front walk.

"Hey, Mom. Hey, Dad," Kenny said.

"'Hey' is for horses, Kenny. We say 'hello,' remember?" Chip corrected.

When he saw Kenny was not alone, he cleared his throat, a signal to Ilene. The couple straightened up in tandem, flashing smiles that would have impressed a photographer.

"Howdy, all," Chip said with a noticeable change in his voice as well.

"Afternoon, boys," Ilene said.

We smiled and waved awkwardly.

"Is it me? Or is this crew growing in height—and numbers?" Chip asked.

"You know Paul and Matt," Kenny said, before gesturing to me. "This is Jayson. He just moved in across the street."

"Ah, the new kid on the block. I'm Chip off the old block." He let out an amused snort and grabbed my hand. "I never get tired of that one."

I forced a smile to humor him. Chip wasn't much taller than Paul and based on his iron grip, I wondered if he was trying to compensate for his lack of height.

"Jayson, we just dropped off some muffins and church literature at your house," Ilene said. "Your mother is absolutely lovely."

"Aw, thank you kindly. And yes, she is," I said. Just then something caught my eye in the window behind her. A silhouette behind a curtain.

"Our pleasure, dear. We'd love to have you all join us at services someday," Ilene said.

"Sure thing," I replied, trying to stay focused.

"Would you consider yourself a pious person, Jay?" Chip asked.

My attention diverted to whoever or whatever was inside the house. Was that a hand pulling the curtain back?

"Jay?" Kenny nudged me.

"Ahh, no, sir. I believe it's important to treat everyone the same, no matter what their race," I answered. As Chip gave me a sideways look, Paul tugged on my sleeve.

"He's been out in the sun a lot this weekend," Paul said. "We should probably get him some water."

A few minutes later, we retreated to a green electrical box at the bottom of Moss Hill. It was wide enough for all of us to sit on. The guys were still chuckling as I peeled a faded Wacky Pack sticker ("Never Ready" batteries) off the side of the humming unit.

"You do this foot-in-mouth thing often?" Paul asked.

"When I'm distracted," I said, trying to rationalize. "I thought he said '*biased*'…I was only half-listening."

"Obviously," Matt said. "What was the other half doing?"

"Looking inside the house," I explained. "I could swear there was a ghost or something. None of you saw it?"

"It was probably my sister," Kenny said with a chuckle. "She can be scary, but she's no ghost."

The guys laughed some more. Good times at my expense but I didn't mind. It was the most fun I'd had in a long while.

"Are you gonna be at school tomorrow, Jay?" Paul asked.

"Don't think so," I answered. "I have to get a shot and a physical."

"Ugh, the ol' scrotum squeeze. I'd rather be doing algebra," Matt said.

I had a million questions about school, but Chip's voice shattered the late afternoon quiet: "*Kennyyy! Diiiinnnerrr!*"

Kenny shook his head in mock humiliation, and we shared one final laugh for the weekend before slapping five and heading our separate ways.

When I arrived at my side door, something dawned on me. I had covered nearly every acre of land in the neighborhood the last two days, and yet I'd spent hardly any time on my property. I took a step back and admired our house and our lot. Mom and Dad had done all right.

I was startled out of my trance by a horn—Dad steering the Skylark into our driveway. He turned off the engine, climbed out, and gave me a bemused look.

"What's going on? You lose something?"

"I'm just kinda taking it all in," I answered.

"I see," he said. "Well, how 'bout you help me take in these groceries?"

That evening we ate on the screened porch, sitting comfortably at a patio table the previous owners had graciously left behind. We talked and laughed, and when we had finished Mom's delicious meal (which included Ilene's tasty muffins), we sat back and listened to the sound of crickets. Darkness descended and fireflies appeared. Everyone was content, and I realized something.

No one had spoken of Pennsylvania at all.

6

By Wednesday Justine and I were cleared for school. We had made it through our appointments the previous day with our new pediatrician, Dr. Cronyn. I got vaccinated against some disease I couldn't pronounce and endured the standard physical with all the uncomfortable parts (as Matt implied). On that note, Mom straight out asked the doctor if puberty was on the horizon for me. Dr. Cronyn responded that I might be a "late bloomer" but there was no cause for concern. And yet, as we left the office, she had nothing but concern on her face

"Why are you so worried about me?" I asked.

"Well, because my brother developed late, and he was teased a lot," Mom replied.

"Jay already gets teased a lot," Justine said.

I frowned and she giggled. Uncle Sam was Mom's younger brother—her only sibling. He had been in LA for years, trying to make it as an actor, but he made a living working in restaurants and doing odd jobs.

"Is that why Uncle Sam likes other men?" Justine asked, just as another family passed us in the parking lot.

"In the car, kiddos," Mom said with a clenched smile.

As she withdrew her keys and unlocked the Skylark, I opened the rear door for Justine and slid in beside her in the back. Mom settled in behind the wheel and took a breath to gather herself.

"What? Is it bad to say that?" Justine wondered.

"Maybe just not in public," I cautioned.

I couldn't blame my sis. It wasn't exactly a family secret anymore. Uncle Sam was open about spending time with men, and even sent photos of himself with his "friends." Sometimes one, and sometimes a group. Dad had a tough time looking at them and said that's what happens when people move to Los Angeles—they get a little "light in the loafers."

"Mom...?" Justine persisted.

"Just—what your brother said, sweetheart. Family matters are best discussed in private."

7

According to the calendar, Justine and I had precisely seven weeks and two days of school left at our new school until summer vacation. We set our alarms for 6:45 on Wednesday morning, but Mom and Dad still woke us when it was dark outside. They wanted to make sure we looked presentable and had a hearty breakfast before driving us in.

As we climbed into the back of the Skylark with our backpacks, I glanced over at Justine. Even though we were old pros at switching schools, I still sensed some jitters. That was a cruddy thing about moving in the middle of the year—you'd have more than one first day of school. I tried to distract her by quizzing her on something I'd read on the side of a Dixie riddle cup.

"Hey, if an athlete gets '*athlete's foot*'...what does an astronaut get?"

Justine turned away.

"You okay?" I asked.

"You're lucky," she said. "At least you'll know people already."

She had a point. I'd be seeing all my new Moss Hill friends, although I'd learned Matt and Kenny were fifth-graders. Paul was in sixth in Mrs. Walker's class, and I had my fingers crossed that's where I'd end up.

"You'll do fine, Justine. You always do…" I said, squeezing her hand.

The drive to Winnicott Elementary was a short one, barely long enough to hear a special news report about Americans being evacuated from Saigon, the capital of South Vietnam. Dad grumbled, turned off the radio, and parked in a yellow zone in front of the school.

"Okay, boys and girls…off you go," he said, stepping out of the car. He gave us quick hugs and wished us luck. I noticed he left the engine running as a not-so-subtle hint to Mom, who would be escorting us inside—be quick about it.

In the school lobby, we took a moment to gaze at a statue of the school's namesake, Alexander Winnicott. Evidently, Alex was a local patriot who fought the good fight against the British some 200 years ago before perishing in battle. After some hasty introductions and signatures in the administration office, Mom hugged us goodbye. She and Dad were headed to Boston for an appointment with her new rheumatologist.

The school's principal, Mrs. Bishop, and vice principal, Mr. Stowe, escorted Justine and me out to the lobby where two wings converged to create an "L" shape.

"All set, young lady?" Mr. Stowe asked Justine.

"Yessir," she said, putting on a brave face.

Mr. Stowe began to escort her down the hallway to our right but then Justine stopped on a dime and turned back with a knowing grin.

"Hey, Jay," she said. "*Missile* toe."

"What's that?" I asked.

"The answer to your riddle," she said before resuming her walk.

If an athlete gets an athlete's foot, what does an astronaut get? I smiled.

Moments later, Mrs. Bishop and I arrived at my classroom. The name "Nelson" was engraved on a handcrafted wood sign beside the door frame. So much for being in Paul's class.

"You'll love Mr. Nelson," she said as if reading my mind. "He's one of our most experienced teachers."

Mrs. Bishop knocked on the door and pushed it open without waiting for a response. Inside, the students quieted down and became apprehensive, the way they always did when the school's principal made an impromptu visit.

Mr. Nelson hopped off a stool. I noticed he was holding a paperback copy of *Jonathan Livingston Seagull*. My new teacher sure did look experienced—white hair, a ruddy face, and a crooked but friendly grin.

"Ahh, you must be Jayson. Glad yah heeeya," he said warmly.

I froze. That accent.

Mr. Nelson gestured to an open desk near a kidney-shaped table.

"Entah, young man. And yah welcome to say a few woohhhds if ya so desiiiiha…"

I shook my head. Mrs. Bishop placed a reassuring hand on my back.

"Go on," she said.

I inched forward. Mr. Nelson spread his arms apart wider.

"I undahstahhnd-yah-prahbahbly-gaht-the-fehst-day-jittahs, but—"

"Can't…*accent*," I stammered. Color rushed to my face as I realized all eyes in the classroom were on me.

"I think he said he had an *accident*," a beefy boy with shaggy blond hair said from a nearby seat. The other students erupted in laughter.

"That's enough, Mista *Gottnah*," said Mr. Nelson.

After sitting at a corner desk all morning and feeling even more like an outsider, I was desperate to find a familiar face at lunch. Sitting alone in class was one thing, but eating all by yourself at a cafeteria table is probably the single worst experience a student could have at school. Well, either that or somebody walking in on your stall while you're doing "number two." Not that that had ever happened to me. But who knew? I still had six years until graduation.

As panic began to set in, I felt a tap on my shoulder.

"Over here, my man," Paul said.

I felt relieved and followed him to a long retractable table, where he had already set down his tray. He asked how things were going, and I told him everything, starting with my deer-in-headlights entrance.

"Who was the smartass?" Paul asked.

"I'm pretty sure he said 'Gottnah,'" I said.

Paul looked off in thought and shook his head. "I don't know that name. Wait!" His eyebrows arched as he looked across from me. "Do you mean *Gartner?*"

"Beats me," I said with a shrug. "The teacher sounds like a Kennedy."

Paul chuckled and explained it had to be Scottie Gartner. He was pretty much a jackass to everyone—at least until he got to know them. Paul said the two of them had an ongoing beef the year before that nearly blew up into a full East Wing/West Wing brawl. Fortunately, they ended up on the same little league team and worked things out.

On cue, Scottie and a few of his cronies approached our table. He rested a boot on the cafeteria bench beside me and looked at Paul.

"What's goin' on Paul?" Scottie asked.

"Not much, Scottie," Paul replied. "What's up with you?"

"So, the new kid—he with you?" Scottie asked, nodding at me.

"Yeah, he's cool," Paul said.

Gartner took his foot down and straddled the bench next to me.

"What's your name again?" he asked, looking me over.

"Jayson," I answered. "Well, Jay, actually."

"All right, 'Jay *actually*.' I'm Scottie."

Despite his sarcasm, Scottie extended his hand. Part of me expected him to pull it away, like "Moe" from *The Three Stooges*. But when I put mine out, Scottie shook it.

The handshake may have seemed like a small thing, but it was a big moment for me as I entered our school's orbit. Being accepted by the "Kings of the Wings," Paul Boucher and Scottie Gartner, made my transition a heck of a lot easier. Students in the upper grades, especially, went out of their way to help me with the school essentials, like where I could find drinking fountains with the coldest water, or which cafeteria workers gave the biggest servings of food. Matt and Kenny tried to do their part, as well, showing me several wrinkled issues of *National Geographic* in the library that featured photos of topless tribal women.

In time, I began to understand Mr. Nelson better. A classmate named Dave Talman, whose desk was next to mine served as a de facto translator. Dave was a quirky and bright guy. Aside from introducing me to new vocabulary words, including "de facto," he shared a strategy for understanding the Boston accent.

"It's like a Math formula. Bostonians subtract the letter "r" from the words ending with "r" and substitute the *sound* "ah." And then they'll substitute that "r" sound for words that normally end with an "ah" sound. So, for example, the word 'Cluster' becomes '*Clustah*.' But the name 'Hannah' will sound like '*Hannar*.'"

"Why?" I asked, dumbfounded.

"*Why*? I don't know," he explained. "It's always been that way."

"It's giving me a headache," I said.

"You said you wanted help," he said.

"Hey, how come you never sit with us at lunch?" I asked.

"Because present company excluded, I prefer to be in the company of individuals with an IQ higher than a thermostat setting."

I looked around, hopeful that Scottie or his crew hadn't overheard his comments. Lunchtime *had* become a little stressful. Scottie gave me grief about Mom scrawling my name with a heart on my lunch bag until he saw what she had packed inside—Slim Jims, Doritos, and chocolate pudding. After that, he turned all nice and wanted to trade every day. While I wasn't exactly drooling over the carrot sticks or fruit loaf he offered in return, I swapped with him from time to time, just to get along.

On the home front, things started to fall into place. Dad rolled up one night after work in a shiny '75 Chevy Impala, his new company car. This meant that Mom would get to drive the Skylark full-time. Mail arrived, including a property tax bill which had Dad muttering about "*Tax*-achusetts." Justine and I received postcards from Uncle Sam in California and Dad's sister, Aunt Patricia, who lived in Wisconsin. Uncle Sam didn't write a lot of words, but he did amazing little sketches of cartoon characters. He could draw characters like Charlie Brown or Superman, and always tried to work my name into their thoughts or actions.

Aunt Patricia never failed to ask how her "favorite" nephew was doing. It was an inside joke because when we had visited her previously, I pointed out that I was her *only* nephew. She acted surprised but then said that I would still be her favorite if she had a million nephews. I was a sucker for praise, so this always made me smile.

The moving trucks showed up, a little later than expected, but all our clothes, furniture, and televisions were intact. Of course, Justine and I couldn't wait for Dad to set up our big Zenith color TV. We were in business once he extended the rabbit ears (the in-house antenna) and tuned in the dial. While Justine liked *The Electric Company* and *Zoom*, my favorite shows were *Happy Days* and *The Six Million Dollar Man* ("Fonzie" and "Steve Austin" were two different kinds of cool). I also watched the Red Sox whenever I could to get up to speed on the players and their stats.

When Mom and Dad thought we'd had enough TV, Justine and I listened to the big cabinet stereo in the living room. We cranked up WRKO and Dale Dorman because he was funny and played all the hits. I also listened to the station on my bedroom clock radio and the Sox.

One night Paul joined us for dinner and even volunteered to wash dishes afterward, which impressed my parents. Afterward, we went up to my room and he helped me unpack the last of my belongings. He wasn't such a prince, though, when it came to some of the items—shouting "Discard!" whenever he saw anything with a Philadelphia team logo. He also rolled his eyes at some of my records like The Carpenters, America, and Bread.

"Who do you like?" I asked, trying not to sound offended.

"Ever heard of Jethro Tull?"

"I think so. Is he American?"

"It's *they*. And they're *British*," he said, rolling his eyes.

"Okay, okay," I said. "Let's talk about something we can agree on—women. Who do you think is sexy?"

"Daphne," he said.

"Daphne *who*?" I asked.

"Daphne from *Scooby Doo*," he replied.

"You're warped," I said. "But I know what you're saying."

We shared a laugh.

"Okay, how about Raquel Welch?" he asked.

"Absolutely," I countered. "But what about school? Anyone?"

"No one at school stands out. But there is someone…" Paul said with a sly grin. "I feel bad saying it…"

"C'mon, out with it, man…" I demanded, unable to take the suspense.

"Kenny's sister," he said, holding up his hands.

"The *ghost*? Does she exist?" I wondered.

"Oh yeah. She's a knockout, but I wouldn't get any ideas," he cautioned.

"Why? Because she's Kenny's sister?"

"More like she's *Chip's daughter*," Paul said.

He then filled me in on a local "suburban" legend. Word had it that Chip once pulled a snub nose .38 from his glove box after a panhandler leaned on the hood of his car at a red light in Boston. When the light turned green, Chip honked. The guy still didn't move, so Chip, irate, stepped out and pressed the muzzle under his chin. The panhandler was so scared, he peed his pants and some of it trickled onto Chip's loafers. Chip, disgusted, stepped out of his shoes and drove home barefoot.

My jaw dropped. "Kenny's dad? *Christian* Chip?"

"The one and only," Paul said.

After Paul left that evening, I took a handful of the discarded items down to the garbage bin in our garage. As I lifted the lid, I caught a glimpse of a pamphlet resting atop the garbage heap. It displayed a cross on the front with a simple message: *"Loving and Living for Him."*

I put two and two together and figured 1) it had to be the church literature that Chip and Ilene dropped off, and 2) that Dad had been the one in our family who had given it the heave-ho.

The irony was that while one man *appeared* devout, and the other was agnostic, they were the same in one way: they were both missing the message.

9

One fun thing about Winnicott was that when outdoor recess was canceled because of inclement weather, students were sent into the gymnasium for a dodgeball extravaganza. I didn't know this until we were hit with showers at the end of April for four straight days. Since Mrs. Bishop was wary of old rivalries being renewed, she instructed the PE teachers to divide the sixth-grade boys and girls alphabetically, not by classes. Students with last names "A" through "M" would be on one side, and those with names "N" through "Z" would be on the other. This meant that my squad would be facing off against a team featuring Paul and Scottie.

Since I was agile and had a good arm (as previously noted), dodgeball was right up my alley. After the first game, I sent almost a dozen students to the sidelines. Even though I didn't hit Paul or Scottie, our team won because we had more players left on our side when time expired.

The next day, it was more of the same, and this time I drilled Paul and Scottie. *Bam, bam.*

"Down goes, Boucher! Down goes Gartner!" Mr. Stowe screamed into a megaphone, sounding like Howard Cosell.

As our side stacked up win after win, players on both sides started calling me the "Eliminator." Of course, this made me a target. Fortunately, no matter how hard everyone tried, I avoided being hit. I was the last man (okay, *boy*) standing and Mr. Stowe raised my hand like I was the heavyweight champion of the world.

Unfortunately, during the fourth and final game of the week, I knocked a petite girl named Andrea off her feet with a side-arm throw and she landed awkwardly on her wrist. Hearing her shriek made me feel awful. I apologized to her a hundred times while she was on her way to the health office. I even wanted to go in with her, but I was rerouted to the principal's office.

Mrs. Bishop, who seemed to have no recollection of meeting me just weeks earlier, wanted to make sure there was no intent on my part. I promised her that it was just one of those things that happen in the heat of battle. Mr. Stowe vouched for me: "This kid could give Nolan Ryan a run for his money."

Mrs. Bishop was not a baseball fan. Or maybe she just wasn't impressed. After she directed me back to Mr. Nelson's classroom, she picked up the intercom and announced there would be no more dodgeball for the rest of the year.

As I returned to my seat, all eyes were on me the way they were on the first day of school. Except this time, instead of blank expressions, there were dirty looks.

"Nice going, 'Eliminator,'" Scottie snarled.

With one fateful throw, I had gone from hero to zero.

10

As the skies cleared and the terrain dried, the guys and I headed back to the field regularly. Baseball was known as "America's pastime" and that's how we passed our time that spring. The problem was the afternoons flew by and we'd be having so much fun we wouldn't hear our parents' calls for dinner. Chip and Ilene finally resorted to ringing a cowbell as a signal to Kenny.

Sometimes Paul's dad, Ed, would let us borrow his transistor radio on the weekends and we'd listen to Ned Martin call the afternoon games as we played our own. Nothing dominated the Boston sports landscape more at this time of year than the surging 'Sox.' It looked like they even had enough pitching and hitting to keep the dreaded Yankees at bay. A couple of rookies named Fred Lynn (my favorite) and Jim Rice (Paul's favorite) stood out. This duo soon became known as the "Gold Dust Twins." They fit right in with long-time favorites Carl Yastrzemski ("Yaz"), Carlton Fisk, Dwight Evans, and Luis Tiant.

Still, not everyone was sold on the Sox as contenders. Ed grumbled, "They're like a beautiful woman you swoon over, but then with time you realize they're nothing special" (given that Ed was married, I hoped he was talking hypothetically).

"Dad, this team is different," Paul argued.

"Talk to me in September," Ed replied with a dismissive wave.

Since I'd arrived too late in the year for Little League sign-ups, I wasn't eligible to take part. This was the only downside to the 1975 baseball season. Sometimes the guys would have practice on the weeknights, and they almost always had games on Saturday.

"Just look at it like you're on the Disabled List," Paul said. "You'll be back next year."

Of course, Paul's outlook wasn't so rosy after he was selected to the Yankees 12-and-under team. Seeing him in that gray uniform with black socks and a NY cap was a strange experience.

"Don't start," he moaned. "I'm surprised my skin isn't burning."

When the guys were at practice, I'd rely on my imagination to pass the time. Since our basement was so large and barren, I grabbed my street hockey stick and ball and headed down the steps. I worked on my stickhandling and practiced taking shots at the unfinished fireplace (which had dimensions that were similar to those of a hockey net). The cement floor and walls were practically indestructible. That made the basement a great spot for any kind of indoor training. If I got bored with hockey, I'd bring my basketball down so I could practice dribbling and passing (slinging the Spalding off the wall for the ol' "give and go").

One evening I put on a basketball "talent show" for my family. I changed into my athletic shorts, tank top, and white Converse sneakers (I even slipped on a headband, for good measure). Not only was I the star of the show, but I was an usher, instructing my parents and Justine to sit in the row of folding chairs I'd set out. I called for a volunteer and Justine's hand shot up before the words were even out of my mouth. Of course, it was all prearranged—Justine was always the second fiddle in these productions, and she never disappointed.

As Sis took her seat in a special "guest" chair, I dribbled around her like I was Curly Neal from the Harlem Globetrotters. The kicker was when I started whistling "Sweet Georgia Brown" while showing off my skills. My parents laughed and applauded. Dad even did the super loud whistle with his fingers in his mouth. That was another adult thing like winking that I just hadn't figured out yet.

Although I loved my sports equipment, my yellow Raleigh Chopper was still my favorite possession. Surprisingly, I had yet to take it for a spin since the rest of our belongings had arrived. That changed one afternoon when I looked out a front window and noticed a pretty, blonde teenager heading down the hill to our left. It was probably more wishful thinking than a family resemblance, but something told me it was Kenny's sister, the mysterious Kelly DeSantos.

I hurried into the garage, opened the overhead door, and jumped on my chopper. I steered down the hill in the direction she'd gone, but when I came to the first street, Sage Lane, there was no sign of her.

I could turn left, into another cul-de-sac, or go straight—which would lead me into some woods—or I could turn right. Decisions, decisions.

A hunch told me to turn right. Just as I was picking up momentum, I saw two shirtless, long-haired teenagers sauntering along the road toward me. One carried a skateboard over his shoulder and the other puffed on a cigarette. I stomped on my brakes, burning rubber, and that gave me away. The dudes looked up.

"Young man? Are you going to tend to that skidmark? We like to keep our streets clean in this neighborhood," the smoker asked.

I ignored him and wheeled my chopper around.

"Hey, brother!" the other dude hollered. "Is that a bike or a very large banana?!"

I pedaled furiously back up Moss Hill, toward the safety of home. I heard their laughter over the sound of my breathing as I cruised into my garage.

I was 99% sure I'd just had my first encounter with the "Big Kids."

As much as I loved summer, Mom despised it. When the temperatures and humidity rose, her arthritis flared up and she needed to take more naps and pain relievers. One thing I didn't understand was that her arthritis-strength aspirin only came in child-proof bottles. How in the heck was someone with weak and painful knuckles supposed to open that? When Dad wasn't around, yours truly (a child!) ended up with the task. Mom said this was "the very definition of irony."

Although Dad could be frugal, he made some concessions to help Mom. We ate out when she felt too tired to cook, and he agreed to hire a housekeeper. One of his coworkers referred him to a woman, Diane, who cleaned homes in our area. My folks spoke with her on the phone first, as if they were taking turns talking to a relative, and after that, they invited her over for an interview. Diane impressed them even more in person: she seemed trustworthy and even offered to bring her own cleaning supplies. I liked her because she was friendly, and she knew a lot about sports, like the fact that "Yaz" had won baseball's triple crown in 1967.

There was one mind-boggling development that arose from Diane's hiring—"Mom Boss" appeared for the very first time. She instructed Justine and me to thoroughly clean our rooms the night *before* Diane was scheduled to arrive for her first visit. She requested Dad vacuum the house (which, after hearing her tone, he did without raising so much as an eyebrow). At breakfast, moments before Diane's arrival, Mom sprayed Lysol into our kitchen trash can, even though Dad had taken out the less-than-full Glad bag to the larger bin in the garage.

"Mom," I said. "It's a trash can. It's not supposed to be clean."

"Well, it doesn't have to smell," she responded.

It was pretty obvious Mom didn't want Diane to think we were slobs. It mattered to her what people thought about her and her family (take Uncle Sam and his lifestyle choices, for example). That said, as harsh as it may sound, she was also a compulsive clean freak. We'd recently gone to one of those restaurants where you're allowed to throw peanut shells on the floor, and Justine and I were practically in heaven. What kind of restaurant allows you to be messy? But Mom's stomach was in knots. The debris on the floor might as well have been cockroaches. Even though she enjoyed the peanuts, Mom couldn't bring herself to litter. She placed the shells on a napkin, balled it all up, and left the tidy little package for the server as Dad paid the bill.

When Mom had good (or at least better) days with her arthritis, Dad made a point to schedule some family outings. For a kid who despised moving, I didn't mind day trips. Some of the places we visited were close, like Concord (one time home to Henry David Thoreau) and Lexington (where I think ol' Alex Winnicott met his unfortunate end). It was cool because we had read about these battles in Mr. Nelson's class and even took a field trip to a park with famous monuments.

Of course, our first family trip to Boston was the highlight. I was no expert when it came to urban culture, but it reminded me of Philadelphia, New York, and Detroit—all the metropolitan areas that were within driving distance of our former homes. Maybe all cities appeared similar for the simple reason that everyone and everything was loud and, in a rush—people, cars, you name it. City dwellers all seemed to have a purpose, just like the pigeons and seagulls that overwhelmed the sidewalks.

I don't know why, but tall buildings always fascinated me—maybe because of all the planning and courage it took to work on them hundreds of feet above the ground. In Boston, the tallest skyscrapers were the Prudential Building and the Hancock Tower. They were both insurance companies, Dad said, which meant nothing to me. He even shared a gory story about a pane of glass falling from the Hancock a few years back, decapitating a pedestrian.

The problem with Dad telling us that story was that I began looking up every block, just to see if anything was going to fall on us. At one point I lagged so far behind that I got caught in an intersection when the traffic light changed. A big guy behind the wheel of a big Cadillac leaned on the horn and zipped around me.

"Ain't got all day, nitwit!" The driver shouted.

Dad tugged me up onto the sidewalk.

"Masshole!" I yelled as the Caddy zoomed past.

Justine giggled, finally understanding the meaning of the term. My parents just shook their heads and grinned. The good vibes lasted maybe ten minutes until we bogged down during Mom's endless window shopping.

"How much longer?" Justine asked.

Dad stepped in, trying to buy her time.

"Hey, did you know there was a famous song written about this city?"

"'Dirty Water?'" I asked.

"No, not that one," Dad replied. "It's a story about a guy named 'Charlie' who didn't have enough money to get on his next train, so he had to ride around under the streets of Boston forever."

"Forever?" Justine asked.

"Yup," Dad said.

"How much money did he need?" I asked.

"I don't know…five cents?" Dad shrugged.

"A lousy nickel?!" I bellowed. "Who wouldn't let him off for five cents?"

"The conductor," Dad replied. "It's a song, Jay. Don't get your knickers twisted."

A while later, we walked the Freedom Trail—which was red-painted bricks that led you down a path "rich with history," as the guides would say. Along the way, we stopped and gazed at things like the Old North Church (from Paul Revere's Ride), the old gravesite of Sam Adams, and the exact spot where the Boston Massacre took place. We also did a tour of the USS Constitution, which was an old battleship from the War of 1812 or something. The thing that stood out about that was the doorways were no higher than six feet. Even Dad had to duck going through. They must have had short sailors back in those days.

I didn't mention it to my family, but, recalling Paul's story, I kept my eye out the entire time for a street dweller with loafers. You'd think someone like that would stand out, but unfortunately, no luck. Most of these guys had tattered boots or tennis sneakers if they even had shoes. Sometimes the shoes didn't match, either. Maybe Chip's victim had moved, or he needed to trade them, or… something worse. At some point, I began to hope Paul's tale wasn't even true.

Either way, I was glad when my parents chose a restaurant closer to our hometown for dinner. I would have felt guilty eating a fancy meal in front of those poor souls. By the time we got home, it was close to ten o'clock. Everyone was exhausted and went straight to bed.

Even though I was full, and my feet were tired, I still had trouble falling asleep. My mind wandered like it often did. I knew it was only a song, but I couldn't shake the image of Charlie riding around and around on the subway.

I wondered if they would finally take him off the train when he died.

12

The last Monday of the school year was also the most awkward. It was the day all sixth-grade students had to attend the AGE workshop. AGE stood for "Adolescent Growth Education." Or, as it was more commonly known—Sex Ed. The teachers had a corny joke about this: now that we were of a certain "age," we were ready for the presentation.

"Did you guys have it in Philadelphia?" Paul asked on our morning bus ride.

"Sex?" I joked. "No, we were too young."

"Funny guy," he said, punching me on the shoulder.

After the usual Pledge of Allegiance to start the day, Winnicott's sixth-grade boys were summoned to the cafeteria. All the tables and benches had been folded up and moved aside, and students were instructed to sit on the floor. Paul was already there with Mrs. Walker's class and gestured for me to join him. I asked Mr. Nelson if I could and, to my surprise, he allowed it.

We sat close to a large screen that was set up against one wall where a man in a white lab coat, looking like a pharmacist, conferred with Vice Principal Stowe. There were no girls in attendance. They were having a similar presentation in the library, supervised by Mrs. Bishop.

After being introduced by Mr. Stowe, the lab coat guy did his spiel. We were going to see a movie, he said, but before that, he had some gifts for us. He then asked a few of the male teachers, including Mr. Nelson, to help pass out deodorant samples.

"Did you bring any cologne?" Scottie Gartner asked. There were a few chuckles in the crowd.

"No, no cologne. Why?" The lab coat guy asked.

"It seems like you're getting us ready for a date," Scottie said.

"Well, in a way we are," the guy admitted, which led to more laughter. "But hopefully one that will occur quite a few years down that road."

"Amen to that," Mr. Nelson quipped.

More chuckles. When everyone settled down, Mr. Stowe flicked on the film projector. Even though it was in color, the movie looked dated and choppy—maybe because it had been played about 5,000 times throughout our great Commonwealth.

"Think we'll see any babes in this?" I whispered to Paul.

He held up two hands with crossed fingers.

It turned out there were only two characters in the film—a teenage boy and his father. There wasn't much of a plot either. The father and son were on a camping trip, and after they set up their tents, they went fishing in a nearby stream. Later, they sat around a campfire eating trout or whatever it was they caught. The silence was awkward until the father commented on how his son's voice was getting deeper. He also implied that other changes were going to occur soon. Hint, hint…

Well, a big change happened inside the son's tent later that night. One moment the kid was sleeping soundly and the next he bolted upright as if he'd been grabbed by the Grim Reaper. The son reached into his sleeping bag, panic-stricken at what he discovered.

At that moment, the picture froze on the son's horrified expression. The film's narrator interjected with a serious voice, like something out of a Nazi propaganda film: "What Johnny has just experienced is a "Nocturnal Emission" (a graphic on the screen clarified "Wet Dream"). Of course, there were "yucks" and "ughs" from our audience. Once again, the men in the room had to shush everyone down. I don't remember how the movie ended, other than the father and son loaded up the truck the next morning and headed home.

As the lights went on, I whispered to Paul.

"I hope they ditched that sleeping bag."

"I know. And what's the moral of the story? Don't eat fish?" he asked.

I chuckled, unaware that Mr. Nelson was standing behind us.

"Something amusing, you two?" he asked.

"No, Mr. Nelson," Paul said.

"Thoughts on the film, young man?" The lab coat guy asked me.

"Ahh, not really," I said, my cheeks burning in embarrassment.

"Well, now's the time to ask. Unless maybe your father or another male family member has had this talk with you?"

"No, sir," I said. "Our only serious talks are about moving."

Even though I wasn't trying to be funny, everyone laughed. Fortunately, Mr. Nelson knew me well enough by then and didn't hold a grudge. When he handed me my final report card a few days later, I was elated to see straight A's. Dave looked at my grades and went off the deep end when he noticed my penmanship grade was an A, compared to his A-.

He insisted at the very last minute on the very last day of school that he and I have a "good old-fashioned writing contest" (as if there was such a thing) in front of Mr. Nelson. I don't know if he was trying to boost his grade or knock mine down, but Mr. Nelson was not going to indulge him. With his dry humor, he told Dave that he wasn't the only one who had a summer vacation waiting. Over Dave's protestations, he ushered us out the classroom door.

"Fayahwell, gentlemen. It's been a plejahhh," he said.

"Thank you, *Mistah* Nelson! Have a great *summah*!" I hollered back.

Yes, *that* accent. I had it down.

13

With the arrival of summer, playing baseball went from an after-school routine to an all-day engagement. The field became our home away from home. We developed our skills and strengthened our bonds. And yet as much as we enjoyed the extra time together, there were drawbacks. The weather was getting hot, so not only did we perspire more, but we'd return home covered in dirt, grass, or burrs.

"Now you know why we call this the 'mudroom,'" Mom said as she shook out my socks in the laundry sink. The area was like a delousing station, where I had to sanitize before being allowed into other parts of the house.

After I took off my shirt, Mom moved closer, as if picking up a scent.

"What are you doing?" I asked.

"I thought I caught a whiff of body odor. Wondering if you've hit puberty." The way she said puberty sounded like *poo-birdy*.

"Mom, you're freaking me out," I said.

"Oh, heavens. We can't have that," she said sarcastically. "Let me see the back of your neck. It looks like you have some kind of bite."

It was funny what concerned parents. When we were out of the house all day, unsupervised, they weren't worried about child abductors or rabid dogs. But insects? That was a whole different story.

That same night Ilene discovered a wood tick on Kenny's neck and word spread amongst the families like wildfire. Mrs. M., the nurse, knew a thing or two about Lyme Disease. She suggested we wear white clothing so it would be easier to spot the little black critters. Before you knew it, the guys and I were outfitted in white from head to toe.

Mom was starting to follow the Sox, too, and she offered us a red permanent marker so we could write numbers on the back of our tee shirts. I chose 19, Fred Lynn's number, while Paul scribbled 14 for Jim Rice. Kenny went with 8 for "Yaz," and Matt scrawled 27, the number for Carlton Fisk.

We strutted to the field one gorgeous Saturday morning, looking like milkmen in our brilliant whites. As we began our descent down the clearing, Paul held up a hand. Voices. I craned my neck to get a better view. Three scruffy-looking teens were tossing a baseball around on the field. *Our* field. Two of them were the guys I'd seen while taking my chopper out for a spin. The other one bore a strong resemblance to Paul.

"The 'Big Kids…'" I said in a foreboding tone.

Paul nodded. The one who looked like him suddenly gazed up at us and flashed a wolfish grin.

"What's up, brother? Hey, boys!"

"Chris, what are you guys doing?" Paul asked, heading down towards the field. We took our cue from him and followed close behind.

"Better question—why are you guys dressed like orderlies?" one of the other teens joked. "You come to take Dallas away?"

"Fuck you, Brett," Dallas said with a laugh before whipping the ball at him.

That filled in the picture for me. Brett was the skateboard guy with curly blond hair like Roger Daltrey from The Who. Dallas had sideburns, long dark hair, and a brooding look.

"Seriously, why are you here?" Paul asked. "You guys don't play ball."

"Like hell, we don't. How about a little game? You even got an extra player—the new kid."

"Banana Boy!" Brett exclaimed with a salute.

"Wanna beat it?" Kenny asked under his breath.

"No, let's do this," Paul said, pounding his mitt.

A few minutes later the game was on. Chris was the pitcher, Dallas positioned himself around second base (wearing flip-flops, I might add), and Brett was somewhere between left field and third base. Since we had four on our side, we supplied the catcher—in this case, Matt, who was happy to volunteer. My scouting report had been accurate.

Paul made our batting order, with me leading off. I grabbed a bat and dug in at home plate.

"Overhand or underhand?" Chris joked.

"Just throw," Paul said.

"All right, kid. You ready?" Chris said, peering over his glove.

I tapped home plate with the bat and nodded.

Chris reared back and—*whack*—his fastball drilled me above the left elbow. I dropped the bat and grabbed my throbbing arm. Tears flooded my eyes.

"Jerkoff!" Paul barked at Chris while rushing to my side.

"Swear to God, wasn't trying to hit him," Chris said, holding up his hands innocently. "You okay, kid?"

I gritted my teeth so hard I couldn't speak. Paul blocked Chris's view and checked out my arm.

"I know that hurts like a sonofabitch, but never let them see you cry," he said.

I shook out my arm and took a deep breath. The pain reminded me of a wasp sting, but I'd live.

"You can do this, right?" he asked.

"Yeah, I'm okay," I said, stepping back up to the plate. I gripped the bat and stared back at Chris.

"You good?" he asked.

I nodded and tapped the plate again, this time with more force. If this was a Hollywood movie, you know how things would play out. I'd smash the next pitch over Dallas's head. Dallas might even trip on the berm as he turned to track the ball and then my teammates would holler as I hustled around the bases for a homer.

But this was real life. After taking two balls outside, I got under a fastball down the middle of the plate and popped it weakly to Chris. That's pretty much the story of the game. The "Big Kids" had too much power and speed. We were down something like 7 to 2 before the older guys said they were hungry. As we picked up our gear, they wanted to know my real name.

"Jay," I said.

"Like the J. Geils Band?" Dallas asked.

"Yeah, kinda like that."

"'Banana Boy' still sounds better to me," Brett said.

"Is that because of my chopper?" I asked.

"Maybe," said Brett. "Or it could be your blond hair and long face."

"Long face—yeah, right," I protested, shaking my head.

"You guys hearing this?" Dallas scoffed. "It's gotta be the first time in history a dude's upset about being called 'long.'"

The guys laughed and I finally caught on. I wasn't in Pennsylvania anymore, that was for sure. I soon found out my pals already had nicknames. Kenny was "Nature Boy" because he looked like a woodland creature. Matt was "Mocha" for obvious reasons, I guessed. Paul had been dubbed "Cracker" because of the expression "Pauly wanna cracker?"

Maybe "Banana Boy" wasn't so bad.

14

Despite our rocky start and age differences, Brett invited all of us over to his house after the game. His parents weren't home, which was probably a good thing. Chris flipped on the family stereo and found WAAF at the end of the FM dial. Aerosmith's "Sweet Emotion" blasted through the speakers. Dallas popped a Marlboro into his mouth and held the pack out toward us. We shook our heads and he shrugged. Brett, meanwhile, was busy being the host in the kitchen. He tossed a cold six-pack of Coke on the counter, and then, using a switchblade, ripped open packages of deli meat, various kinds of cheese, and chips. He returned to the fridge and grabbed an armful of condiments in one hand. With his other hand, he gulped from an open bottle of Chablis.

"Alkie!" Dallas called out from across the room.

Brett wiped his mouth and shot him the middle finger. Satisfied with his spread, he called us over for the grub.

"Dig in, boys!" he roared.

We didn't need to be told twice. Each of us had worked up an appetite and everything was devoured in seconds. After lunch, Brett gave us a tour of his house. The most interesting thing was his parents' waterbed. He even let us each have a turn flopping around on it. Meanwhile, Chris flipped through an issue of *Playboy* he found on a night table. He came to the centerfold in the middle of the magazine and let it fall open.

"Go ahead fellas, take a gander. That's what 'beaver' looks like."

Matt's eyes grew wide. He reached out for the magazine, but Chris snatched it back. "Uh-uh, Mocha. Look, don't touch."

It wasn't all gutter talk and nonsense. In the basement, there was a ping-pong table and an air hockey machine. Brett also showed us his collection of Wacky Pack stickers and a few baseball-themed board games, including Strat-O-Matic and APBA. Although the rules were different, they both featured dice, markers, and player cards—which were based on actual statistics. You could tell by looking at certain numbers which roll of the dice would produce a home run, a hit-by-pitch, or an out.

As the guys and I became more engrossed in all the player cards, the "Big Kids" called us "dweebs" and went outside. They were doing something far more productive like throwing firecrackers at one another.

"We gotta get these games," Paul said. "Perfect for a rainy day."

Just as we finished reading the instructions and started to set up the game board, Brett opened the basement door.

"Hey girls, I just looked at my watch. You need to hit the road. My old man's gonna be back from work soon."

"Can we borrow this game?" Paul asked.

"Yeah, I don't give a shit. Just haul ass," Brett said, gesturing for us to hurry up.

A few minutes later, as we sauntered up the incline from Brett's house, someone near the top of the hill began a descent toward us on a bicycle.

"Here comes trouble," Matt said.

A young woman, the same one I'd seen walking down the hill a few days earlier, slowed her red Schwinn.

"There you are," she said.

"What is it, Kelly?" Kenny asked.

My hunch had been correct. It was the famous Kelly DeSantos.

"You didn't hear the bell?" she said, encircling us, like a shark sizing up prey.

"No, we were inside Brett's house and lost track of time," Kenny explained.

"Great. Mom and Dad will love that," she said before glancing my way. "Is this the new kid?"

"His name's Jay," Paul said.

"Jay? Like the bird?" Kelly asked.

"No one ever gets your name," Kenny said, giving me a playful shove.

I was quiet, thinking of something clever to say.

"Does he talk? Or is he, like, a foreigner?" Kelly continued.

"I'm American," I said. So much for being clever. The guys burst out laughing.

"Okay, 'American.' Nice to know ya," Kelly said with a smirk before pedaling back up the hill.

15

One Saturday afternoon in June, I was upstairs in my room reading a *Thor* comic book when the phone rang. Dad took the call and while I couldn't exactly decipher his words, I could tell he was exchanging pleasantries with someone. When he hung up, he and Mom had a brief discussion, and then I heard him climbing up the stairs. Within seconds there was a knock on my door. Dad poked his head in.

"Hey, Kiddo. Got a minute?"

"Sure," I said, lowering my comic book.

"Mary Monetti just called. She said Matt would like to invite you to their house for a sleepover tonight," he said.

I tossed *Thor* aside and sat up. "Aw, cool. Can I?"

Dad sat on my bed. "Well, how do you feel about it?"

"Fine," I shrugged. "I went to sleepovers back in Pennsylvania."

"Sure," he continued. "But this is a little different…"

"Why?" I asked, although I already had a feeling what he was going to say.

"Well, let me put it this way," Dad said. "Back in my day, it wasn't something that happened often. You know, a white boy sleeping over at a Black boy's house, or vice-versa."

"I thought we weren't supposed to talk about skin color," I said.

"No, we shouldn't. I just wanted to see if you're comfortable with it."

"I am," I said. "So, is that it?"

"I suppose," Dad said, still wrestling with something. "It's just sometimes one doesn't know how people are going to react."

I wondered which people he was referring to. Maybe they were closer than I knew.

"No, I guess one doesn't," I said. "So, what time should I head over there?"

16

I arrived at the Monetti's house in time for dinner. Mrs. M. cooked cheeseburgers for Matt and me and served them with beans, tater tots, and salad. After we finished our meal, she told us to just leave the cups and plates in the kitchen sink. My folks had reminded me about 28 times to thank her, so I made sure I told her how good everything was and how much I appreciated the dinner and the invitation. She replied, "No worries, doll," which caused Matt to roll his eyes as we headed up to his bedroom.

Although Matt was a baseball fan, his real passion was hockey. He had a matching Boston Bruins pillow and bedspread. Above his headboard, there was an autographed Bobby Orr poster. Matt's room had a similar layout to mine, but his had an extra window. I noticed I could see my house across the street and Kenny's house next door.

"How come you get an extra window?" I asked.

"I don't know," he said, changing his voice to sound like Vincent Price. "All the better to spy on you with."

Matt put the Beatles "Revolver" album on his turntable and tapped on his thigh to keep the beat. I looked at his record collection, which was a lot more impressive than mine.

"Hey, I'm sorry about what happened with your dad," I said.

"Which one?" he joked.

"The one who passed away."

"Ah, thanks, man. Yeah, cancer's a bitch." he said.

"How about your other—what did you call it—biological father?"

Matt shrugged. "Canada, last I heard."

"Do you ever think about connecting with him?"

"Not until I'm 18. That's what the agreement says. We'll see."

There was an awkward silence.

"Since we're getting all deep, have you lost anyone?" he asked.

"Yeah, three grandparents. My mom's mother is still alive," I said.

"You go to the funerals?" Matt asked.

"Nope. I thought it was because it was too much money, but Mom said it's because my dad doesn't want us to see him get all emotional."

"Parents," Matt said, rolling his eyes. "Always keeping stuff from us. I think my mom's bopping my uncle."

"No way," I said.

"Come with me," he said, hopping to his feet. "Be the lookout."

Matt opened his door, and I followed him out of the room. He glanced down the stairwell to make sure the coast was clear and then trotted into his mother's bedroom. I waited in the upstairs hallway while he rummaged around somewhere. Seconds later he reappeared.

"Catch!" he said, flinging a small, flat, rubbery object to me.

I caught it and took a closer look. It resembled a tiny rubber frisbee.

"What is it?" I asked.

"A diaphragm," he said.

"A what?" I asked.

"You know. A birth control device," he explained. "It's like a shield, so the little army of men can't get to the prize."

"Ewww," I said, tossing it right back to him.

He snorted in laughter as I wiped my hands on my pants.

"Matt? Jay?" Mrs. M. shouted from the bottom of the stairs.

"Shit," Matt said under his breath before disappearing.

"Hi, Mrs. M.," I said, realizing I was looking at her in a different light.

"Where's Matthew?" she asked.

"Um, in the bathroom I think," I replied.

"Do you boys want any ice cream?" She asked.

"Ahh…" I hesitated, not sure if I had an appetite.

"Sure, Mom," Matt said, appearing by my side. "Sounds delicious."

An hour later, after we'd finished off our chocolate fudge sundaes, Matt and I reclined on the floor and watched the *Rockford Files* on his family room TV. Mrs. M. told us she'd had a long day, wished us a good night, and added the usual parental footnote— "Don't stay up too late." Matt assured her we wouldn't but didn't sound convincing. A minute later he was in the kitchen rifling through cabinets and drawers.

"Now what?" I asked. "You gonna show me rubbers?"

He laughed and pulled out a pack of Winston cigarettes.

"Care for a smoke?" he said, now imitating James Bond.

"Your mom smokes?" I asked.

"She used to, but not this brand," Matt said. "More evidence to support my theory about her and my uncle."

"Right," I said, looking back to a scene in the show where Jim Rockford was trying to get a straight answer from Angel.

"So, seeing Dallas the other day got me thinking. You wanna try it?"

"No, thanks," I said. "Weren't we just talking about cancer?"

"Just *one*. Outside." he insisted.

"I'm fine," I said.

"Come on. It won't kill ya," Matt persisted.

"If my dad finds out, it might," I said.

He stared at me and held open his hands. Finally, I just shrugged.

Moments later we were in the dark woods between the back of Matt and Kenny's properties. Matt had snagged one cigarette along with a lighter. He lit it up, inhaled, and passed it to me.

"Did you know in England they call these 'fags?'" he asked.

"Nope," I said.

"Yup. So, take a drag of the fag," he said, cackling to himself.

I took it and inhaled. It felt like somebody had pumped car exhaust into my mouth. I coughed twice and Matt snorted laughter.

"Your face!" he shrieked, pointing.

"Yeah, my face. All right, I tried it," I said and headed back to his house.

"Lightweight," he said, taking another puff. "Leave the door unlocked.

The next morning, I strolled down Matt's long driveway toward my house. Mrs. M. hadn't said anything at breakfast about doors opening or closing the previous night. Nor had she mentioned that either of us smelled like smoke. My mother, on the other hand, had a nose like a basset hound. I was wondering if I should take a detour around the block when—

"Hey, American..."

I turned to see Kelly standing beside her mailbox, a newspaper in hand.

"Hey, Kelly," I said, sounding a little too neighborly.

"You remembered my name," she said.

"Not that hard."

"Would you prefer I call you 'Jay?'"

"Seems to work for most people," I said.

"All right, Jay," she said with a grin. "You guys have a fun sleepover?"

"Um, yeah," I said, caught off guard. "How'd you know?"

"My mom thinks she saw you and Matt smoking last night."

"Oh yeah? Where?" I said, realizing I was hardly issuing a denial.

"Out in the woods. The thing is, it did sort of look like you two," she said, sounding like Nancy Drew.

"Interesting...*smoking*?" I wondered. "Hey, I should probably get—"

"For what it's worth, I told her it wasn't you. She wasn't wearing her contacts, so she believed me."

"Thanks," I said. "I guess I owe you one."

"Don't mention it," she said. "So, did the guys tell you about 'neighborhood games?'"

"No, what's that?" I asked.

"Ask them," she said, and then her voice changed. "It's a good way for all of us to...get to know each other. You know what I mean?"

I did. "Sounds fun," I said, my mouth suddenly dry.

"It can be," she said with a grin, before flipping her hair and starting back down her drive. "Catch ya 'round, Jay."

You can bet I asked my friends about "neighborhood games." I wanted to know everything. The guys took turns telling me it was a Moss Hill tradition, dating back to the days when Paul's oldest brother, Tony, was in grade school. It was Mrs. Boucher, who taught the original neighbor kids how to play the games, which included old-time favorites like "Kick the Can" and "Capture the Flag."

According to Paul, the games usually started after dinner and went on until dark, which meant they could last three to four hours. Without revealing my ulterior motive, I suggested we give them another trial run. The guys all agreed, and we decided on the following Friday at 6:30 in the circle by Boucher's house. At that point, it was just a matter of spreading the word.

When Friday evening rolled around, we had a good-sized turnout—over a dozen boys and girls from various age groups, including Chris, Dallas, and Brett. I even talked Justine into playing. Most of the participants were from Moss Hill and vicinity, but others came from surrounding neighborhoods, including a girl named Maura who used to be in Kelly's seventh-grade class. And speaking of Kelly, she was the last to arrive. It was hard not to stare. Not just for me, but all the boys.

On her way to greet Maura, she whispered to me. "Nicely done, Jay." While I tried to remain cool, I noticed Matt raise an eyebrow at me.

Since Chris was the oldest, he decided we would play 'Kick the Can.' After taking a few minutes to explain the rules, he brought out a can and a handful of sticks. Everyone 12 and over would choose one stick. Whoever drew the short stick would have to start the game as the 'spotter.' Not only did the spotter have to search for people, but he or she had to holler out the names and locations of the "hiders." Once the person hiding was called out, they became a "prisoner" and had to go sit inside a large chalk-drawn circle (aka the "jail") near the can. You couldn't be a pushover if you were a spotter—you needed to be alert, have good eyes, and run fast.

Brett drew the short stick in the opening round, and of course, there were all sorts of jokes and jabs from Chris and Dallas about having the "shorty." He started to reply, but to his credit, thought better of it with the youngsters around.

"All right, good people! Take your positions!" he shouted.

When everyone was ready in their sprinter stance, Brett stepped to the nearest tree, and started the countdown…"30…29…28…"

By the time he reached 15, mostly everyone was out of sight. Some of the neighborhood dogs barked at the commotion. When Brett hit zero, he pushed away from the tree and set off to find the hiders.

"Ready or not, here I come!" he shouted like a demon.

Within ten minutes, he had caught more than half the group, including Kelly. I could see him from my hiding spot behind a log pile. I had been watching and knew he was a bit of a gambler, meaning he would stray from the can. When he wandered off in the opposite direction, I sprinted out of my hiding place. Kelly cheered me on excitedly. As Brett realized what was happening, he dashed back toward the can.

Too late. I beat him there by a foot and kicked the can down the road. Pele would have been proud.

"Damn you, Banana Boy!" he shouted as he went to retrieve the can. All the prisoners, including Kelly, bolted. *"Jailbreak!"* she hollered.

I hightailed it into the woods beyond Paul's house, skidded down an embankment, and stopped in a thicket of trees close to the field. Brett returned the can to its proper spot and began counting down again from 30. To my left, I saw a flash of movement—Kelly.

"My hero!" she whispered, bouncing up and down on the balls of her feet.

"Hey," I said, trying to catch my breath. "Think we're safe here?"

She peeked back at Brett and shook her head.

"We need better cover. Over here," she said, grabbing my hand and leading me behind a big rock.

"That was close," I said, realizing she was still holding my hand.

"I think you should be rewarded," she said.

Before I could respond, she kissed me on the lips. It was soft, sweet, and exhilarating. I kissed her back, closed my eyes, and just as the magic of the moment charged my entire body, there was a familiar voice from nearby.

"Jay?!"

Justine.

"Your sister?" Kelly asked softly.

I nodded and stayed silent. What kind of brother was I?

"*Jay!* I saw you. I think I'm trapped in poison ivy. And something just moved in here," Justine cried.

"You better go," Kelly said, kissing me one more time for good measure.

As difficult as it was, I set off to look for Justine. I found her not far away, frozen in a patch of ivy.

"I'm here, Sis," I said, reassuringly.

I looked around, grabbed a large branch, and beat down the Ivy. Following my instructions, she tiptoed on the same branch until she reached my outstretched hand.

When we entered our house a few minutes later, our expressions couldn't have been more different. She looked miserable and I was on cloud nine. Mom ran a cool bath for Justine and set out a bottle of Calamine lotion. I had a reddish color, too, but it was an entirely different reaction to the evening's events.

All I wanted to do was replay the events with Kelly. I had kissed a girl before in a game of "Truth or Dare," but I had never kissed a girl like *that*—meaning as beautiful as Kelly, but also in that *way*, with such passion.

My heart raced and I felt like my stomach was going to float out of my body. It must have been 3 a.m. before I finally nodded off.

19

The next morning, since I was too young for coffee, I drank a Carnation Instant Breakfast at the kitchen counter. With my adrenaline levels returning to normal, seeds of doubt entered my mind. What if the night before was a fluke? A one-time, spur-of-the-moment thing? Part of me wanted to tell everyone, but I also knew I could tell no one. I was a little concerned about what Kenny would think, but if *Chip* found out…

Just then the phone on the wall beside me rang. I tugged the receiver off its base and answered.

"Jay?" Kelly said.

"Yes," I said, trying to play cool.

"Say you have the wrong number, hang up, and then meet me at my mailbox in five."

"You have the wrong number," I said. "See you soon."

I hung up, realizing I had flubbed my instructions. At least no one in my family overheard. And I didn't mess up the part about meeting Kelly. She had a smirk on her face as I approached her outside.

"You'll never make it as a spy. Were you followed?"

I turned and looked towards my house. The coast was clear.

"No," I said.

"I can see you weren't, Jay," she teased. "You're a fun one, aren't you?"

By this point, I had given up on wondering if I was blushing. Kelly didn't seem to mind. She leaned in and whispered her plan to me. As if reading my mind, she also whispered her Dad was out getting an oil change and would be gone for a while.

It took us about three minutes to arrive at our destination—the stable. Straight down the hill and through the woods we went. Of course, you tend to move faster when you're practically walking on air.

After letting 'Star' nibble some oats out of our hands, Kelly led me to a ladder, and we climbed up to a hay loft. Within seconds we were rolling in the hay, as corny as it sounds. It's hard to call myself a gentleman in this context, so I'll just say it was romantic and daring, and yet we somehow knew when it was time to stop.

I strode up Moss Hill later, alone, but with a spring in my step. As my yard came into view, I noticed Matt leaning against our lamppost. He had something in his hands.

"Well, well…where have you been?" he asked with a raised eyebrow.

"Just took a little walk," I said.

"How come your eyes are red?" he wondered.

"Could be…pollen," I guessed.

"Or maybe *hay* fever?" he suggested.

I shrugged, wondering if he was insinuating something. I nodded to the device he was holding.

"What do you have there?" I asked.

"A new Polaroid camera my uncle gave me," he replied. "Check it out. You just click and shoot."

He aimed the camera at me and pressed a button. Sure enough, there was a click and a flash. The camera spit out a square of glossy paper. Matt pulled it out by the corner and in seconds it developed, right in his hands, into a color photo.

"How cool is this?" Matt asked.

The photo captured my bemused expression, red eyes, and several strands of *hay* on my shoulder.

"It's cool, all right," I said, fearing that Matt was on to me.

"Isn't it?" Matt said. "Imagine the possibilities."

I wasn't sure I wanted to.

20

My 12ᵗʰ birthday was a week later, and my folks gave me the best present I could have imagined: a ticket to my first Red Sox game. To be precise, there were four tickets. Since Mom's arthritis was acting up that morning, I brought Paul as my guest.

The minute we passed through the turnstiles, I discovered there were professional baseball stadiums—and then there was Fenway Park. One thing that always struck me about professional baseball diamonds was how vivid the colors were—from the emerald, green grass to the bleach-white bases. Of course, what made Fenway unique, as most baseball fans know, was the enormous, 37-foot "Green Monster" in left field.

As for the game, the Sox played the Minnesota Twins. All our favorites were in the line-up for the home team and contributed. Fred Lynn made a diving catch in center field and hit a double, while Jim Rice walloped a towering home run over the monster. On the other hand, none of the Sox pitchers could figure out Rod Carew, who was arguably the best hitter in all of baseball.

The only thing that ruined the experience was a couple of stoners in front of us—acting like they were at a 'Deep Purple' concert. They passed a joint back and forth and shouted gibberish like "Carew the Jew!" By the seventh inning, Dad couldn't take it anymore, and we were out of the park before the crowd finished "Take Me Out to the Ballgame."

I was glad Paul joined me because the following week he was off to a baseball camp. This just happened to overlap with Matt going to a hockey camp, which coincided with Kenny and Kelly going to camp in the Berkshires.

Justine was happy to have me around and for the next few days, we played two-square in our driveway, rode our bikes up and down the street, and ran through our backyard sprinkler to cool down. That's what families did when they didn't have a pool.

When Mom took Justine along for her hair appointment one afternoon, I headed down to the hoop near Paul's house with my basketball. I'd been practicing my dribbling in the basement, but my shot needed work. After three misses, I finally sank a bank shot.

"Banana Boy for two!"

I turned to find Dallas and Brett lumbering out of the woods. Dallas scooped me up like a sack of dog food and spun me around. He reeked of marijuana and body odor.

"Playin' with all your friends?" Brett asked, gathering up my swish and bricking a two-footed, two-handed layup off the backboard.

"What are you guys up to?" I asked as Dallas set me down.

"We're thinkin' about swimming in McKelvey's pool," Brett said.

"I take it they're not home," I said.

"Correct-a-*mundo*," Dallas said, imitating "The Fonz" from *Happy Days*.

"Wanna join us?" Brett asked.

Despite a little voice nagging me to decline, I shrugged and picked up my ball. It was the same voice that nagged me about smoking. At some point, I needed to listen to it...

The McKelveys lived up on a hill in the woods behind Brett's house. The pool was in the backyard, surrounded by a high wooden fence. The three of us worked our way to a cluster of pine trees about ten yards from the property.

"There's a gate around to the side. Usually unlocked," Brett said.

"Okay," I said.

"What do you say, Brett? Streak in, streak out?" Dallas said.

"Shit yeah. The only way to go." He winked at Dallas, then turned to me. "You know what streaking is, right?"

I nodded. It was stripping down to your birthday suit and running to, or through, something to make a scene. There was even a streaker at the Academy Awards a few years back.

"All right let's do it," Brett said, clapping for emphasis. "We each find a tree and get outta our clothes. I'll count down, just like 'Kick the Can.' When I hit zero, we bolt to the side gate."

The three of us scattered to find our own personal changing tree. I went behind a large oak and stripped down.

"10...9...8..." Brett began.

Three seconds and I was out of my clothes.

"7...6...5..."

Three more and I hung clothes on a branch.

"4...3...2..."

I was ready.

"And *one*! Let's go!" Brett cried.

I sprinted towards McKelvey's backyard in all my glory, as the saying goes. Just then ol' man McKelvey himself opened the pool gate with a large water pitcher, whistling a merry tune. I froze in my tracks.

Mr. McKelvey's jaw dropped when he saw me. And then his arms did, too. Water cascaded onto his work boots.

"Good lawhhhd, young man!" he shouted.

I pivoted, just in time to see Brett and Dallas, fully clothed, racing with *my* clothes toward Paul's house.

"Assholes!" I yelled, giving chase.

As they vanished in the distance, I cursed myself—wondering why I trusted those two delinquents. I felt myself start to tear up in frustration, but then I recalled Paul's words— "Never let them see you cry." Exhausted and exposed, I ducked behind an old fern and plotted my next move. Did I take a chance running home? Or should I look for something on a nearby laundry line to steal? Suddenly, there was a shuffle of leaves off to my left. Brett and Dallas.

"It's okay, BB," Brett said.

"We ain't *that* cold," Dallas said, tossing my clothes to me.

"You sure can haul ass, though," Brett said.

"Yeah, thanks. Real funny, guys," I said, putting my clothes on.

You'd think anyone with an ounce of common sense would have marched home and never talked to these guys again. Well, maybe common sense was overrated.

A few minutes later I was sitting on a stool in Brett's kitchen, sipping from a can of A&W root beer and munching on some deli meat. Dallas snatched up the kitchen telephone.

"Who wants pizza?" he asked with a mischievous grin.

"Come on man, not again," Brett pleaded. "They're gonna trace the number."

Dallas ignored him and punched in a number by heart. On the other end, a woman said, "Pizza Palace."

"Yes, I'd like to order three large pizzas, please," said Dallas. "All sausage."

Brett shook his head in dismay.

"Yes, the name's Dick," Dallas continued. "D-I-C-K LaVurr. The number is—"

He made a curious face and then set the receiver down in the cradle. "She hung up."

"No, shit…*really*?" Brett said sarcastically.

Before I left his house that afternoon, Brett offered me a peace token—a large assortment of *Playboy* photos, including some centerfold pictorials. I accepted them eagerly, with a quick "thanks" before the "Gallant" voice in my head could issue another warning.

I entered my house with the stash tucked under my arm and quietly tiptoed past Mom, who was napping on the family room couch. Dad was at work, and Justine was out of sight, so I hurried up to my room.

The next hour or so I browsed through Brett's collection. It didn't take me long to conclude that "Miss May" of 1974 was my favorite. Her name was Stacy, she dotted her 'i's' with hearts, and her turn-offs were rude people.

Of course, I needed a safe place to hide my stash. I thought about putting them under my mattress, but that would be an obvious place for Mom or an experienced housekeeper like Diane to look. Then I zeroed in on a little door in the corner of my room. I knew from my first day in the house that it opened to a small attic space above the garage. I pulled the knob, peered inside, and was hit with a blast of hot, dry, insulated air. There were rows of planks that covered insulation, stretching back into darkness. So many planks. So many options.

Hello, hiding place.

21

The guys and I reunited in the field the following Monday. Everyone had stories to share. Paul met Jim Bouton at his baseball camp and admitted he was a decent guy, considering he was once a Yankee. Matt skated with Phil and Tony Esposito. Kenny, meanwhile, went water skiing and saw James Taylor in concert.

I wanted to ask Kenny about Kelly but didn't want to appear too eager. The guys were curious about my week, and I relayed that it was uneventful. There was no way in hell I was going to tell them about my exploits with Brett and Dallas.

After a few days of not seeing or hearing from Kelly, I grew restless. I wondered if she had mentioned our so-called involvement to anyone. If so, had she been warned to keep away? Or was she waiting for me to initiate our next rendezvous? After all, I was the guy.

As I lay in bed one night with my mind going in all sorts of directions, I decided to be bold. I threw on some clothes, slipped into my shoes, and tiptoed downstairs.

A moment later I was outside. The night was quiet, but not dark enough for my liking. The full moon illuminated the sky and most of the houses had their streetlights on. I crossed the road and stopped by a tree on the DeSantos property.

"What are ya doing?" A voice asked.

I whirled around and discovered Matt, dressed in black from head to toe.

"Jesus, you scared the crap outta me," I said, my heart thumping. "What are you doing up? And in a Cat-Burglar suit, by the way?"

"I told you I can see everything from my room," Matt said. "Looks like a stealth mission is underway. Give me the 411…you going to visit Kelly?"

"Why do you say that?" I asked.

"Just had a hunch, because ya know, hay is for horses."

"All right, congrats, 'Columbo,'" I said.

"How far did you get with her? First base?"

"Listen, it doesn't matter—"

"Second? She does have some ripe looking tatas," Matt said, forming shapes with his hands.

"Matt, enough," I said.

"Let me go with you," he said. "Maybe she'll be in something revealing, you know."

He held up his camera and made a "click-click" sound. I rolled my eyes.

"No, no '*click-click*.' Just a quick hello and not a word to *anyone*."

"Quick hello. Got it. Scout's honor," he said, holding up his right hand.

We ducked into the woods and cut across the side lawn on the west side of the DeSantos property. I approached Kelly's bedroom window and noticed the lights inside were off.

"It's dark. Maybe we should—"

"Stop being a pansy," Matt said and then tapped on the glass.

The blinds drew back, and the window slid open. Kelly leaned out wearing an oversized "Sonny and Cher" tee shirt.

"Hey, you," she said before noticing Matt and changing her tone. "What's he doing here?"

"Nice to see you, too," Matt deadpanned.

"Just wanted to say a quick 'hello,'" I said. "How was the vacation?"

"It was fine. Can we maybe catch up later?"

"Sure, no problem," I said.

"Don't you guys want a picture?" Matt said, holding up a new camera.

Just then the front door of the house swung open, and the porch lights flashed on.

"Who's out there?!" Chip hollered, voice booming through the night.

"You guys need to go, like *now*," Kelly whispered.

Matt and I backed away from the window and hightailed it into the woods.

"I'm gonna call the cops unless you show yourself. Or heck, maybe I'll get my damn gun!" Chip shouted.

Matt and I stood our ground. While I pointed home, he shook his head, dropped the camera, and stepped out onto the lawn.

"It's Matt Monetti, sir."

"Matt? What's going on out here? Who else is with you?"

Matt remained quiet. He was taking one for the team.

"I asked, 'Who else is with you?' Do you want me to go wake your mother?"

Although I was terrified, I couldn't leave Matt hanging.

"Coming out!" I exclaimed, holding up my hands. I stepped into the light next to Matt.

Chip was standing inside the door frame, holding a wooden baseball bat, and wearing nothing but boxer shorts with red hearts.

"It's me, Mr. DeSantos," I said.

"What in God's name…*Jayson*," he said with disgust.

He stared at both of us for what seemed like an eternity.

"I can explain, sir…" I began.

"We were just going to—" Matt interrupted.

"I don't want to hear it!" Chip snapped.

Matt and I shut our mouths, while Chip closed his eyes. I hoped he was praying. If he wasn't going to listen to us, maybe he would listen to God.

"Get on home, both of you," Chip finally said, opening his eyes. As we slowly backed away, he slammed the front door so hard that the foundation of the house shook.

22

The next day we were scheduled for our last family outing of the summer—the New England Aquarium. I knew the right thing to do was tell Mom and Dad about the events from the night before. But I also knew coming clean would derail our plans, and Justine and I had been looking forward to this trip more than any other. My compromise was to tell my folks after we had returned home.

It must have been the full moon because crazy things seemed to be happening everywhere. On the way to the Aquarium, I noticed graffiti of a penis scrawled on a bus bench. A few blocks down the road we passed a man dressed like an American Indian screaming to anyone who would listen: *"I am the son of the living God!"*

The Aquarium was great and all that—the electric eels, sting rays, and sharks sent chills down our spine—but the most unnerving sight came after our visit. As Dad pulled out of the parking garage into bottle-necked traffic, we noticed a group of white teenagers—at least a dozen—congregating across the street. They were shouting at a school bus full of Black children at a traffic light.

"Go back to fuckin' Roxbury!" One of the white guys hollered from the sidewalk.

It looked like the children inside the bus were wearing summer camp uniforms. They raised their voices and gave it right back.

"Do you want to pull over so I can call the police?" Mom asked.

"No honey, stay inside. The driver probably has a radio," Dad explained.

As the tension escalated, the guy who looked like the ringleader began pushing the side of the bus. Soon some of his delinquent friends joined him. The bus began rocking, almost going up on two wheels. The driver, an old Black man in his 60s, yelled and honked his horn, maybe as a plea for help. The angry passengers began throwing trash out the open windows.

At last, the traffic signal turned green, and the driver accelerated through the intersection. One of the teens picked up a rock and threw it at the back of the bus. CLANK! It missed the rear window but left a dent in the emergency exit door.

Dad took his foot off the brake and merged into traffic.

"Why were the white guys getting so violent?" Justine asked.

"Well, we don't know what started it," Dad said.

Well, we kinda do I thought, but I didn't say it.

"Everyone okay back there?" Mom asked.

I looked down and noticed Justine was gripping my arm.

"Yeah," I said.

"I know it might not sound nice, but should we feel lucky that we're not Black?" Justine asked.

"Oh, Justine, honey," Mom said. "Let's try to put that out of our thoughts for now. Maybe we can discuss it later."

"But it might not be in my thoughts later. I mean, we just saw it," she said.

Mom glanced at Dad, and he shrugged. He was more focused on merging onto the Mass Pike entrance.

"The way I see it, we're all God's children. Different qualities make us unique. We're all blessed in our own way," Mom said.

"But would the passengers on that bus feel blessed?" Justine wondered. "They may go through life wondering if a person who isn't their color is going to like them or not."

So much for everyone being "okay." My sister had just seen a snapshot of race relations in Boston—and too many other places in our country. Dad tuned back into the conversation and assured Justine that her feelings and questions were understandable. However, with everyone still a little unnerved, it would be better to continue the conversation later with a fresh perspective. That's when it occurred to me that my parents often played their version of Kick the Can—punting uncomfortable discussions down the road, so to speak.

Unfortunately, I couldn't do the same with my situation. I needed to fess up about the previous night's encounter with Mr. DeSantos. As Dad drove up Moss Hill, I glanced at Monetti's house. I wondered if Matt had already told his mom and if he'd received any kind of punishment.

After we made our way inside our house and began hanging up our jackets, I cleared my throat.

"Hey, Dad? Mom? Can I talk to you for a second?"

Just then the phone rang. Mom held up a finger and hurried to the kitchen. She picked up the receiver with a cheery hello. It wasn't long, however, before her voice tightened and she looked my way.

"I see, Chip," she said. "Okay, thank you."

Mom looked at Justine.

"Justine, sweetheart, please go upstairs and change into your jammies, I'll come up in a while," Mom said.

"What about Jay?" Justine asked.

"He'll be up later," Mom said. "Right now, he's going to have an important chat with your father and me."

"Uh-oh," Justine said, before disappearing.

Uh-oh was right. I sat in the nearest chair and awaited my fate.

23

The verdict was short but not so sweet. I was grounded for a week. Technically, it was a "work week," from Monday morning until the following Friday night—which meant Saturday morning when you got right down to it. Not great, but better than your standard seven-day suspension.

After Dad left for work on Monday morning, I enlisted Justine as a spy to find out if Matt was disciplined (I cleverly dropped a note in a sock down the laundry chute). Ever dependable, she kept things hushed and reported back, sliding a note under my bedroom door, that he wasn't. If I had to guess, he told his mom that he saw me heading over to Kelly's and wanted to tag along. And to think I could have slipped out of the woods and left him alone to deal with Chip. I instantly thought of the saying "No good deed goes unpunished."

The rest of the day dragged on while I took up various positions in my bedroom, feeling like a caged bird. I turned on my clock radio and flipped through various pop stations to cheer me up. As I lay on my floor, I strangely recalled Dad telling me about the origin of our family name. I'm pretty sure he said Zimmerman was German for "room man." Well, that pretty much described me and my predicament.

As the hours crept past, I flipped through my various books and magazines and yes, my new stash of photos—but only when I could tell no one was home. If my family was around, I turned to "safe" reading, like old issues of *Highlights* magazine. I had outgrown it, but I still had my favorite parts like "The Timbertoes," "Hidden Pictures," and "Goofus and Gallant." The latter was a cartoon about two boys who were like night and day—like the *Odd Couple* but for kids. Gallant was a perfect little boy who said "please" and "thanks," and did things like hold the door open for old ladies and pick up trash off the ground. On the other hand, Goofus was pretty much a slob, who only looked out for himself. I had to admit, though, some of the stuff he did would crack me up. It dawned on me that I'd been a lot more like Goofus since our move than Gallant.

I practiced tricks with my yo-yo and shuffled my new deck of cards (another birthday present) to pass the time. Mostly, though, I closed the shades in my bedroom and put a pillow over my head. It was tough to see my friends running around the neighborhood, especially with their caps and mitts on.

Dad would occasionally check in and ask if I wanted to read the newspaper, especially the sports pages because he knew I liked to check out the box scores. One afternoon, though, he began a lecture about consequences having "real life" implications. As I began to tune out, figuring it was nothing I hadn't heard before, he hit me with the hook. Ed had bought tickets for his three sons to attend an auto show in Boston that evening. And who were the special guests at the show? None other than the "Gold Dust Twins."

After Dad left with a "you made your own bed" look, my heart sank. *Thud.* Pretty soon my stomach hurt. On my way back from the bathroom I caught a glance of Kelly through our guest room window. She was standing by her mailbox, sorting envelopes. I lifted the window, yanked a white case off a pillow from the nearby bed, and waved it frantically outside. It took a few seconds, but my improvised flag caught her eye.

"Are you surrendering?" she asked.

I held up one index finger to my lips for "shush" and the other to show "one second." I dashed back to my room and found a piece of notebook paper and a marker. I scribbled "SO SORRY/MISS YOU," raced back to the window, and held it up for her to read. She crossed into our driveway, squinted, and held up her hands. No good. I quickly folded the page into a paper airplane—classroom experience coming into play—and flung it out the window. The note soared and landed gently at her feet.

Kelly picked it up, unfolded the flaps, and read my message.

"It's okay," she said to me, oddly reserved. "Let's catch up later."

I gave her a thumbs up and watched as she put my note on top of her mail and walked back into her garage. I may have been infatuated with Miss May, but it was nothing compared to the feelings I'd developed for Miss Across-the-Street. But then reality hit. Kelly crumpled up my note and tossed it in a trash bin! In a distant corner of my mind, I heard Paul's voice ("Discard!"). The DeSantos garage door then descended and landed with a *thud.*

Thud, thud. As they say in boxing, I had been hit with the ol' one-two.

24

The next morning, I lay in bed, thirsty and hungry, but with no desire to move. I had no desire to do *anything*, not even look at my clock. It had been a restless night and I wasn't sure what hurt more—my head or my heart. Just then there was a light knock on my door.

"Still sleeping," I said.

"You're not sleeping if you're talking to me," said a familiar voice.

"Paul?" I mumbled, sitting up. "Come on in."

The door swung open, and Paul entered.

"Jeez, you look like shit," he said.

"What do you expect? I haven't seen the sun in days," I said, leaning back to roll up my window shade. "What day is it?"

"Saturday," he said.

"Wait. So that means I'm—"

"A free man. Your dad said it was cool for me to come up."

I rubbed my eyes and tried to get my bearings.

"How was the car show?" I asked.

"It sucked," he said with a miserable expression.

"You're full of it," I said, throwing a pillow at him.

Paul broke into a grin and gave me the scoop. He told me everything about Jim and Fred, from what they wore to how they acted. He then took a small piece of white paper out of his pocket.

"Freddy wanted me to give it to you," he said, passing me the paper.

I glanced at it and my heart started racing. It was Fred Lynn's autograph, and he'd also scrawled #19 under his name.

"No way!" I cried, jumping off the bed. "My man! You're the best!"

I hugged Paul about five times and then tacked the paper to a small bulletin board that Mom had attached to the wall above my desk. When I looked back at him, however, his smile had disappeared.

"What's wrong?" I asked.

"You might want to sit down for this," he cautioned.

"Okay," I said, taking a seat on the edge of my bed.

"So…you know how Matt has that fancy new camera?"

"Yeah. Did he ever get it back after our run-in with Chip?"

"Yeah, he did. For better or worse," Paul said.

"What do you mean?" I asked.

"Well…" he sighed and took an Instamatic photograph out of his pocket. "Sorry, man, but I thought I should be the one to show you."

He handed me the photo and every organ in my body seemed to freeze.

"Kelly?" It was like her name got stuck in my throat.

Paul nodded. "And Dallas. Matt followed them."

Kelly and Dallas. There they were seated on a motorbike together, somewhere in the woods near the field. Kelly in front, Dallas behind her. He was kissing her neck, his hands inside her shirt.

"When?" I asked as if it mattered.

"A couple of days ago, I guess," Paul said.

I handed the photo back to him, collapsed back onto my mattress, and stared up at the ceiling. Paul gave my shoulder a tap.

"Women…ya know?"

"Yeah," I said.

But I really didn't.

Part Two: Middle

25

I felt like a fool. The first day of middle school I was in the principal's office before I'd even made it to my classroom. The worst part? I was sitting next to Kelly. We looked down at our shoes while Principal Lucero leaned against his desk, muscular arms crossed, waiting for an explanation. He was tall and well-built, with dark wavy hair. He handed me a clean tissue.

"You still have a little…" he said, putting his finger to his face, showing where I should dab.

As the British might say, the entire morning had been a "bloody mess." More to the point, *I* was the bloody mess. It had all started like a normal day; well, normal for the first day of school at least. Kenny, Matt, and I met up at our bus stop at the bottom of Moss Hill, with new clothes, new haircuts, and new backpacks. Kenny and Matt were still going to Winnicott as sixth graders now, but we would ride the same bus because Evergreen Middle School was right across the street. The district had started combining bus routes during the "Gas Crisis" to conserve fuel and save on driver salaries. Even though the crisis appeared to be over, reconfiguring transportation was not a priority for our district's superintendent.

Since I'd been grounded for the last week of summer, I hadn't seen much of Kenny at all. If he knew something was going on between his sister and me, he hadn't addressed it. And yet that morning, he seemed uncharacteristically low-key. I wondered if someone had spilled the beans. I knew Paul wouldn't. Besides, he was in Rhode Island for a funeral. Matt? That was a different story.

Meanwhile, I cast my eyes towards Kelly who was on the opposite side of the street. I tried not to look angry, or sad. I just looked. She was chatting with her friend Maura, who seemed to look my way. Were they talking about me?

I was startled out of my thoughts as a shiny yellow school bus rolled to a stop beside me. The doors swung open with a hiss, and everyone lined up. The guys and I lumbered past a female driver and strode to the back of the bus. All the seats were available because we were the first stop on the route. Matt sat in the last row, and I took the seat in front of him. Kelly, the old hand at this, plunked down across the aisle from Matt, while Kenny slid into the seat in front of her. Even though all the students had boarded, the bus sat idling. In the visor mirror, I noticed the bus driver peering back at us, smiling.

"What's with driver-lady?" Kelly mumbled.

"You don't recognize me?" The bus driver asked, talking to me.

"Um, not sure," I said. Her voice sounded familiar, but I didn't recognize her face until she lowered her sunglasses. It was Diane, our housekeeper.

"Oh, hi, Diane," I said, sounding surprised and apologetic.

"How are you, kiddo?" she asked.

I flashed a thumbs up and there were a few snickers. Diane lowered her shades and shifted the bus into gear.

"*Hi Diane*," Kenny mimicked under his breath.

"Get up on the wrong side of the bed, Kenny?" I asked.

"Must be nice having a cleaning woman," Kenny said.

"Not exactly breaking news," I replied. "What's goin' on with you?"

Kenny glanced at Kelly and then back at me.

"You weren't gonna tell me?" he asked.

"Tell you what?" I asked.

"About you and my sister?" he said, moving closer. "I had to find out from the gossip chain?"

"Hey, I resemble that remark," Matt interjected.

Well, that solved that mystery.

"All right, touché. But now you know how I felt when I found out about Kelly and Dallas."

Kelly glared at me and then Matt.

"What?" Kenny asked.

"Ask your sister. Apparently, I wasn't good enough," I said.

"Sit down, Kenny. We can talk about it later," I said.

"Screw you," Kenny said, thrusting his finger at my face.

I stood and pushed his hand away, hoping that would be enough to deter him. Instead, it enraged him. He balled up his left fist and took a swing. I pivoted right and the punch deflected off my left shoulder. Feeling more anger than pain, I spun and countered with a right to the sternum that doubled him over.

"Guys!" Matt hollered.

"Stop it!" Maura screamed.

The bus lurched to a stop, and I lost my balance. Bodies were lunging, tumbling, and ducking. Out of nowhere an arm wrapped around my face and jerked me down into the aisle. For a few seconds, there was blackness, and I couldn't breathe.

"Get off him, young lady!" Diane hollered.

Young lady? Oh no.

I was released and as my eyes adjusted, I saw Kelly sliding back into her seat. Her cheeks were red from exertion. Kenny, meanwhile, was trying to catch his breath, tears in his eyes.

"Enough! All of you!" Diane shouted.

Her voice was commanding, and no one moved a muscle. I wiped my nose and saw a line of blood. Diane inspected my face and handed me her bandana. She then leaned over to check on Kenny.

"Looks like you're both gonna live," she said. "At least long enough to talk to the principal."

After hearing various accounts of the morning's events from various parties, Mr. Lucero let Kelly and me know that we were banned from the bus for the rest of the week. It would be up to our parents to get us to and from school. There'd be no detentions or suspensions, but notes would be placed in a discipline file. Mr. Lucero also expected us to apologize to each other, as well as Diane, who was waiting in the outer office.

Kelly and I followed through on his directive and then we were escorted to our classrooms. I handed my new homeroom teacher, Mr. Brennan, a note and, ignoring the stares, took a seat at the desk I'd been assigned. As much as the first-day procedures and protocol were important, I couldn't focus all morning. I had just been in a brawl with my ex-girlfriend (could I even call her that?) and one of my best friends.

After a school fight, there are the inevitable stares and whispers, speculation and exaggeration. It's not *always* a bad thing, because sometimes a fight leads to a certain amount of respect or credibility.

Not in my case, though. Not when the male is involved with a female. Sure, the tussle started between Kenny and me, but once Kelly became involved, that changed the narrative.

I happened to run into my old classmate, Dave, at lunch and he voiced what I imagine everyone was thinking.

"Is it true?" he asked.

"What?" I asked.

"That you got beat up by a girl," Dave said.

"She jumped me—and it was a headlock," I protested, before turning and walking away.

"Okay. How was your summer, by the way?" he asked.

"Fine," I said.

"We could still try doing that handwriting contest if you want," Dave said.

I kept walking, not even sure where I was going.

The one saving grace from the bus fiasco was that Diane called Mom after that afternoon to offer her take. She stressed that I wasn't the instigator—I was just defending myself. She also said that she had applied for a different bus route to avoid any more potential problems.

I went to bed early that evening and Dad arrived home late. I knew after the customary kiss for Mom, there was going to be a conversation. This usually occurred as Dad made a martini to unwind,

As Mom spoke over ice clunking into Dad's glass, I slid my bedroom window up as far as it could go. Even over the crickets' chirping, I could pick up on her words and the undertones of distress. Different subject, but it was reminiscent of our last evening in Pennsylvania.

"Sneaking out at night, now this incident on the bus…" Mom was saying. "Do you think it's these kids he's hanging out with?"

"Well, Paul seems to have a good head on his shoulders," Dad said. "I mean, he could use a haircut, but other than that…"

"I'm not laughing," Mom said.

"All right," Dad sighed. "Should we just move again?"

I sat upright in my bed.

"Would you please be serious? Our son is almost a teenager. That's going to be a lot for me to handle when you're not around."

"He's still adjusting, Louise. We all are," Dad said.

"I understand. But maybe if you took some time to interact with him more it would help. You often say how you wished you were closer to your father, right? Well, here's a chance to grow closer to your son."

Mom's words had hit home. Dad had no reply. As I heard his footsteps on the stairs, I held my breath. I wasn't upset with him, but I just didn't want to explain myself anymore. The day had been long enough. Dad paused at the top of the stairs. I could tell because his shadow blocked the crack of light coming in from under the door.

After a moment, the footsteps resumed, and Dad made his way to his bedroom.

Dad must have taken Mom's words to heart after a good night's sleep. The next week was like a father-son montage from an "ABC Afterschool Special." He asked me to play chess, took me to buy some new Boston merchandise at Herman's Sporting Goods, and invited me to hit golf balls with him at the driving range in town.

One day he asked if I'd like to invite Kenny to see a movie with us.

I told him I'd be fine with it, but I wasn't sure if Kenny was "free"—meaning not grounded. Dad said not to worry, that he'd take care of it.

The next thing I knew, he walked over to the DeSantos home to talk to Chip who was watering his lawn. After a brief discussion, there were smiles, followed by a handshake. A few minutes later, Dad was back and said we were on for the movies later that night. My jaw dropped. This was what Dad did for a living, but I was still shocked. I would bet my baseball card collection that Dad could get a German Shepard to meow like a kitten if you gave him five minutes alone with the two of them.

The film we saw was called *The Other Side of the Mountain*. It was a bit of a downer because it was about this promising female skier named Jill who had a horrible accident. She ended up being paralyzed and just like that, her skiing dreams were shattered.

Dad wanted to see the movie for a couple of reasons: first, because he was a former ski racer and instructor, and second because he had received a nice reply from the real-life Jill after he'd sent her an uplifting letter.

Later that week, Justine complained that she wanted to be part of these excursions, too, so my folks agreed to plan another family outing (but not to Boston). Mom's favorite season was fall, and once the cool crisp air arrived, she was in her element.

"Isn't the foliage beautiful here?" she'd ask, glancing out our kitchen window.

I agreed it was nice to look at, but I never liked autumn. Or was it fall? Why two names? Winter was winter, spring was spring, and summer was summer. It was the only season that didn't know what it wanted to be called. What's more, all those pretty leaves fell to the ground at some point, and it was up to me to rake them up. Let's just say I had issues with the season.

Fortunately, I was given a reprieve from raking one Sunday in late September when my parents woke Justine and me early. They had planned an outing to Old Sturbridge Village, a popular tourist attraction where colonial life was recreated.

After paying our entry fee, we were matched up with a pretty tour guide named "Abigail." She wore a long dress and bonnet and led us on an informational tour of various exhibits. I noticed she didn't have the Boston accent, but she liked to throw around the word "ye" instead of "you."

Of course, Mom ate it all up. She'd inquire about craftsmanship and the tools. I swear, she even had a ten-minute conversation with "Elijah the Blacksmith" on how to forge metal as if this is how he presently made his living. When Mom and Justine moved on with Abigail, Dad and I hung back to chat some more. We discovered "Elijah" was really "Frank Riccardi," an AC/Heating repair specialist from Medford. When Dad mentioned that he might need a heating guy to check our airflow "Elijah/Frank" looked around surreptitiously before reaching below his table and giving Dad a business card.

28

Whenever our family was out in public, Dad was always on his best behavior. And that's what he expected from us. Impressions were important to him.

Back at home, it was often a different story. Dad was consumed a lot—either thinking about his job or taking care of responsibilities around the house. Eventually, work and travel began to require more of his attention and time. It wasn't long before things returned to the status quo. In other words, I had free time on my hands once again. That meant hanging out with the guys.

Paul was happy that I was back in circulation. The Red Sox regular season had ended, and they were headed to the playoffs. We watched every inning together as they swept the Oakland Athletics to win the American League pennant. Boston was going to be playing in a World Series for the first time since the 1967 "Impossible Dream" team. Even a recent convert like me knew they hadn't won the title since 1918—back when Babe Ruth was the star of the local Nine.

Long-time Sox fans like Ed were still pessimistic. They'd had their hopes dashed too many times. Besides, Jim Rice wouldn't play because of a hand injury. And yet some held faith and believed they could defeat the Cincinnati Reds and go all the way (on that note, Dallas bragged that his new girlfriend promised him she'd go "all the way" if the Red Sox won it all. Of course, Brett asked if she had a sister—hah!).

Most baseball fans know how the series turned out. Despite many incredible highs (Game 6, when the Sox tied it on Carbo's homerun, and won it on Fisk's "if it stays fair" liner over the wall in extra innings), there was still a crushing defeat in the end. The Reds won the series four games to three. I'll admit it, I cried like a baby when it was all over. Freddy was not his MVP/Rookie of the Year self. "Yaz" was solid but not spectacular. Tiant was tremendous, but it was asking too much to expect him to win three games in such a short stretch.

All that joy in the region building up to the World Series dissipated overnight and many locals were left stunned, bitter, and angry. This was especially true at school. Disrespect towards students and teachers intensified and the waiting area outside Mr. Lucero's office was always full.

In just a few months, cliques had already formed. For many students, this would define their social status through 12th grade. I imagine the breakdown was the same at our school as it was anywhere in the country: jocks, burnouts, and the regular kinds of kids (like me) who were content to fly under the radar.

Then there were the students who had it rough—those from different ethnic backgrounds, or ones who didn't come from much money. Both the jocks and the burnouts would bully these kids for amusement. A boy in my homeroom, Henry Witherspoon, was often teased for wearing the same hooded sweatshirt every day.

One morning Mr. Brennan postponed our rotations. He gathered us in a circle and spoke solemnly.

"As some of you know, one of your classmates is having a challenging time. Does anyone know who I'm referring to?"

Whether it was too early in the day, a lingering Red Sox depression, or just that no one was in the mood to volunteer, the room remained silent.

"No one knows? I find that hard to believe. This boy has had a rough—"

"—Henry Witherspoon?" I blurted, trying to move things along. There was stunned silence in the room. My classmates shifted uncomfortably.

"Fuck you, Jay!" I turned to find none other than Henry Witherspoon glaring at me from a "blind spot" to my right.

"Okay, take it easy, Henry. Jay...?" Mr. Brennan gave me an expectant gaze.

"Sorry, Henry...didn't see you," I mumbled, before burying my head in my arms. I'd done it again, putting my foot in my mouth. There were chuckles all around.

"All right, settle down class. I'm talking about Lao Xi." Everyone looked around to see if Lao Xi had somehow entered the room. "Lao is not here. He's presently in the office."

Mr. Brennan shared Lao's story about being a refugee from Cambodia. I tried to listen but at the same time, I could still feel Henry's burning gaze lingering on me.

29

As the weather turned cooler and the days became shorter, it was time to say goodbye to our field for the season. The new hangouts were our homes, as we transitioned to indoor board games like Strat-O-Matic (which we had borrowed from Brett). With our parents' permission, we all chipped in some of our allowance money to order the football version of the game. After a wild summer, our folks weren't going to complain. Having the "Fearsome Foursome" (Mrs. M.'s nickname) inside made it easier to keep track of us.

The best part about "Strat" wasn't the playing board or the set of dice or the game pieces—it was the player cards. Since the numbers on the cards correlated to a player's actual season statistics, the stars of MLB and NFL were now stars in our living rooms. The games could sometimes last three hours and often had the back-and-forth drama of a real-life game. Aside from the thrill of competition, we were exposed to new teams and players. For example, in football, I became a fan of the Raiders and Packers, two teams that I "owned." We also developed a knack for setting line-ups and calling plays, the way a baseball manager or head coach in football would.

Of course, these matchups would strengthen, but sometimes test, our bonds of friendship. Being in close quarters for hours at a time gave us insight into each other's quirks and habits. The guys, for example, gave me a tough time about the way I chewed my bubblegum when I was tense ("like a cow," they'd say). Paul would not only crack his knuckles but his shoulders as well—linking his hands behind his back and raising them until they were level with his neck! Matt chewed toothpicks and did imitations of Hollywood legends. Kenny played Elton John records for good luck, and he also had a peculiar talent for mimicking people.

Sometimes I'd ask him to mimic the TV or radio if they were on in the background. It was almost like he knew what the announcers were gonna say. One time I even asked him to mimic Mom (what kind of son does *that*). She was a good sport about it, though.

"Okay, well, what am I supposed to say?" she'd ask.

"*Okay, well, what am I supposed to say?*" Kenny said before she even finished her thought.

"Ooh, that's pretty impressive, Ken," she said.

"*Ooh, that's pretty imp—*" he began before I pulled him out of the room.

For some reason, Strat-O-Matic materials weren't sent via the regular postal service—only by UPS. As a result, whenever one of the large brown delivery trucks would enter our neighborhood, we'd perk up and drop everything.

"*Ups* truck! *Ups* truck!" We cried, purposefully botching the acronym. Then we'd charge outside like madmen, chasing after the truck, hoping the driver would stop at one of our homes. Even the neighborhood dogs looked at us like we were ridiculous.

One evening Paul and I were playing a baseball game between my Orioles and his Mets that went into extra innings. I don't remember what he rolled or what player it was, but it ended up being a game-winning grand slam.

As he raised his arms to celebrate, I noticed something.

"Is that armpit hair?" I asked.

"Yeah. Why?" he asked, pulling his tee shirt back and looking at the tuft of brown hair.

"When did you get hair?"

"I dunno," he shrugged. "I've had it for a while. You don't?"

"No."

"Nowhere?" he asked, implying other parts of the body.

I shook my head.

"So, you haven't had the dream or been able to—" Paul stopped when he saw my face cringe.

"Been able to what?" I asked.

He looked around and then lowered his voice. "Like the movie we saw, you know? Except when you're awake."

I shook my head as a realization hit me. "Oh God, now I know what Dad meant. When I was taking a long shower last week, he asked if I was playing with myself."

"Yikes. Were you?" Paul asked.

"No, well...I mean, I was kind of playing. I was trying to juggle bottles of hotel shampoo," I explained.

Paul rolled his eyes.

To say I was disconcerted by my friend's development, or my lack of it, was an understatement. Later that night I positioned myself up close to the bathroom mirror and inspected my underarms, legs, and yeah, my private areas. I was looking for something, anything—even just the length of an eyelash. But there was nothing.

The next morning, I met up with Matt at his mailbox. We were still waiting for Kenny before heading down the hill to our bus stop.

"All right, this is gonna sound weird," I said. "Can I ask you about hair?"

"Aw, man, if you're thinking about an afro, don't do it. Even I have trouble," he joked.

"No," I said. "I mean *body* hair. Under your arms and other places, you know?"

"You're right, this is weird," he said.

"Just be honest. Like overall, would you say you're more like a 'Slippery Stu' or a "Hairy Gorilla?'"

"I dunno," he said. "Maybe a 'slippery gorilla.'"

As I contemplated his response, Kenny joined us.

"Hey, Kenny... 'Slippery Stu' or 'Harry Gorilla?' Jay wants to know."

"Huh?" Kenny asked.

"Never mind. Not important," I said.

The thing was—it was important. Was this why Kelly developed an interest in Dallas? Because he was more physically mature?

At school I began observing some of my classmates, looking at their facial hair and listening to their voices. Some were deeper than mine and some were not. The best way to tell, of course, was in the locker room when we changed for PE.

One day as I was changing out of my gym shirt, I glanced at a new seventh grader named Brian who was rolling on deodorant a few lockers down from me. I squinted to see if he had any underarm growth.

"Are you looking at him? Whoa, gay-wad alert!" A voice bellowed.

I turned to find Scottie Gartner arriving at a locker across from me.

"What?!" I asked, startled.

"What?" asked Brian, clueless.

"My man, Jayson right here was checking you out," Scottie explained to him.

"Shut up, Scottie. I was gonna ask him about his necklace," I fired back, I was pleased with myself for quick thinking and yet disgusted for having been busted staring.

"What about it?" Brian asked, touching his shark's tooth necklace.

"Did you get it in Hawaii?" I asked.

"My parents brought it back from Tahiti," Brian said.

"Cool," I said.

I gathered up my belongings, As I passed Scottie on my way to the exit, he shook his head at me,

"Whatever you say, Jay," Scottie said.

30

If sixth grade was the year of mischief, seventh grade was shaping up to be the year of humiliation. Instead of wallowing in it, I needed to act. I began lifting, using Dad's free weights in the basement. Even if I couldn't see the results right away, I would at least feel better about myself.

One afternoon I had just completed a set of curls when Mom and Justine returned from the store. Mom called me upstairs to help unload some groceries. As I removed some items from the bags, she leaned toward me, nostrils flaring.

"Wait," she said. "I think I smell something."

"Mom, give it a rest," I pleaded.

"No, it's there. Body odor!"

She couldn't have looked happier if she'd won the Mass lottery. I sniffed my underarms, too—what the heck. Yup…there was BO, all right.

Justine entered from the porch with two bags of groceries but then stopped dead in her tracks at the bizarre sight.

"Your brother just hit puberty!" Mom exclaimed. Again, it sounded like *poo-birdy*.

"Wow. Should we bake a cake?" Justine asked sarcastically.

"You may laugh but I've been waiting for this day," Mom said, before reaching high into a cupboard and retrieving a drug store item.

"What's that?" I asked.

She handed me a brand-new deodorant roll-on in white and red packaging.

"*Tussy*," I said, reading the label.

"Yes, indeed."

Tussy. Not Speed Stick or Right Guard. This was equivalent to my folks buying me white figure skates at a garage sale back in Pennsylvania. Sometimes they seemed clueless about what it was like to be a guy, having to hang around other guys. At least Justine could use my figure skates someday.

Heck, I'd be happy to let her use my Tussy, too.

31

As I lay in bed that night, I wondered if the "nocturnal emission" fairy would soon visit me. Then I would have everything out of the way in one day, like a two-for-one deal on adolescent growth. If not, I could ask Paul what to expect. I felt bad that I was starting to think of my new best friend as a type of crash test dummy—but the truth was, I could find out what affected him and prepare accordingly.

Believe it or not, there was an even bigger revelation on the home front that week. I was working on a final draft of an English paper and messed up, so I asked Mom if she had any liquid paper. She had me check the top drawer of her "stationary," which was like this tall, narrow, antique desk. Even though my parents had lived in many states, they were raised in the Midwest which meant they had funny names for things: a 'Davenport' referred to a couch, a 'sack' meant bag, and so on.

I didn't find any liquid paper in the top drawer, so I kept looking in the remaining drawers. When I got the last one, I saw stacks of photographs, including my fifth-grade class photo from Pennsylvania. I suddenly felt nostalgic and kept digging through the photos.

I came to the bottom of the drawer and pulled a photo out of some parchment paper: a photograph of Mom in a wedding dress close to Dad. Except, when I looked closer, I realized it *wasn't* Dad. Blonde crew-cut hair, broad shoulders, big smile, straight white teeth. Who was he?

I glanced at the woman in the photo, hoping my eyes were playing tricks. She was younger, and her hair was styled differently, but the rest—eyes, nose, and smile—was exactly the same. It was Mom, no doubt. So, there I was cross-legged on the floor, staring at a photograph of my mother with another man in wedded bliss.

My world suddenly rocked, I jumped to my feet and tracked down Justine. She was in the dining room, sketching at the table. I placed the photo in front of her.

"Hey," she protested.

"Do you know who that is?" I asked.

"Mom and Dad," she said.

"Look more closely at the man," I said.

She did and her eyes welled with tears. "Mom has another husband?"

"No, silly. But I think she *did*."

I was relieved Dad was out of town. What would his reaction be? Or did he already know? We confronted Mom with the photo and asked her, in the politest way possible, about the other man. After a long sigh, she told us to take our seats at the kitchen table.

She didn't sit right away as she chose her words. Her voice was thick with emotion, and she finally explained that the man in the photo was, in fact, her *first* husband. His name was Chet Parsons.

Mom paused because she saw our expressions. I mentioned that I thought Mom was Dad's first love, and vice versa. She held up a finger and resumed filling us in. Chet was a popular guy, well-liked by her family and friends. He was a captain of the football team at Oberlin and a Deacon in the church. He earned a degree in Engineering and planned to go into the Army...*until* he was diagnosed with leukemia. He died in '62 before any of us were born.

"Does Dad know this?" Justine asked.

"Yes. Although it's a sensitive subject," Mom replied.

"How come you didn't tell us?" I asked.

"I was waiting for the right time, when I thought you were both old enough to understand," Mom explained, taking hold of our hands. "It's not something I'd want to get around...for Dad's sake than my own."

"You can trust us," I said.

"So, if Chet didn't die, you wouldn't have met Dad," Justine said. "And that means we wouldn't have been born, right?"

"That's one way to look at it. People say things happen for a reason."

"Did you love him more than you love Dad?" Justine asked.

Mom seemed taken aback.

"Sweetheart, you can't compare love. People love in different ways. Here's what I want you to know: Chet was my life then, but you two and your father are my life now. And I wouldn't trade what we have for anything."

32

During the winter break, our maternal Grandmother, Marjorie, flew in from Ohio for an extended visit. Without a doubt, the Christmas season was my favorite time of year. It wasn't about the gifts—it just put me in a mood like nothing else. The sights, the sounds, and the scents, especially when Grandma Marjorie was baking, lifted my spirits. People were kinder to one another than they were when the Sox were headed to the World Series, but this event was *guaranteed* every year. And no one personified kindness like Grandma Marjorie.

The only drawback with these visits was communication. Grandma Marjorie didn't hear well, even with her hearing aids. Instead of saying "Excuse me" or "I beg your pardon" when she couldn't make out what we were saying, she'd ask *"What is it?"*

When something was important to her, she would look at us carefully and read our lips. Sometimes as she did this, however, her lips would start moving along which was a little disconcerting. I wasn't sure if she was trying to tell me something, so I'd stop out of respect, and then she'd stop, and we'd have to start all over again.

One evening as Justine and I were setting the table for dinner, I gazed out the window and saw a colorful bird with spotted wings and a long tail in our backyard.

"Dad, look at this bird. Is that a pheasant or a quail?"

Dad walked over from his reading chair, paper in hand.

"Not sure, but it's a beauty," he said and then waved at Grandma, as if she was blind, too. "Marj, do you want to take a look?!"

"What is it?" Grandma asked from the couch.

"I said, '*Do you want to take a look at the bird?*'" Dad said in a booming voice.

"I know it's a damn bird," Grandma retorted. "I want to know what *kind!*"

Justine and I stifled a laugh. It was the first time we had seen our grandmother be anything other than sweet. And it was the first time I could recall Dad being speechless.

A few days later, Grandma Marjorie was knitting in the rocking chair by our family room fireplace. She looked at her watch and turned to Dad.

"Would you mind turning on the TV, Joel?"

"Not at all," Dad crossed to the set. "What would you like to watch?"

"I think *Jeopardy* is on Channel 5," she said.

When Art Fleming appeared on the screen, Dad returned to his seat.

"Thank you, Chet," Grandma said.

Oops. Dad did a double take while Justine and I froze. Mom interjected from the kitchen.

"You mean *Joel*, Mom," she hollered.

Grandma Marjorie blushed and shook her head. Justine and I traded subtle looks and then looked down as if we didn't hear a thing.

"For heaven's sake, I don't know why I said that. *Joel*, I'm sorry." She then glanced at Justine and me. "Your ol' Grams is getting up there in age, kids."

Make that *twice* in one week Dad was speechless.

The Zimmerman Christmas celebration usually started on the 24th when we feasted on beef fondue—a once-a-year treat in our household. Dad cut the tenderloin, Mom prepared various dipping sauces, and Grandma Marjorie made cornbread.

When the oil was hot enough, we loaded up our skewers with raw meat, set them into the boiling oil, and then watched as the tender meat sizzled. While we dined, Dad played an assortment of Christmas records, from the old favorites (*Christmas with Conniff*) to the new (*A Partridge Family Christmas*).

After dinner and dessert, we returned to the family room to open our stocking gifts. If Christmas was the entrée, then the stocking gifts the night before were the appetizer. The one thing that always tugged at my heartstrings was that Mom took the time to individually wrap every one of these items—ranging from dental floss to Chapstick to baseball cards, just as she would a $500 watch (not that I'd ever want a gift like that). The thought of her doing this with knuckles that resembled a boxer's made it even more endearing.

While we were cleaning the wrappers off the floor, our telephone rang. Dad hustled into his office to answer it from his desk phone.

"Probably my sister," he said.

"If it's Auntie, I wanna talk to her," Justine said from across the room.

I wanted to talk to her as well, so I moved closer to the office door. Dad's voice grew quiet and then somber, and he didn't say anything at all. When he spoke again, his voice was choked up... "Hold on a minute, please."

Dad appeared in the doorway. There were tears in his eyes as he called out to Mom.

"Honey," he said, choking up. "Your brother..."

Mom was distracted, delivering Grandma Marjorie a cup of decaf coffee.

"Okay, tell him I'll be right there," Mom said.

Dad's jaw tensed. "It's *about* your brother. You better come now."

33

I had always wanted to go to California, but I never expected Uncle Sam's death would be the reason for my first journey. The man on the phone was somewhat vague, saying there was a hit-and-run accident involving a car. Dad was annoyed that the caller couldn't tell us more, but maybe the guy had other people to call. And it wasn't exactly the easiest news to break.

One of the hard parts about death I realized, is when you see someone else learning about the loss of a loved one. We looked sympathetically toward Grandma Marjorie, but she didn't need to read lips. She could read the room.

"Is it Samuel?" she asked.

Mom nodded and our Grandmother clasped her hands, looked down, and shook her head. She didn't cry. Instead, she voiced a stream of thoughts.

"Oh, dear. So young. My goodness. Never got married. He may have become an Atheist…"

Mom caressed her arm, trying to soothe her, and then she stood with a look of determination.

"We're going to pay our respects in person," she announced. "Mom will fly out with us from Logan."

"Honey, I don't know if there's any need for the kids—" Dad started.

Mom turned to him with a glare that could peel paint off the walls. "It's my brother and I want my children to go. When it's been your family, you made the choice," she said.

That was the end of that. Mom wasted no time in making the arrangements. Justine and I packed our suitcases ("Two nice outfits, shoes included!" Mom commanded). Less than 24 hours later, Grandma Marjorie, Justine, and I were in adjoining hotel rooms at the Beverly Hilton Hotel. Dad stayed behind for work and to "hold down the fort," which didn't seem all that difficult considering all the soldiers were on a mission.

The day after Christmas there was a "celebration of life" for Uncle Samuel at a park in Santa Monica, high on a bluff overlooking the Pacific Coast Highway and the ocean beyond. It was a beautiful day, with a vast blue background dotted by white sails.

The four of us sat in the front row of chairs that had been set up near a makeshift podium. To our right, there was an enlarged black and white photo of Uncle Samuel on an easel (one of the guests called it a "headshot," which was ironic because that was the cause of death after the car clipped him). The only thing missing was Samuel's body. To Mom's surprise, Samuel's wish was to be cremated, with his ashes scattered in the waters around Catalina Island. He did not want, under any circumstances, to have a memorial service in a church.

We learned all this from a man named Jeremiah, the one who spoke last and longest at the podium, even after Mom said a few words. It turns out he was also the one who broke the news about Sam to Dad over the phone. Jeremiah was older than my uncle by at least ten years. I liked him because he was calm under the circumstances, and confidently waved away a portable microphone someone offered him. He told some funny stories about my uncle—stories I'd never heard, but that I'd always remember.

One was about Sam chasing down a purse-snatcher, beating up the perpetrator, and then returning the purse to the stunned female victim. But here's the catch: the victim was a male dressed in drag—and Samuel realized he knew him! In fact, he even owed Samuel money. So, what did Sam do? He took $40 out of the wallet and then threw the purse back at the lady, or, um, guy.

Later that afternoon, a restaurant in West Hollywood called "Eat Up" closed its doors so the guests could gather and continue Samiel's life celebration. My uncle had worked there as a manager, among his many other gigs.

Grandma Marjorie decided to skip this event because she was exhausted and wanted to rest back at the hotel. I had no doubt she was tired, but I also had the feeling she wanted to grieve in private. When Mom dropped her off in our rental car, she assured her we wouldn't be gone too long.

There were far more people at the restaurant than at the park. Mom said that was probably because many of Uncle Sam's friends were night owls. Jeremiah stopped by our booth and asked Mom if he could get her anything. I hardly ever saw Mom drink, but she said she would have a glass of Chardonnay. Just *one*.

"How about you two darlings?" he asked us, tapping his fingers on the tabletop.

"Can we have Shirley Temples, Mom?" I asked.

"If that's what you want, sure," Mom replied.

"Are they good here?" Justine asked.

"You bet! Best I've ever tasted," Jeremiah answered.

Over the next few hours (so much for not being gone too long), we drank and talked. It seemed every few minutes Uncle Sam's friends visited us—a colorful assortment of neighbors, co-workers, classmates from acting class, classmates from art class, and even ex-boyfriends. They all had wonderful things to say about my uncle. Most of them offered stories, not condolences, which I appreciated. Justine asked why all the people were hugging Jeremiah and Mom explained that it was *his* loss, too.

"Oh," Justine said. "Like what you said to…*not* talk about?"

"Right, sweetheart. But it's okay to talk about it here," Mom replied, finishing the last bit of wine in her glass.

Jeremiah returned then with another glass of chardonnay for Mom and two more Shirley Temples for Justine and me.

"May I join you all?" he asked Mom.

"Of course," she said.

He sipped his magenta-colored drink and smiled at Justine and me.

"You know, you two have grown up a lot," he said.

"How would you know?" I asked. "You've never met us before today."

"Well, your uncle had your school photos up on his refrigerator.

"How did he get them?" Justine asked.

"I sent them, silly girl," Mom said.

"But I thought you didn't talk that much?" Justine asked.

"Well, talk—not so much. But we wrote to each other often," Mom said.

"Oh, he *loooooved* your mom's letters," Jeremiah said. "And he loved hearing what you both were up to. Of course, he needed a new address book on account of you all not being able to stay in one place very long."

He pantomimed tearing up a book and tossing it over his shoulder. Justine and I giggled, and Mom laughed like it was the funniest thing she'd ever heard.

"You are a card!" she said, slapping Jeremiah's shoulder.

"What's a card?" Justine whispered to me.

"A funny person," I replied.

"Justine, honey, I need to use the ladies' room," Mom said, leaning over the table. "Why don't you come with me? And I should call the hotel to check on Grandma."

When they exited the booth, Jeremiah stood politely and then sat back down.

"I can see the similarity between your mother and Samuel…in the face. It's, I don't know, comforting. And you, too, a little bit."

I smiled, flattered.

"Jeremiah, can I ask you something? Did you and my uncle live together? Or…?"

"We did not live together. It was more of the 'or' situation…" he said, with a grin. "I don't want to say anything that anyone may deem inappropriate, but let's just say I loved him very much."

"Me, too. My mom says I was like him in some ways, like kind of a late bloomer."

"Well, cheers to late bloomers," Jeremiah said, clinking his glass against my Shirley Temple glass. "There's nothing wrong with that. The longer you view the world from a child's perspective, the more beauty you see."

34

We returned from Los Angeles just in time. A big storm, what the meteorologists called a "Nor'easter" was supposed to hit the region in less than 24 hours. Dad set his boots out in the mudroom and told Justine and me to get our parkas and gloves ready. Mom, meanwhile, made sure our flashlights had new batteries and took out some candles, just in case. I knew a blizzard was a huge headache for most people, but as I went to bed that night, I crossed my fingers that school would be canceled in the morning.

There were two ways parents and students would receive this news. The first was to be awake and alert at 6 AM because, if it was a "snow day," the fire engines at town hall would blast their sirens. The second, more foolproof, method was by tuning in to the local TV or radio stations where newscasters read the names of towns and/or schools in alphabetical order. Since the first letter of our town was near the end of the alphabet (just like my last name!) it could be a little anxiety-inducing. Sometimes we were dressed half in our pajamas and half in our school clothes—ready for any outcome. Naturally, once Justine and I heard our town mentioned, as we did that January day, we broke into a celebratory dance.

Just like the autumn leaves, the winter snow in New England was beautiful. And yet I was reminded that what came down must be picked up—or, as was the case of accumulated snow, shoveled aside (another one of my chores). Fortunately, our driveway wasn't long, at least in comparison to the Monetti's. Also, Dad and Justine pitched in with the shoveling.

The following week we had a warm stretch, followed by a day of rain, then more freezing temperatures. The only good thing about these cold snaps was that our local ponds would freeze over. That meant ice hockey.

I was a horrible skater, but I was a happy participant. I confided to Paul that I had a "figure skate" issue and without any judgment whatsoever, he loaned me a pair of old hockey skates. From his house, we ventured down to what was known as Pat's Pond looking like mountain climbers with all our gear. After throwing a large rock onto the ice surface to figure out if it was safe, we laced up our skates on the frosty edge of the pond.

"So, who's Pat, anyway?" I asked.

"Some old guy who lived in Paul's house before they moved in," Matt said.

By this point, the guys and I were ready to test out the ice. The surface color left something to be desired, but at least it was smooth. Matt, Paul, and Kenny easily glided onto the ice. I tentatively stepped on and tiptoed around the perimeter a few times. After a while, I found my balance and even a little bit of stride.

"There you go," Paul said, offering encouragement.

"Must be the skates," I replied.

Matt, a goaltender on his bantam team, had all the goalie proper equipment. It was only logical for him to step into our hastily assembled goal (two gloves about six feet apart). He tightened his plastic facemask and banged his stick on the ice.

"All right, boys! Careful with the 'slappahs,'" he shouted in a faux Boston accent.

Paul, Kenny, and I grinned and then formed a line. We skated in, one at a time, doing breakaway drills. With every save, Matt blurted out "Gilbert!" (Pronounced as *Jhil-bare*) in honor of the Bruins' goalie. When one of us scored, we'd raise our sticks in celebration like Phil Esposito or Bobby Orr.

For a few days, Pat's Pond was the winter equivalent of our beloved field.

The New England snow returned in February which worked out well because Dad had booked a condominium for us at a popular ski resort in Maine. One morning, while Mom and Justine were finishing breakfast in the lodge, Dad and I hit the slopes. After a handful of successful runs on the beginner slopes, Dad convinced me I was ready for a more challenging trail which meant a longer ride on the chairlift. I soon realized why he wanted the extra time.

As we rose in the crisp air above the white powder, Dad cleared his throat.

"How's middle school going?" he asked.

"It's okay," I replied.

"Growing pains?" he asked. "That's what I recall."

"Yup. You could say that," I answered.

"Any girls you're interested in?"

"Nah, not really." It was the truth. No one had caught my eye since Kelly.

"Well, when the time is right, as they say," he said. "And on that note, your mother's been hounding me to talk with you. You know, *the* talk,"

"Oh," I said, eyes stretching wide behind my goggles. "I'm all set. We saw a movie at school last year. On the, you know, topic."

"That's good," Dad said before doing a double take. "A movie?"

"Yeah. This kid and his father go camping," I said.

Dad gave me a sideways look.

"Interesting. Was there anything the movie didn't cover?"

"Can't think of anything," I answered.

"Look, I'm trying here, Jay. We're getting near the top and we both know Mom's gonna ask me what we covered."

I started to feel bad for him, so I searched in my brain for something.

"Okay," I said. "Does it feel *good?*"

To his credit, Dad kept a straight face. "*Verrrrry* good."

We were seconds away from the exit ramp. I bit my lip, stifling a grin, as Dad lifted the safety bar.

"Here we go, my boy. Tips up, get ready to push…*now!*"

Dad pushed out and glided down the ramp. I stayed in, paralyzed by silent laughter.

"Jay!" Dad hollered when he saw I'd missed my departure.

I gave Dad the okay sign as the lift swung me around and back down the mountain. Like a swimmer holding his breath, I finally let all my laughter out.

It was so loud, I thought I was about to cause an avalanche.

Winter soon gave way to spring, and I was ecstatic. No more leaves, no more snow, and no more dreary darkness at 4:30 in the afternoon. Spring meant baseball. In the field, and the region. Hopes were high for the Red Sox again after coming oh-so-close in the last World Series. On the local sports scene, I was determined to play Little League, having missed out the year before. Open sessions were in April and without going into the whole tryout process, I landed on the Braves. Sure, I would have preferred the Red Sox, but at least the Braves used to be the *Boston* Braves. Paul wound up on the Mets ("No escaping New York," he said).

Having lived and breathed baseball since our move, I knew I could hold my own. I was a decent hitter, and a good fielder, and no surprise—I had a strong arm. My goal was to be a pitcher, but Coach Henderson's son, Todd, had the inside track on taking the hill. The coach was open to the idea of me being a reliever, but after seeing me field a few grounders he reconsidered.

"Kid, with that glove and arm, I'd rather put you at third base. I bet you could handle that hot corner like Brooks Robinson," he said.

Around the same time, I was able to show off my arm in front of a different audience. At school, our PE teachers were preparing seventh graders for the state-mandated physical fitness test. This consisted of a ¼ mile run, pull-ups, the standing broad jump, and a softball throw. Students who excelled, meaning those who placed in a certain overall percentile, would receive certificates of recognition from the Governor.

Things didn't start with a bang. Even though I was quick, my endurance was below average. There was no recognition for my ¼ mile run (one full lap around the school) unless you count the concerned teacher who asked if I was lost.

I did okay in the next two categories: 14 pull-ups and a broad jump that exceeded six feet. Last was the softball throw. Although I was used to tossing a baseball, I still ended up with the longest distance for our grade. I even outgunned Paul and Todd.

"You gotta cannon there!" Mr. Ackerman, the eighth-grade PE teacher, exclaimed.

Although my result in the distance run sunk my chances of earning a fancy certificate, I felt good about being the best in something.

When I headed back inside the school through the side doors, I almost collided head-on with a student rushing outside. I couldn't see his face, but he was in the standard PE uniform.

"Move it, pussy!" he yelled as he barreled past.

"Who the hell was that?" I said to no one in particular.

"Ahh, first, let's watch the language. Second, that would be Ricky Catano."

I looked up to see Mr. Lucero descending the stairs from the second floor.

"Sorry, Mr. Lucero," I said.

"It looks like he's taking a shortcut on his fitness run, too," he added, continuing to watch the guy through the window.

"Who's Ricky Catano?" I asked.

"He's one of our recent transfers. Let's hope that's your last run-in with him, no pun intended," he said.

37

In 1975 the Red Sox had won us all over, but a year later it was the Celtics who captured our imagination. They cruised through the playoffs and defeated the Phoenix Suns in the finals, which included a thrilling triple-overtime game. The local sportscasters joked about how it was always up to the Celtics to pull Boston's psyche out of the dumps after yet another winter mourning the Sox.

That NBA Championship wasn't the only celebration in town. My Braves turned out to be a powerhouse and won the league title. To give credit where credit was due, Todd Henderson was a heck of a pitcher. You could say I did my part with some timely hitting. For what it's worth, Paul had an incredible season on the Mets, but his team's pitching didn't hold up and we beat them in the final.

Being the champions of anything that year meant your team was invited to take part in our town's 4th of July parade. Keep in mind, this was not your ordinary Independence Day. *This* was the "Bicentennial." Big word, bigger event. That's all you'd see and hear that summer. It was on TV, radio, license plate brackets, and stamps. The good ol' U-S of A was turning 200.

Dad wasn't all that impressed. "I bet there are people in the mountains of Peru that are almost that old."

"Then let's invite them to the parade," I joked.

On the morning of the fourth, Justine was in uniform, as well. Her Girl Scout Troop had been invited to march, and she was going to carry a flag. Dad and Mom were genuinely excited to see us take part in a historic parade and Dad even bought a new Kodak film camera for the occasion.

After we spent what seemed like 200 years searching for a parking space, we stepped out of our car to a riotous noise. The streets were flooded with revelers dressed in red, white, and blue, waving American flags. Music and noisemakers drowned out an announcer trying to give instructions.

My parents hurried us to the local supermarket, the parade's designated starting point, and Justine and I quickly met up with our groups. Coach Henderson told Dad we were planning to march two miles along a route that would take us to the town hall where there would be even more festivities.

The fire engines roared to life and the parade started with brass bands, jugglers on unicycles, and funny cars that could raise their two front wheels and spin around. Many participants wore the attire of Founding Fathers (carrying rolled-up documents) and Militiamen (holding muskets).

I marched along with my coaches and teammates, waving and smiling to the crowd of onlookers on both sides of the street. Keeping a smile in place was exhausting. I had no idea how movie stars did it on the red carpet for all the paparazzi. I kept my eyes on the crowd and finally caught a glimpse of my parents ahead when—

TAT-TAT-TAT!

I jumped in fright, suddenly engulfed in smoke. *Firecrackers.* I managed to catch my breath and shrugged it off as part of the crazy celebration. Realizing I'd lost a few steps, I hurried up to my team and waved to Mom and Dad. Dad kept the camera rolling and waved back with his free hand. Mom leaned forward, over the cordon.

"Are you okay?" she shouted.

"Yeah! Fine!" I hollered back, with a thumbs up.

It was only the next day when Dad brought in the local paper that I realized what had happened. There was a two-page spread inside with an assortment of photographs devoted to the historic event. Lo and behold, I was in one of the photos—just before my scare.

As I focused on the crowd in the background, I noticed Henry Witherspoon and a familiar-looking guy, holding fireworks called "cherry bombs." As I zeroed in on their faces, it all came back to me…Mister *"Move it, Pussy!"* himself…

Ricky Catano.

38

After all the festivities settled down, it was just another hot and muggy New England summer. My parents joined a country club after weighing recommendations from Dad's work colleagues. I had mixed feelings, to be honest. First, a housekeeper, which Kenny had already jabbed me about, and now a country club membership?

When I told my friends, they gave me a little grief, but not as much as I expected. Once again, their summers were booked with travel and camps, which also cost 'beaucoup bucks,' as Paul conceded. After the previous summer's high jinks with Brett and Dallas, I was looking forward to having legitimate access to a pool.

Dad and Mom had different ideas, though. Since Justine and I were mediocre swimmers to put it kindly, they signed us up for lessons. I was registered for Intermediate Swim and Justine would be in Advanced Beginner.

My instructor, a college sophomore named Donna, was friendly and nice to look at in her one-piece suit. What impressed me the most about her, though, was her patience. She kept up the encouragement as I struggled with the fundamentals like the breaststroke and elementary backstroke. My classmates, some of them two years younger than me, picked things up with no problem.

"You'd have better luck keeping a couch afloat," I said, moments after I'd finished another aquatic splash session.

"Nonsense," she said. "You're doing great."

One of her next activities required us to retrieve a half-dozen "donut" weights from the bottom of the pool in 30 seconds or less. I was the last to go and it took me so long that all the other participants were allowed to go to the snack bar as I submerged repeatedly.

Another task was to transform our clothes into flotation devices. It may have sounded easy, but here's what was required: jumping into the deep end fully clothed, disrobing (to your swim trunks), making knots in these items, whipping them over your head to inflate, and then using them to float—all while treading water. Piece of cake, right?

I told Donna I didn't remember my parents signing me up for the Navy SEALS. She laughed and reminded me that if I could save my own life, I might be able to save others. When it was my turn to take the plunge, I flailed away as expected. Donna eventually had to jump in to guide me through the steps and didn't blink when I accidentally whipped her in the face with my shirt.

When I climbed out of the pool, exhausted, Donna passed me a certificate. I looked and then looked again. Somehow I passed the course! When I asked her the obvious question—*how?* —she responded that I met all the standard criteria.

"But the Navy SEAL stuff..?" I asked.

"That's part of Junior Lifesaving. Just wanted to see what you had in store for next year," she said with a wink.

In contrast, tennis was a cakewalk for me. There were no lives to be lost or saved in racquet sports. After Dad and I finished hitting on the courts one afternoon, we headed over to the cooler by the Pro Shop for a drink of water. A notice on the bulletin board soon caught his eye.

"Hey, they have tournaments for kids," he said.

Before I could respond, he already had a foot inside the door. I followed him into the shop and overheard the tennis pro say the only slots left for the 12 - 14 age group were in the mixed doubles event taking place the next day. Players who didn't have pre-arranged partners (like me) could give their names and be matched by a random draw. Dad asked if I was interested, I told him I was, and we completed the paperwork.

The next morning, we returned and looked at the chart which listed the pairings for the tournament. It turns out I was matched with a girl named Andrea Hayes. The name sounded familiar, but I couldn't picture her face.

At noon, all participants were instructed to sit on the bleachers with their parents for an explanation of guidelines, procedures, and seedings. Everyone was already broken up into pairs, except me, so I stood off to the side with Dad.

"Maybe she bailed out," I said.

"Let's give her another minute," he replied, checking his watch.

Just then a middle-aged man and an attractive teenage girl approached from the parking lot. She looked familiar—light brown hair, tan skin, and a slight yet athletic build. When we made eye contact, she slowed her stride and then smiled in recognition.

And that's when it all came back to me...

Winnicott Elementary.

Rainy April days.

Dodgeball.

The girl I'd injured.

And she was *smiling*?

Dad gave me a tap on the arm, stepped forward, and introduced himself to the girl's father. I heard the man say something like "Stan," but I was still fixated on my partner.

"Andrea," I said aloud.

Andrea smiled. "How are you, 'Eliminator?'"

"Doing well, thanks," I replied. "How's the wrist?"

"It's healed, as you can see," she said, holding up her tennis racket like a mighty goddess.

Dad and Stan exchanged puzzled looks.

"I don't know what any of this means," he said,

"Me neither," Dad replied. "Are you two good?"

Andrea and I looked at each other and nodded.

Moments later we strode onto the court where an actual umpire was waiting in a highchair. There were also line judges. I seemed to lose track of who, and where, I was—like an out-of-body experience. I collected myself just as we arrived at the net to greet our competition.

"Jayson," I said, extending my hand over the net.

Andrea shook hands as well and then did the whole "up or down" thing, spinning her Wilson racket to see who would serve first. It came up "W" which allowed us the opportunity to serve first.

As it turned out, that was one of our few 'W's of the day. We lost the match 6-1 and 6-2. The pair we squared off against were siblings—and the defending mixed doubles champions, no less. Sure, they were impressive, but I couldn't help but marvel at Andrea. She was determined and poised throughout. And in defeat, she showed grace.

"Thanks, Jay. It was a pleasure," she said.

"No, thank you. I guess I'm a little better at dodgeball than tennis," I said.

"Hey, at least no one got injured," she said with a smile.

I smiled back, thinking of something else to add. I had nothing.

"Well, I better run," Andrea said. "Stan's not exactly known for his patience."

She gave me a wave and turned towards the exit by the bleachers.

"Andrea?" I asked.

She turned back.

"Good job."

Andrea flashed that beautiful smile until she was intercepted by her father who had come to retrieve (or perhaps, save?) her.

As I watched them embrace, I reviewed the last line in my head. *Good job?!* That's what you'd say to someone who helps you carry a piece of furniture.

I *really* needed to work on my game.

39

While I had been misfiring on the tennis court, Mom was connecting with ladies from the club. She joined a bridge group and even got the green light from Dad to host the inaugural game.

While I had read some books on poker and played "Crazy Eights" with Grandma Marjorie, I didn't understand the game of bridge. I knew that people played with partners and sometimes a certain partner had to be the "dummy." Who would want a gig with a name like that? Besides, the dummy was allowed to get up and walk around. If I was playing, you can be sure I'd be on the lookout for the dummy—who knows if they might try to look at my cards.

Bridge night was always a lively affair from the moment the doorbell rang. Almost all the ladies, except for Mom, drank like sailors on shore leave. And I'd say at least half of them smoked. Our porch was the designated smoking area and that meant those old ashtrays from Pennsylvania could finally be excavated from storage.

Dad, meanwhile, managed all the drink orders. When I marveled at his cocktail-mixing skills, he reminded me that ski instructors back in the old days didn't make a lot of money, so he sometimes needed to earn a little extra cash. Bartending at night was one way to do it.

Mom also joined a book club with several women in the neighborhood, including Mrs. McKelvey, who turned out to be a nice lady. I don't know who chose the books but some of them, at least based on the covers, looked downright racy. One, a paperback called *Fear of Flying*, had me sneaking a peek whenever I could.

At some point, Mom, Mrs. M., Mrs. Boucher, and Mrs. DeSantos thought it might be fun to have a neighborhood softball game/picnic with all the families in the area taking part. They decided on a date and sent out invitations. The guys and I were ecstatic. We'd get to show our stuff against our parents.

The event was held at the baseball field at Winnicott School on a Sunday afternoon in August. The weather was perfect, and the turnout was better than expected. Mrs. McKelvey brought her husband along which gave me a huge scare. Much to my relief, the man of the house didn't seem to recognize me (probably because I was *clothed* and wore a cap). Dallas and Brett didn't show up, but their parents did. I don't know what I expected, but both couples seemed clean-cut and cordial.

A bonus was having both of Paul's brothers, Tony and Chris, play on the "kids" squad (big kids were still kids). Naturally, that tilted the odds in our favor and the game ended up being a rout. Tom hit two homers and Chris hit one. The best part was robbing Dad of extra bases in the outfield with a sliding catch, just like Fred Lynn himself. Dad dropped his bat and shook his head in disbelief.

"Hope you can find yourself a ride home, son!" he hollered in jest.

When the post-game snacks and beverages were polished off, Mr. DeSantos called everyone in to join him at the pitcher's mound. Ilene, Kelly, and Kenny went to his side, and he looked to the sky to gather his thoughts.

"Here comes the 'Heavenly Father,'" Matt whispered.

But then Chip surprised us. He announced the family was moving to Chicago. We shifted our eyes to Kenny who gave us a subtle nod in confirmation.

"Chicago?" Ed asked, cocking his head.

"Chicago," Chip said.

Ed threw up his hands.

"Aww Jeez. Just like Bobby-friggin'-Orr!"

There was a ripple of laughter that seemed to lighten the mood. Bobby Orr, legendary Bruin, had recently signed as a free agent with the Chicago Blackhawks.

Mrs. Monetti stepped forward and cleared her throat.

"Well, I just want to say, I'm gonna miss you. You've been terrific neighbors." She then turned back to the other adults in the group with a grin. "Too bad I can't say that about the rest of you!"

There were a bunch of "Hey now's" and "To the DeSantos clan" cheers as the adults moved into a tight circle around Chip and Ilene. As hugs and handshakes were exchanged, Kenny and Kelly wiggled their way out of the throng.

"This sucks, man," Paul said, pulling Kenny in for a hug. Matt and I took turns after Paul.

"Thanks, guys. Yeah, I wanted to tell you, but my pop said he should be the one," he said.

Out of the corner of my eye, I noticed Kelly had taken a seat on one of the benches. I ambled over to her.

"Hey," I said, approaching with caution. "I just wanna say 'good luck.'"

"Thanks, Jay," she said with a smile.

"Last summer, for a while anyway, was like the best time of my life."

"Aww, come on," she said.

"I'm serious," I shrugged.

"You're a good guy. You weren't just using me," she replied, standing. "And I should have said all this earlier so we could have stayed friends."

"We are friends," I said.

For a split second, her tough façade dropped, and she stood up to hug me.

40

By the end of summer, I counted out all the cash I'd earned from helping shovel driveways and cutting lawns. It came out to almost $600. Of course, I broke the cardinal rule by boasting to my folks about how much I had earned.

Mom and Dad recommended that I put the money in the bank.

"You never know, Jay, you may misplace it," Dad said.

"It could be stolen. Or, God forbid, what if there's a fire?" Mom added.

I twisted my face in doubt. When had any of those things ever happened to us? But now that my parents had warned me about all the possible calamities, I felt I'd been jinxed.

Dad scheduled an appointment on a Saturday morning with the manager down at First Bank. As I clutched a manilla envelope that held all my savings, Dad opened the passenger door and encouraged me to slide in. I was stunned. It must have been the way people felt when they were bumped up to first class on an airline. I had more legroom and could experience the ride better. Dad even let me search for radio stations if we could agree on the music. Maybe there were some advantages to the maturing process.

On the drive into town, Dad explained another benefit to opening a savings account: my money would make money.

"It's called 'interest,'" he said.

"Why would the bank do that?" I asked.

"Because it's a way to say thank you for putting your money in their bank," he said.

"Why don't they just send a card?" I asked.

"How about we just go in and see how it works?" Dad said as he pulled into a parking space.

The moment we entered through the lobby doors, the branch manager, Mr. Cavanaugh, approached us with a smile. After brief introductions, he escorted us to a desk situated near the teller windows.

"Have a seat, please" he said, gesturing to a couple of chairs.

Dad and I sat as Cavanaugh grabbed a form and a pen.

"So, we're opening a savings account?" he asked.

"Yes," I said.

"With…?"

"Jayson," I said.

"I meant, with checks or cash?" Cavanaugh asked with a smile.

"*Cash*," Dad said, not bothering to hide his impatience.

He then tapped my leg and I realized that was my cue. I pulled out the manilla envelope and handed it to Cavanagh. He withdrew bills, separated them, and then counted front to back and back to front again. I was amazed at how quick his hands were, like a card dealer's.

"Yes, indeed," he said happily. "Somebody's been busy."

After Dad and I signed a few forms, Cavanaugh handed me a receipt and a little book called a register.

"You are all set, young man. Thank you for your business," he said, tucking my money into a drawer.

As Dad stood, I remained seated. I couldn't help but feel I was getting ripped off. This Cavanaugh guy had just taken all my hard-earned cash and all I got back was paper.

"Your money's safe," Dad said, sensing my uneasiness.

"What if they get robbed?" I whispered to Dad.

Cavanaugh raised his eyebrows.

"He's got an imagination, this one," he said.

"If you only knew," Dad replied.

We said our goodbyes to Kenny and Kelly over Labor Day weekend. They'd loaded up their car to maximum capacity and hit the road with waves and tears. I had to admit it was strange to be on the opposite side of things, saying farewell to a family while I stayed behind.

It felt like a double wallop of grief because summer was also over. Kenny's absence was even more conspicuous at the bus stop on our first day of school. It seemed like ages ago that he and I (and Kelly!) scrapped on the bus and yet it had only been a year.

Fortunately, there was no drama on my first day of eighth grade. Mr. Brennan was still my homeroom teacher, and the same cast of characters was present for the most part, including Henry Witherspoon.

"How was your Fourth, Jay? Did you have a blast?" Henry snickered.

"Great, Henry," I replied. "Best one ever."

I bumped into Dave later in the day and found out he'd had his Bar Mitzvah a few weeks back. I was a little surprised I wasn't invited, but then again, we hadn't been as close in seventh grade. Dave told me he'd received over $2,000 in cash from relatives.

"Are you going to put it all in the bank?" I asked.

"Heck, no. I'll never see it again," he replied.

My face sagged when he told me that, but then I thought about how sweet a couple of grand would be.

"So, how does one become Jewish?" I asked, raising an eyebrow.

"Yeah, nice try," Dave said with a smirk and walked away.

The beginning of the school year was mundane compared to years past. Justine and I woke up early and watched *Partridge Family* reruns on a small kitchen TV, while Mom prepared breakfast. She *still* packed our lunches with care, scrawling our names with hearts on the brown paper bags. It wasn't necessary, but I didn't have the heart to tell her not to do it anymore.

That fall I wanted to show my appreciation to her by making a colonial-style wall sconce for her birthday. I thought it was just okay, but Mom was so touched that she asked Dad to hang it from the wall in our living room. She even put a candle on it, which came in handy one night when we lost our power during an autumn storm.

This was right around the time Dad asked me to help him move the dehumidifier down to the basement. A minute later, he asked me to carry up the humidifier for winter. I hesitated. Didn't the two machines cancel each other out? Wouldn't it have been the same if he bought neither?

"What's the matter?" he said.

"Nothing," I said, grabbing hold of the machine.

My parents still had their club membership but there wasn't much to do in the cooler weather except golf, for a few more weeks anyway, and eat at the clubhouse. Golf didn't interest me that much and Dad wasn't too eager to change my mind. He had tried to teach me guitar over the summer and that didn't go so well. Golf, he said, was ten times harder than playing guitar and a hundred times as expensive.

Of course, no one had to twist my arm to eat. The clubhouse didn't have an official name or anything, but It was a lot fancier than a typical dining room where you'd expect the specialty to be a Reuben. The head chef, Mick, had been hired away from a fancy restaurant in Cambridge, and the dining room was always packed. The menu featured an assortment of steaks, seafood, and pasta, but all I ever ordered was a big bowl of French Onion soup—the kind that had melted cheese flowing over the sides. Whenever Mick stopped by the table, I told him his soup was my favorite meal on the planet—other than our traditional Christmas Eve fondue. He joked that he'd have to get the recipe from Mom so that he could add it to the menu.

One night, as we were leaving the restaurant, we ran into Andrea and her family. The dads, who had gotten to know each other from tennis and golf, greeted each other like they were long-lost brothers.

"Joellll!" Stan exclaimed.

"Staaaaaan!" Dad gushed.

The moms, meanwhile, exchanged pleasantries before turning a cheek to receive a kiss from the other's husband.

"You must be Jay," Mrs. Hayes said, turning her eyes to me.

"And you must be Andrea," Mom said, looking across to Andrea.

Andrea and I smiled at the adults and then shared a knowing (*"this is awkward"*) look with each other. She looked stylish in a blue beret, leather jacket, and slacks.

"Who is this little angel?" Mrs. Hayes asked, touching Justine's shoulder.

"This is our youngest, Justine," Mom said.

Sis was shy and tried to wedge herself between Mom and me.

"Aww," Mr. and Mrs. Hayes murmured as if they were being shown a photograph and not a live person.

Stan gestured to Andrea and me.

"Well, you two don't have to let us do all the talking."

Great. A dog and pony show, I thought.

"Hi Andrea," I said.

"How have you been, Jay?" she asked.

The adults watched the back and forth like it was a ping-pong match. It was annoying as hell but who knew when—or *if*—I'd see Andrea again.

"I'm doing well. Hey, I didn't ask over the summer--what school do you go to?"

"Pine Haven," she replied.

"All girls," Stan chimed in, "if you get my drift, Joel." He gave Dad a playful jab with his elbow.

"I hear you," Dad replied, tousling my hair. "Military school for this one if he doesn't shape up."

I rolled my eyes and Justine tugged on Mom's arm. "Caweeepleeesgohhh?" Justine whispered.

"I think translated into English that means, 'Can we please go!'" joked Mom.

"Aww," Mr. and Mrs. Hayes said.

43

For Halloween that year, Paul, Matt, and I dressed as bank robbers, and our loot was candy. Lots of it. The three of us had started with our empty pillowcase and by 9:00 pm all three were overflowing with sweets. We had even eaten a bunch, too. Not only that, but we each had finished a can of Schlitz that Paul had lifted from Ed's garage refrigerator (he took his role as criminal seriously). The sugar and alcohol seemed to be affecting us in strange ways as the conversation turned nonsensical.

"What if it's like an alien invasion?" Matt asked. "What are the odds of three Hollywood stars having glass eyes? Peter Falk, Sandy Duncan, and Sammy Davis. Right? And that's just the people we know about."

"So instead of *Invasion of the Body Snatchers*, it's like 'Invasion of the Eye Snatchers?'" Paul asked, humoring him.

"Exactly," Matt said and then burped for emphasis.

"And then what are they doing with all the eyes they're snatching?" I asked, playing along.

"That's the mystery," Matt insisted.

"Maybe next year we should dress up as Peter, Sandy, and Sammy," Paul suggested.

"I'm down. But hey, don't make me be Sammy, just because I'm Black," Matt said.

"Well, I don't think Sandy Duncan says, 'I'm *down*,'" Paul said.

Just then we heard what sounded like the clatter of bells on a nearby road, followed by an eruption of laughter.

"I know that laugh," Paul said.

We picked up our pace and made our way toward the commotion.

"I know that smell," Matt said.

I smelled it too—the unmistakable aroma of marijuana. Paul flicked on his flashlight revealing Chris, Dallas, and Brett kneeling behind a stone wall.

"Hey, girls! Long-time no-see!" Brett said. His eyes were bloodshot in the cone of light.

"What was that noise?" Matt asked.

"You know how we play Kick-the-Can?" Dallas said. "This is like, '*Drag*-the Can.'"

He could hardly finish his sentence before he broke into laughter. Chris, the only one who didn't look stoned, tried to explain. Even then, there were giggles and snorts.

From what I understood, the guys had strung two dozen cans together with a long fishing line—a dozen on one side of the line, and a dozen on the other. Next, they stretched the line across the road, knee height, and attached the ends to shrubs on opposite sides of the road. When a car came zooming along, the line would get caught on its bumper and the cans would rattle along in tow.

"Genius," Matt said with genuine admiration.

"We think so. The women freak out and the dudes get all pissed!" Brett said, baked out of his mind. "Who's out there?!" he crowed, imitating an angry old man.

As one would expect given the cloud of smoke still hanging in the air, the "Big Kids" had the munchies. Chris inspected Paul's bag and made us an offer: two candy bars for every swig of the evening's beverage. We traded looks and shrugged. Why not? We had plenty to spare.

Chris stepped over to a tree stump and retrieved a two-liter bottle that had its label removed. The container was about half-full, with an orange liquid that looked like Tang.

Paul unscrewed the top and, without any hesitation, took a gulp. His eyes bulged and he shook his head.

"What the hell *is* that?" Paul asked.

"Lighten up, brother," Chris said. "It's Orange Fanta with a splash of vodka and triple sec. Won't kill ya."

I'd heard those words before, so I stepped back and deferred to Paul. He guzzled some more and passed the bottle to Matt. He chugged away until Brett had to put a hand on his arm.

"Easy, Mocha," Brett said.

Matt offered the bottle to me, and I shook my head. The beer earlier had made me bold, and I had something damned important to say.

"Hey guys," I said. "About that nickname for Matt…"

All eyes were suddenly on me.

"Jay," Matt said. "It's okay."

"No, hear me out. Maybe it's no big deal to you but there's so much prejudice around here and—"

Paul gave me a tug on the arm. Everyone was staring. I suddenly flashed back to seventh grade when I'd put my foot in my mouth about Henry.

"You know why we call him 'Mocha?'" Brett asked, tapping my chest.

I looked at Matt. He was grinning. Why was he *grinning*?

"It's because the first time they met me I had ice cream on my nose," he explained.

"So, we asked him what flavor it was," Dallas said.

"And I said 'Mocha.' True story," Matt said.

"That is a good story," I agreed in a subdued voice.

"Damn, Banana Boy, you trying to kill our buzz?" Chris asked.

"Forget about it," Dallas said, taking a can of Skoal out of his front pocket. "Have you guys ever tried 'chew?'"

He held out the can and I stepped forward, aware that I had an opportunity for redemption. I pinched out a few tobacco leaves and dropped the wad between my "cheek and gums," just like Walt Garrison said to do in his famous commercial. Suddenly, liquid fire filled my mouth.

I looked over at Paul and Matt to wave them off it, but they had tried it too—their faces contorted like reflections in a funhouse mirror. Chris and Brett chuckled. Dallas, meanwhile, looked reflective.

"Hey, BB, hope there are no hard feelings about Kelly."

I couldn't speak because my mouth was filling up with volcanic saliva. The pressure made my eyes water. Dallas noticed.

"Damn, man, I didn't know she meant that much to you. I swear, that was the only time. I just caught up in a moment."

I held up my thumb as if to say, 'All good.'

"Spit it out, my man," Brett exclaimed, giving me a whack on the back.

I let it all fly but as I inhaled fresh night air, saliva and granules of chew trickled down my throat. Instant hacking cough. Not only that but my sphincter was opening and closing like the mouth of a goldfish.

"Gotta run, guys!" I stumbled away from the group and started my trot home. I swear it must have looked like I was in a potato sack race.

I'll spare the ugly details, but I recall needing a safe place to throw my soiled underwear that night. I decided once again on my personal attic space. I was in no condition to crawl in, so I put my not-so-tidy-whiteys on my finger and flipped them deep into the darkness.

I closed the door and leaned back against it as if guarding all the secrets the space concealed. In a matter of seconds, I was asleep.

44

Not that I deserved it given my antics, but two wishes came true that Christmas. The first was that "Santa" delivered the famous Farrah Fawcett pin-up poster that seemingly every teenage boy in America had—or wanted. (My folks thought Justine still believed in Santa. Justine thought "Santa," if he did exist, was a dirty old man).

As for wish number two? My parents finally got us a dog. The day after Christmas they brought home a fluffy Golden Retriever puppy.

When I suggested the name 'Farrah' for the new pup I was voted down.

"How about Daisy?" Justine suggested.

Mom and Dad looked at each other with raised eyebrows.

"*Daisy*," they said in unison as if they needed to hear how it sounded coming out of their mouths.

"I like it," Mom said.

"Me, too," I seconded.

"Then Daisy it is," Dad said.

For the next few days, neither Justine nor I went anywhere after school. We'd wolf down a Hostess cherry pie or some other snack and play with Daisy in the backyard until we were all exhausted.

After dinner, when we'd watch our favorite shows (*Charlie's Angels* for me if there was any doubt), Daisy would wedge herself between us. At night, Justine and I would rotate evenings with Daisy in our rooms. Mom and Dad said it was okay as long as we set some newspapers down.

Justine wrote a cute poem in her honor, which Mom stuck on our fridge with a magnet.

Daisy the dog is an amazing beauty.
With her bark and walk—she's such a cutie.
But don't try to bathe her…
Because she will get snooty!

Shortly after Daisy's arrival, a new couple, Martin and Sally Burke, moved into Kenny's old house. They seemed nice, around late-40s, and low-key, almost studious. Paul, Matt, and I were hopeful they'd have a child around our age, but we soon found out their three "children" were grown up and scattered around the country. According to Mom, this made the Burke's "empty-nesters." It was kind of sad when you looked at it that way.

Mr. Burke was a Raytheon engineer and didn't look like he was in the best shape, so he asked if I would be interested in shoveling for him in case we had moderate or heavy snowfall (his adjectives). What defined "moderate" or "heavy?"

Trust me, he had it figured out. Any precipitation that accumulated six inches would necessitate my service.

I guess he had devised a formula that anything less was manageable given the types of tires they had on their vehicles, in addition to the probability of the shallow snow melting. I accepted his offer, but in turn, suggested that if any precipitation exceeded 18 inches, he should look to someone else for snow removal—like Matt or Dallas, whose families owned a snowblower.

After the first moderate snow (nine inches, according to Mr. Burke's measurements), I bundled up for the job. It was rewarding, knowing you were going to be paid by someone else (the basic difference between a job and a chore, you could say). Also, the change of venue was refreshing. As I cleared the Burke's front walk, I glanced at the window where I first saw Kelly DeSantos (or she first saw me). I had a nostalgic pang in my stomach, thinking back to our fun times.

I should add that the Burkes also owned a dog, Hunter—a large and ferocious-looking German Shepherd mix. Fortunately, Hunter was always inside while I worked, but I could still hear him growling and barking like he wanted to chomp one of my limbs off. Dad had seen him, too, and made it clear that we were to keep Daisy away from Hunter until she was older. And then a second later he changed his mind and said it would be best to keep them apart. Period.

I was fine with that, but at the same time, I felt sorry for Hunter. When the temperatures eventually warmed up, the Burkes finally let him outside, but even then he was tied up with a rope…left alone with just a bowl of water.

No wonder Hunter was an angry dog. And maybe it was no surprise that the Burke children had flown the nest.

45

Although I had attended a game at Fenway Park, I'd never been to the Boston Garden, so I was thrilled when Paul told me that he had an extra ticket to a Celtics game against the Milwaukee Bucks. The plan was for Paul's big brother, Tony—the reclusive one—to drive us in one of Ed's cars to Riverside, which was the closest place for us to catch the MBTA. From there we'd take the "T" the rest of the way into North Station and the Garden.

As we rattled along the Green Line into the city, I couldn't help but recall Dad's story about poor Charlie, the guy who never got off the train. I hoped Tony or Paul knew our stop because I didn't want to live Charlie's nightmare. As I glanced at Tony, it occurred to me that he resembled the actor Charles Bronson.

"Hey, Tony, you know who you kinda look like?" I asked.

"Someone who's gonna tell you to shut up?" Tony asked, keeping his gaze on the cityscape that streamed past.

I looked at Paul and he grinned. I took Tony's advice for the rest of the ride.

The "Gahden" wasn't as old as Fenway, but it still had history. Our seats were fantastic, too. Even though we were up on the balcony, we had a view of the entire court. What's more, we were sitting behind legendary announcer Johnny Most. It was the best of both worlds—seeing the game live, while also being able to hear the play-by-play with Johnny's inimitable growl.

If you thought being told to "shut up" was the low point of my evening, you'd be wrong. After drinking two cokes, I needed to go to the restroom. At halftime, the line was too long, so I went during the third quarter. I approached a urinal, unzipped, and began relieving myself.

Just then an older, well-dressed guy shuffled up to the urinal right next to me, even though the restroom wasn't crowded. Soon he started teetering into my space, and I thought he was losing his balance. His shoulder was almost touching mine, so close I could smell the booze on him.

And then, all of a sudden, he craned his neck and gazed down at my "unit." I cursed myself for buying a second soda.

"Niishe one," the drunk slurred.

Completely creeped out, I zipped up without a word. As I hurried toward the sink to wash my hands, I saw Tony standing near the restroom entrance. I had no idea how long he'd been there, but he looked intense.

"Go back to the seats. I'll meet you there," he said.

I walked past him as he stepped toward the urinal. Curiosity got the best of me, and I turned around to see Tony slug the drunk in the gut. The man crumpled to one knee, gasping for air.

"Fuckin' pervert," Tony said.

46

The men's room incident was the first in a series of dramatic events involving the Boucher family over the next few weeks.

One late Saturday afternoon, I heard a motorcycle cruising through our neighborhood. The rider was constantly revving the engine and shifting gears, so I figured it was Ed testing out one of his repair jobs. As the VRROOOOOM became louder, I heard ferocious barking and a horn—followed by a scream and horrendous yelping.

My parents leaped to their feet and headed outside. Justine and I followed. In the middle of Moss Hill, just beyond Burke's house, was a horrible scene—

Mr. Boucher was on the ground, conscious but clutching his leg which was bloodied and burned. There was also a gash on the side of his head. His Honda motorcycle was thrashed, about 15 feet away, with the front wheel still spinning.

Meanwhile, Burke's dog, Hunter, tried to drag himself to the side of the road with a mangled hind leg.

"Hunter!" Mr. Burke yelled, exiting his front door.

"Nooooo!" Mrs. Burke shrieked.

Mrs. Monetti, meanwhile, hurried over from her house, carrying a First Aid kit and a blanket

"Ed, hang tight, we're gonna get you taken care of!" she hollered.

The next few minutes were filled with screams, howls, accusations, human and animal triage, and sirens. While Mom and Dad acted as peacemakers, I took Justine back inside. Through an upstairs window, I could see Ed being wheeled toward an ambulance on a stretcher, while the Burkes wrapped Hunter in Mrs. M.'s blanket and loaded him into their car.

That evening we all let out a collective sigh as we learned the victims, both human and canine, were recovering. Regrettably, the incident created bad blood in the neighborhood. The Burkes were angry because Hunter had been struck by a speeding motorcycle. The Bouchers were upset because the dog's chain was not properly secured, which enabled him to chase after Ed. Mr. Burke threatened to send Mr. Boucher the veterinary bill for Hunter's treatment, which included amputation of the dog's rear left leg. In turn, Ed demanded the Burkes pay for his ER visit, not to mention bills for knee surgery and the physical therapy he would need.

After a while, with my parents and Mrs. M. serving as mediators, cooler heads prevailed. While both victims were hobbled, neither family seemed interested in pursuing matters in court.

Another development soon came to light: Mr. and Mrs. Boucher were having marital problems. It wasn't like Paul had to tell me. I saw it. Terri was already displeased with Ed for a lot of things, but the accident was the last straw. She had warned him about riding without a helmet and testing out his "damn bikes" when there might be kids around.

"There were no kids around!" he shot back.

Paul told me his Dad moved into their Winnebago after that.

47

There were more snow days that winter, which allowed me to earn some extra cash shoveling for Mr. Burke. The guys and I also went back to our old standby, Strat-O-Matic, when time allowed. One morning, after clearing Burke's property and winning an overtime thriller with my Raiders over Matt's Steelers, Matt and I took a break from the action. We called Paul and he joined us as we tossed Matt's frozen Nerf football around.

"Who's that?" Matt asked, nodding towards my house.

I turned and looked. It was Dad, outfitted in stylish ski pants, jacket, goggles, gloves, boots, and hat. Turns out we weren't the only ones enjoying the white stuff that day.

"You've got to be kidding," I said.

Dad stepped into his blue Olin skis, picked up his poles, and gave himself a push. Within seconds, he was zipping down the packed powder of Moss Hill, as if it was his very own slalom course.

"Now *that's* cool," Paul said.

When Dad finished sidestepping his way back up the hill, the guys and I surrounded him.

"How was it?" I asked.

"Short," he joked.

"Looks like a blast," Matt said.

"You boys have skis, poles, and boots? I know Jay does," Dad said.

"Somewhere we do, yeah," Paul said.

Dad encouraged us to get our equipment and we dashed off through the snow like Dancer, Prancer, and Comet. Less than fifteen minutes later, we were back at my mailbox and Dad helped us with our equipment. For the next hour, at least, he gave us free ski lessons—encouraging us to bend our knees, shift our weight, and follow his trail. Soon Mom and Justine came out to watch us, bringing Daisy along to frolic in the snow.

Moss Hill had been transformed into Moss Mountain—and it was our personal winter wonderland, at least until the salt trucks came.

48

At some point, young teens discover a simple, inescapable truth: Middle School is traumatizing. After "Fisticuffs with Friends" on Day 1 of seventh grade and all the awkward growing pains (physically and socially), I thought it would be smooth sledding for me in eighth grade. Well, not exactly…

Take Social Studies, for example. The two films the teacher, Mrs. Neal, showed us in the first month of school were *The Grapes of Wrath* and *Bless the Beasts and the Children*. These tear-jerkers made *The Other Side of the Mountain* look like *Blazing Saddles*. Don't forget, I liked the Carpenters, but if I heard the title track from "*Bless the Beasts…*" one more time I was going to run headfirst into a wall.

The ultimate kick in the pants happened in a class I liked, English 2. My teacher's name was Mr. Lasher. He wore a bow tie, had a beard, and spoke with a booming voice despite his small stature. He was into the arts and spent summers out in the Berkshires acting in plays. I don't know if he was "light in the loafers" as Dad would say, but to borrow another phrase, he was on the "artsy-fartsy" side.

Mr. Lasher would occasionally turn on his cassette player and entertain us with old radio shows, like *War of the Worlds* and *The Twilight Zone*. Whenever he mentioned the names Orson Welles or Rod Serling, you could be certain the word "genius" would spring from his mouth. What I'd like is that he'd turn off the lights, pull the blinds closed, and crank the volume up high. Even Ricky Catano, who was in the class (yes, *that* Ricky Catano), seemed to get into it and was on his best behavior.

It started innocently enough. My favorite *Twilight Zone* episode of all time was "The Hitchhiker." Mr. Lasher chuckled when he saw my face after the episode ended. I must have looked riveted. "I imagine you'll think twice before trying to hitch a ride, Master Jayson."

"More like Master-*bator*," Catano snickered under his breath, which led to a chorus of laughter from those within earshot.

"Something amusing, Master Catano?" Mr. Lasher asked.

"No, sir. Just said he better call a *'cab later,'*" Catano replied.

Mr. Lasher let it go and then assigned us a fun project: create a suspenseful radio show in the proper audio format (meaning audiocassette). That wouldn't be a problem. Dad already had a portable audio cassette recorder and tapes. I just had to come up with a story.

After catching a glimpse of *Butch Cassidy and the Sundance Kid* on TV one night, I decided I'd create a Western radio show. The story would be about two rival bank robbers and their gangs. I recruited Matt for the other role, and a few days later we went up to my bedroom with a script and a few props.   When Matt was ready, I pressed "record." In hindsight, the production could have used more elaborate dialogue. For example, we relied heavily on "Put 'em up" and "Die, you scoundrel!" There were plenty of sound effects, including the popping of plastic bags for pistol shots. At some point, the action scenes got out of hand, and we went crazy flicking drawer handles and slamming doors.

"Hey!" Justine hollered outside my door.

Instead of responding to her, I improvised and screamed, "Save the girl!"

"We're coming to get you, lass!" Matt said, following my lead.

In the end, I got what I deserved. Mr. Lasher gave me a C- on the project. His notes on my script were like a punch in the gut: *This is horseplay (and I'm inclined to substitute another suffix for that word). The battle scene was monotonous, nearly unbearable. Fortunately, you typed your script—otherwise, your grade would have been lower. I know you have an imagination... PLEASE USE IT IN THE FUTURE!*

If that wasn't bad enough, Ricky Catano received an "A" for his project. Of course, he cheated, just like he did on his mile run, recording a passage straight from Disney's "The Haunted Mansion." I knew this because Justine had the same record at home--she'd been playing it for years around Halloween.

What surprised me was that Mr. Lasher had no clue that it was a rip-off. I thought he would have seen and heard everything by now. But no, he lit up as he described the key story points of Catano's "House on Haunted Hill" and all the elaborate effects.

While Catano ate up all the praise, I fumed. The smart-ass bully was gloating about something that he had ripped off 100 percent. Enough was enough.

"Mr. Lasher," I said, raising my hand.

"Yes, Jayson."

"I was just wondering if we could have Ricky bring in some of his narrators and props, and, you know, show us how he put together this amazing production. I think all of us could learn a lot from that."

Catano stared at me across the room.

"Well," Mr. Lasher said. "I know sometimes great chefs don't like to reveal their secret ingredients, but let's ask him. What do you say, Mr. Catano?"

"About what now?" Catano said, tuning into the conversation late.

"Would you be interested in bringing in some of the elements from your production to share? Perhaps for a small scene or two?"

"Oh," Catano said. "Well, a lot of the props and players, as you might say, are no longer accessible, So, sadly, as much as I'd like to entertain my fellow students, I don't think it would be possible."

"Alas, sometimes lightning is only meant to be captured in a bottle once. We have our answer," Mr. Lasher said, looking back at me.

When the bell rang and my classmates gathered up their belongings, Catano veered my way. He stepped in front of my desk, shielding Mr. Lasher from my view, and swung his backpack so it knocked my books to the floor.

"Oops, sorry about that, Jay,"

That afternoon Paul and I boarded the bus, greeted our afternoon driver, Luis, and made our way toward the back row as we usually did. To my surprise, Catano was sitting in the last seat next to Maura, Kelly's old friend, from down the street. Apparently, they were an item—who knew?

Paul and I nodded to Maura as we slid into separate seats a few rows ahead of them.

"Boys," Maura said matter-of-factly.

Catano gave us an amused look as he wrapped an arm around Maura and kissed her forehead. As they snuggled, I kept my fingers crossed that Maura would keep him occupied until we arrived at our bus stop. Familiar landmarks passed by in a blur. I began feeling optimistic, until—

"So that was some bullshit you tried in class today," Catano said.

I ignored him, trying to wait things out.

"So, what? Now you're deaf and stupid?" he continued.

I glanced at Paul, and he was doing a slow burn. I didn't want him involved so I faced Catano.

"Hey, you got an *A*…you should be happy," I said.

"I'd be happier if I kicked your ass," he replied. "Maura says you all think your shit don't stink up on that hill where you live."

"Ricky! I did not!" Maura exclaimed, slapping his hand.

"Is that why you've always been a prick to me?" I asked.

"No," he said. "I just don't like your face."

"Ricky," Maura pleaded. "*Don't.*"

"I just can't believe this pussy lets me talk this way to him," he said.

I began to rise, but Paul put a hand on my shoulder as he stood.

"How about you just shut the fuck up?" Paul challenged.

"Oh, look, the boyfriend. You gonna make me?" Catano scoffed.

Luis braked and I realized we were at our stop.

"Do something, tough guy," Paul said.

Catano charged and swung but Paul ducked and drove him into the side of a bus seat. Catano grimaced but managed to slide an arm around Paul's neck. He pivoted and, gaining leverage from his legs, put Paul into a headlock. Luis was on the spot in a flash and pulled them apart.

"Break it up!" Luis said.

With Paul's shirt riding up his back, Catano gave him a vicious slap.

"You! *Stop!*" Luis yelled, pushing him back.

"Get your hands off me, damn *wetback!*" Catano said.

"Okay, you two," Luis said to Paul and me, trying to keep his cool. "Off now."

Paul and I grabbed our belongings.

"*You,*" Luis said, pointing to Catano. "Back to school with me."

After stepping off the bus, Paul took a moment to inspect his shirt, which was torn. He then craned his neck and tried to look at his back.

"Are you okay?" I asked.

He nodded and we began trudging up Moss Hill. Paul kept his eyes focused on the road. His jaw was rigid.

"You didn't have to get involved," I said.

"Yeah, I did. That's what friends do," he said.

"You think I should have jumped in?" I asked, sensing something in his tone.

Paul shrugged. "Don't worry about it."

"Paul, it was one-on-one. I thought you were about to take him."

He shook his head without comment, and veered down his street, towards his house. I watched him, hoping he would turn around.

But he kicked a stone and kept walking.

49

Later that afternoon, I debated whether I should call Paul to apologize. I knew I'd disappointed him. But part of me was disappointed, too. He'd walked away, rather than talking it out. Of course, he had a lot going on at home. Just as I was about to pick up my parents' bedroom phone, Dad hollered that dinner was ready.

A satisfying meal will almost always lift one's spirits. The food and conversation helped take my mind off Mr. Lasher, Ricky Catano, Paul, and the terrible day I'd had. As Justine and I helped clear the table, I noticed Dad moving items, like the salt and pepper shaker, to the mantle above the fireplace. Things being stowed away? *Hmm.*

"Hey gang, take a seat again. Honey, you ready?" he asked Mom.

She refilled her glass of water and sat down as soon as Justine and I were back in our chairs.

"Well, gang…as you know, I've been spending a lot of time on the road—"

"We're moving," I said, nonchalantly.

Dad threw up his hands. "How does he do this? *Every* time—"

"I don't know. It's uncanny," said Mom, shaking her head.

"So, you mean it's true?" Justine asked.

"Yes," Dad said. "It's true. Once the school year ends."

"No!" Justine cried.

"Justine—" I said.

"What?" she asked.

"They didn't even say where we're moving to," I said.

Justine took a breath and tried to compose herself.

"Right," she said. "So where are we moving this time?"

"Vermont," Mom and Dad said as if they'd practiced the response.

"Vermont," Justine repeated. She then looked at me for my reaction.

"Okay," I said.

"Okay?" Justine asked.

"Could be worse. Can I take Daisy for a walk?" I asked, rising from my seat.

Dad was too stunned to respond. Mom leaned towards me and placed the back of her hand on my forehead as if checking for fever.

"Are you feeling okay?" she asked.

"Yeah." I didn't know if I was or not, but I needed to get outside.

Maybe Paul was right.

I just didn't have the fight in me anymore.

50

A lot had changed in my life. There were changes amongst my peer group, and with my body—*still*. Why not a change of location to top it all off? Besides, it wasn't the way it used to be when I was a little kid. I could see Paul and Matt again. I had their phone numbers memorized. And Vermont was still part of New England—it wasn't *that* far away.

The details about our move were still sketchy. From what I understood, Dad had saved a lot of money—maybe even borrowed some—to purchase an athletic sock company in Vermont. Athletes loved these socks, he explained, because they absorbed perspiration and kept the feet dry.

Dad also revealed that he had plans to develop headbands and wristbands, too. That got me jazzed. I envisioned a commercial where Bill Walton lost his headband and then I threw one of Dad's specials to him from the crowd as a replacement. Big Bill would put it on and at once block a dozen shots and score 80 points, leading his team to victory.

The following Saturday morning, Dad and I loaded our travel bags and family cooler into the Impala. The two of us were embarking on a weekend business trip to a small town outside Montpelier, Vermont. Mom and Justine, on the other hand, would stay home to organize, pack, and look over Daisy.

Once we were northbound on Route 128, Dad allowed me to take control of the car stereo from the passenger seat. I heard a snippet of "Cats in the Cradle" and tuned it in. The late Harry Chapin's voice seemed to cast a quiet spell on us as he sang about a father and son who just can't ever find time to be together.

"Damn good lyrics," Dad said when it finished.

"Yeah," I agreed, surprised by his reaction. "Classic song."

Even though Dad played guitar, I thought he was just a toe-tapper. Was he deeper than I gave him credit for?

We stopped for gas and lunch in Manchester, New Hampshire, which surprised me because its downtown featured a half-dozen tall buildings. I thought the Granite State was all rocky hills.

As we ate our burgers and fries, I worked up the nerve to talk to Dad about something I'd often wondered about.

"Hey, Dad?" I asked. "What's the story with Church? How come you don't like going?"

Dad sighed and fixed his eyes on me. As difficult as it was, I didn't look away.

"It goes way back, Jay. Your mother never told you?"

I shook my head.

"Well, I told her it had to do with a stutter," Dad said.

"Whose stutter?" I asked.

"Mine," Dad said.

"I didn't know you stuttered."

"I didn't."

"I'm confused," I said.

"The thing is, when my parents took me to the Baptist Church for the first time, I was 13. The preacher asked my parents if I would stand up so everyone could welcome me. Well, the truth is, I had been thinking about a beautiful classmate of mine named Emily who was seated in the pew in front of us."

"What's wrong with that?"

"I was thinking about little Miss Emily in ways that weren't appropriate for church. And so, I reacted, if you will, at the exact moment my father pulled me to my feet. It was so obvious that my mother covered it up with the Bible."

"*No,*" I said, partly because I empathized with Dad, and partly because I wasn't sure if I wanted to hear anymore.

"It was just as embarrassing as it sounds. My parents were so ashamed they never took me to church again. This stays between us, right?"

"*Right,*" I said emphatically. Telling friends about Dad having a boner when he was young was not high on my priority list.

We checked into our motel room outside of Montpelier a little after 3:30 pm and by 4:00 we arrived at Comfort Sports, Inc., the sock company. A receptionist named Delores led us through the office lobby. She wore big round glasses and a necklace full of beads over a floral dress. The owner, Mr. Silverberg, stood by her desk.

"Nice to see you again, Joel," he said, extending his hand.

"You too," Dad said, shaking. "This is my son, Jayson."

We shook hands and I noted that Mr. Silverberg's hands were soft and small. He was slender, with white hair, and dressed comfortably—a little like Mr. Rogers. Although he may not have been an athlete, the walls of his lobby were adorned with photos of sports stars, many from the world of tennis.

Perhaps sensing that I was starstruck, Mr. Silverberg took a paper from Delores's desk. It was a personal thank-you letter he'd received from the 26th-ranked men's singles player in the world. He allowed me to read the second paragraph where the gentleman raved about the socks.

"Would you like a pair of those socks for yourself?" he asked.

"You bet," I said, a little too excitedly.

Mr. Silverberg crossed to a nearby cabinet and retrieved a clear package that had a pair of white socks with a single blue stripe. As he handed them to me, I asked Mr. Silverberg if he knew Fred Lynn. He shook his head and said not personally. He was a Mets fan and planned to retire to Florida where he could watch them play during spring training.

While Dad and Mr. Silverberg met in a private conference room, I strolled around outside the building. On one side of the road, there was a stream, and on the other, a large farm. Mom would describe it as "quaint," no doubt about it. I noticed an empty table beside the building, presumably one that employees used for their breaks. I sat on one of the chairs, took my deck of cards out of my pants pocket, and dealt hands for an imaginary game of Five Card Stud.

Dad came out to get me an hour later. On the way back to the motel, we rolled down the windows and let the cool breeze whip around our heads. The surrounding buildings and homes were white and nicely maintained. Dad said every street corner looked like a scene from a Norman Rockwell painting.

After we returned to our room, we turned on the television and found a Red Sox game on one of the UHF channels. They were up on the Rangers 7 to 3. I was overjoyed. Not just because the Sox were winning, but also because we weren't moving to a place where I'd have to root for a brand-new team.

51

When I returned to school on Monday, I informed Dave and my other friends that I was moving. Since I hadn't ordered a yearbook, I asked if they'd be willing to sign a piece of beige construction paper for my scrapbook. Dave obliged and wrote with a calligraphy pen: *If this isn't a fine example of my superior penmanship, I don't know what is.*

Some of the guys asked why. It wasn't phrased in a way that implied "Why are you moving?" but rather "Why do you want my signature?" Those who did honor my request were visibly torn up by the news with messages like "See ya, wouldn't want to be ya," or "To a good kid from a better one." Matt wrote: "Don't eat too much cheese." Once again, I wondered if I had overvalued my friendships.

The only person I still hadn't shared the news with was Paul. Mom told me that his parents were separating, and Mrs. Boucher was moving out. The last thing Paul needed was to deal with another life-changing event, but I wanted him to hear it from me.

The next afternoon, while I was packing boxes in my bedroom, I heard someone dribbling a basketball. I knew where it was coming from and, more importantly, who it was by the rhythm. I hurried downstairs and headed outside to the path behind our house. In less than a minute I stepped out of the woods to find Paul shooting baskets at his hoop.

"Hey," I said.

"Hey," Paul said back.

He took a shot from behind the free-throw line and swished it.

"I heard the news," he said. "You guys getting the hell out of Dodge, eh?

"Yeah," I said. "How'd you find out?"

"The usual suspects. My mother, and Matt," he said.

"Matt," I said, shaking my head.

"Don't hold it against him. I almost had to beat the news out of him."

I chuckled and then turned serious.

"Paul, look, about your folks…I'm sorry."

Paul picked up the basketball and held it against his hip.

"Eh, it's for the best. At least my dad gets to sleep in the house again."

I nodded and he threw me a pass. I hit a short baseline shot and Paul collected the rebound.

"And listen, about not jumping in with Catano, I know I let you down," I said.

"No, Jay, you didn't. I shouldn't expect you to help fight my battles," he said. "I'm sorry I acted like a prick."

I reached into my pants pocket and took out my memorabilia page with some of my classmate's signatures.

"Hey, I got this paper I'm asking people to sign—"

Paul gave me a dirty look.

"Get the hell outta here with that."

"Why?" I asked.

"If I'm gonna write something, I'll need more space than that. Heck, I might even type it. But just my   'John Hancock?' No chance."

"All right then," I said with a grin. "I'll look forward to that."

Paul nodded and stuck out his hand.

"So, I guess this is it?" he said.

I pushed his hand away. "Get the hell outta here with that," I said, imitating his tone.

Instead, I gave him a brotherly hug.

52

The clock began ticking on our move. Dad gave his notice at work, canceled our club membership, and started calling local real estate offices in town and Vermont. Mom arranged to have our mail and magazine subscriptions forwarded to a PO box in Vermont and found a new vet in the area for Daisy. Justine and I, meanwhile, went through our drawers. We were instructed to stuff old clothes into bags for Goodwill and deposit trash into boxes. I discovered a few bucks and some change in various drawers, which reminded me that I needed to ask Dad about my money with Mr. Cavanaugh.

With the items on our checklist complete, our family ate out at the best restaurant in town that night. Although we were all tired when we returned home, no one was ready for bed. We gathered on the screened porch like we did our first night in Massachusetts—and so many others. Dad strummed his guitar softly and I almost dozed off until Mom nudged me with her toe.

"Jay, I just thought of something. Did you remember to clear out your attic space?"

Before I could respond, Dad stopped playing.

"Aw, there's nothing in there except a dirty pair of underwear and some girlie pictures," he said.

There was silence as everyone turned to me. I felt my face turn red.

"How did you know?!" I blurted.

My family laughed hysterically, and I dropped my head in exaggerated shame. The safe space of Miss May and my soiled Fruit of the Looms had been violated.

"What did you do with them?" I asked.

Dad winked. "Tossed out the skivvies, kept the pics."

Mom threw a crumpled napkin at Dad, and soon I was laughing harder than anyone.

Part Three: High

53

It didn't happen. Things hit a snag at the last minute and the sock deal was off. Kaput. Mr. Silverberg had gone from friend to foe. There was no group sit-down to share the news. Justine and I asked for details, but my parents were tight-lipped. It was ironic how whenever we were moving, they were an open book about all the possibilities our new lives would present. Now we were in the dark about how we would return to our old life.

Once again, I had to rely on my ears to pick up tidbits of info when Dad was on the phone or conversing in hushed tones with Mom. As far as I could tell, Dad had pulled out of the deal—something to do with Mr. Silverberg fudging numbers.

"What does 'fudging' mean?" Justine asked.

"Like changing," I replied.

When she gave me a blank stare, I told her that Mr. Silverberg was probably trying to make the company appear more profitable than it was. Dad smelled something fishy, told Silverberg that he wanted out—and demanded all his money back. Of course, Mr. Silverberg refused. He'd already moved to Florida, and I imagine he was counting on Dad's money to sail comfortably into the sunset of his life. The only way things could be resolved was by getting lawyers involved. And that meant one thing: huge headaches for all parties. I knew this because Paul told me not long ago his parents had hired lawyers to duke it out over property and custody. Things could get ugly.

I was thankful that Dad and Mom, while preoccupied, were still a team and united in getting us back on track. If our life were a movie, this is where the reel would be played backward—the way it sometimes was in school when our teachers were in a fun mood. All our careful packing turned to hasty unpacking. As for the upcoming school year? We suddenly went from unenrolled to enrolled.

"What do we say to our friends?" I asked.

"Tell them we had a change of heart," Mom said.

"Can't we tell them Mr. Silverberg tried to fudge us?" Justine asked.

"No!" Dad yelled from his office, cupping his hand over the mouthpiece while on yet another phone call.

When I asked Mom what we could do to help, she simply asked for our patience and understanding. Sacrifices had to be made. No back-to-school shopping, no more movies, or eating meals out—just the essentials.

I could live with that. The only thing I minded was Dad being down in the dumps or MIA from sunup to sundown. Ever since the deal went south with Silverberg, he'd disappear into his office for hours at a time. On the rare instances when he'd reappear, I'd flag him down and ask if he wanted to play chess or go hit tennis balls. He'd shake his head and say something about "having a full plate."

When Justine and I voiced our concerns to Mom, she reminded us that Dad had given up a well-paying position to fulfill a dream, and that dream went up in smoke almost overnight. He was scrambling to get our old life and that took time. I got her point but wondered where she got all her patience and understanding.

It wasn't long before taking refuge in his office wasn't enough for Dad. One night after dinner he grabbed his car keys and said he was going to go for a drive to "clear his head." A few nights later, he did it again, but that drive lasted longer. By the following week, he was gone so long that Justine and I were already in our beds by the time he returned home.

Even though I wasn't sure of Dad's exact whereabouts, I had a pretty good idea of what he was doing. After one late-night outing, I heard him stumble up the stairs, and then curse under his breath. My suspicion was confirmed the next morning when I discovered a cocktail napkin on the garage floor with "Meacham's Ale House" printed around the border.

It felt a little like a science fiction movie because "Mr. Manners," aka Joel Zimmerman, seemed to be developing an alter-ego right before our very eyes.

Mom and I were reading the *Sunday Globe* on the porch one afternoon when we heard Dad searching for something in our garage freezer. *Thump. Bang. Wham.* It sounded like an episode of *Batman*. Instead of pummeling villains, however, Dad was tossing frozen packages around.

"*Jesus H. Christ*…we've got to have chicken," he muttered to himself.

Mom dropped her paper and went to the garage to investigate the commotion. The door remained ajar, and I could hear their conversation.

"What's going on?" Mom asked.

"I'm looking for chicken breasts," Dad replied.

"Well, we might be out," Mom said.

"Didn't we just go to the store?" he asked.

"Yes, we did. But you know we only have so much in our grocery budget," Mom replied.

"So, what then? *Goddamn* pasta again?" Dad fumed.

"That's enough!" Mom roared. I sat up alarmed. Even the insects paused their chirping. When she continued, her tone was more measured. "I'd appreciate it if you wouldn't use God's name in vain."

"Look, Louise…" Dad sighed, "I'm more concerned with feeding my family than appeasing God right now. I don't need to remind you there's no money coming through that door."

"Then you better consider scaling back your evening outings, Joel, and the money that's going *out* that door," Mom replied.

A parental discussion in our house was always serious when my parents called each other by their first names. I wondered if they'd been speaking to each other this way in private.

"Point taken. It just helps me let off steam," Dad explained.

"Does it? Because five minutes ago says otherwise," Mom replied.

I heard the handle turn on the garage door and I quickly went back to my book. As Mom stepped back onto the porch, she cast her eyes on me.

"Not a word about any of that to your sister," she said.

That evening we ate spaghetti for dinner and there was little conversation. I don't know if Justine sensed tension or if she had overheard the argument way up in her room, but she was quiet, too. I quickly went from being surprised, to thankful, when Dad *didn't* go out to clear his head after the meal.

Later that night, as I settled into bed, I was reminded of one important thing: even though Mom had never worked a conventional job outside the home, inside of it she was *the* b

54

By the first of September, Paul's parents and their lawyers had finished wrangling in front of a judge. The divorce was official at last. The way things shook out wasn't great, at least from my point of view. Paul would be going to live with his mother in an apartment closer to Boston, while Tony and Chris would stay in the neighborhood with Ed. Even though Paul said he'd be coming back every other weekend for something called "visitation," he'd be going to a different high school.

Matt and I wanted to say a formal goodbye to Paul, just as we did when Kenny left. Once again, the day before school was set to start, we found ourselves huddled around a packed car. This time it was Terri's, parked in the circle in front of the Boucher house. As she waited behind the wheel of her car, Paul, the leader of our pack, stepped out to give us hugs.

"Bye, again, brother," I said, forcing a smile.

"It's not a 'goodbye,'" Paul said. "Just a 'See ya soon,' okay?"

Somehow, though, as we watched Terri drive away, it felt *impactful*. Things weren't going to be the same. Matt felt it, too.

"So, we've gone from the 'Fearsome Foursome' to the 'Terrible Twosome,'" Matt said.

"Yup," was all I could say.

"You think ol' Ed was cheating?" Matt asked, glancing at the old house.

"Who knows," I said. "Doesn't make any difference now."

"My mom says everyone cheats," Matt said. "One way or another."

"I'm starting to believe that," I acknowledged. "This guy Silverberg cheated my dad."

"That's what I'm saying," he said. "I know that kinda sucks for your family, but if you moved, I'd be flying solo."

The next morning, on the first day of school, I was alone at the bus stop. Same place, but earlier pick-up time. With all the tension at home, and without Paul by my side, my apprehension was higher than ever. Also, I was a *freshman*…the lowest link on the high school food chain.

Within the first hour of the day, I must have heard "What are you still doing here?" a dozen times and "What did I sign that paper for?" Seems like my classmates had gotten used to the idea of me being gone. Guys like Scottie Gartner and Henry Witherspoon muttered it with scorn—as if my presence had ruined an otherwise blissful day. Dave seemed relieved, but that was about it. Some students had no clue I was supposed to be moving, which was better.

The extra attention caught the interest of a clique of older students, and I soon had to endure the further humiliation of being "initiated" (an annoying tradition if there ever was one). A pair of shady-looking juniors locked me out on a second-floor balcony and laughed like it was the funniest thing ever. It could have been worse—I could have been stuffed into a trashcan like Albert Morrison or wrapped up in toilet paper like Benji Cohen (accompanied by "Do you want your mummy?" taunts). I was out on the ledge for only five minutes or so before I was let back in by Dallas, of all people.

"Thanks, Big D," I said.

"No worries, B-boy," he said. "I had to doubletake to make sure it was you. Thought you guys moved."

"No, this old guy tried to fudge us," I said.

"You mean, fuck ya?" he asked.

I titled my head.

"It means, like, screw you over. Rake you over the coals," Dallas continued.

"Yeah," I said. "All of that."

As it turns out, Dave and I were in the same French class right before our lunch block, so we ate together. We picked our food at a table in the middle of the cafeteria. It was an expansive room, with one interesting design feature: an elevated dining area that was accessible by a long ramp on one side and a set of steps on the other. This area, known as the "Ramp," was both exclusive and infamous—a favorite dining/hang-out spot for the school's popular students, while infuriating almost everyone else.

I knew this because Dallas and Brett had clued me in about the school's "hierarchy" over the summer. I also recall them giving Chris grief for sitting up there. As I took my seat, I spotted Chris sitting at one of the Ramp's long tables. In addition to a bunch of football and basketball players with varsity jackets, I noticed Scottie Gartner leaning pulling up a chair.

If you wanted to split hairs, the "Ramp" was a misnomer because the tables were technically on a large platform. I imagine this section was originally designed for disabled students with wheelchair access in mind, but as far as I knew, no one had ever pushed the issue.

As I scanned the crowded cafeteria, I spotted Ernie Fitts, a freshman whom I knew vaguely from eighth grade. He was eating near the base of a Ramp. He was also in a wheelchair with a cast on his leg. A thought occurred to me:

"If you're going to have a ramp, the guy in a wheelchair like Ernie should be the first one up there," I said.

"Well, I heard he broke his leg because he fell out of a tree trying to save a cat."

"What does that have to do anything?" I asked.

"So, it's not like he has polio and he'll never walk again," Dave said.

"I don't think people get polio anymore," I said.

"Well, then some other disease," Dave said. "I mean, he's gonna be out of that cast in a few weeks."

"A wheelchair is a wheelchair," I said. "We could talk to someone in the office. Or better yet, we could just ask him if he wants to eat up there."

"Trust me, if we go to the office or try to push him up that ramp, the two of us will end up in wheelchairs, too."

55

There was finally good news at home: Dad landed a job with his former company. It wasn't his former position (which had been filled) but it was a full-time gig and had all the benefits like health and dental coverage. The only downside was that it was a different department and Dad would be earning about half of what he made before.

Mom did her part, too. After tirelessly going through the "Help Wanted" section of the local papers, she found work answering phones in a local real estate office. Given her physical limitations with her arthritis, it was a bit of a risk, but that told me how determined she was to help us climb out of our financial hole.

With two parents working, Justine and I would be home alone often. We'd have to be more responsible with cleaning, but also sometimes cooking if our parents had to stay late at the office. Mom gave us a crash course on making simple dinners like frozen entrees and pasta dishes (yes, there were still lots of noodles in the cupboard).

One afternoon when I returned home from school, there was a large white Lincoln Continental in our driveway. The garage door was open, and Dad's car was parked in its usual spot in the garage inside,

When I walked in, Dad was behind the kitchen counter making drinks. Opposite him was a man in a suit, sitting on one of our counter stools, with his back to me.

"Is that my boy?" Dad asked almost merrily.

"Hey, Dad," I said and then looked at the man. He had wavy brown hair, green eyes, and sharp features.

"Hi there," he said.

Dad tightened the cap on a bottle of Gordon's gin. Both men had drinking glasses within arm's reach.

"Jay, say hello to Mr. Carney, our new attorney."

"Nice to meet you," I said.

Mr. Carney offered his hand, and I shook it. His grip was firm.

"How are ya, Jay? Jack Carney," he said.

"But you can call him *Mister* Carney," Dad clarified—as if I needed a reminder. "How was school?"

"Fine. Big place," I said with a shrug.

"He's a good-looking kid, Joel. He must get that from his mother's side."

"Jay, say goodbye to Mr. Carney. He'll be leaving now," Dad joked as he pulled a Coke out of the fridge.

Mr. Carney chuckled, and Dad handed me the cold soda.

"Thanks," I said, popping the lid.

"Shall we?" Dad asked Mr. Carney, with a tilt of the head.

Dad explained they had things to go over in his office. I didn't take it personally. As I heard more laughter, I marveled at the change in Dad's demeanor.

If having Mr. Carney around lightened the mood around our house, I hoped we'd be seeing more of him.

Johnathan R. "Jack" Carney, Esq., as his business card said, soon became a fixture at our house. Apparently, '*Esq.*' stood for Esquire. I wondered if anyone could be an Esquire or only a lawyer. Was there a special class taught by an Esquire master? The point was that his cards were everywhere, including our refrigerator, taped above Justine's poems.

Dad and Mr. Carney often disappeared into Dad's office with the door closed for hours at a time. We rarely saw them unless they were refilling drinks or taking a restroom break.

"Do you feel like you have two husbands?" I asked Mom one day.

"Sometimes I feel like I don't even have one," she replied.

Dad mentioned at dinner one night that in the Gaelic language, Carney meant "fighter." More macho than "room man," I had to admit. But I was glad Dad had a fighter on his side against shifty old Silverberg.

Occasionally I'd overhear things between the two that I wished I hadn't: "I gotta tell you, Joel, the craziest thing…I had twin craps this morning. I mean, side by side, you shoulda seen it. Looked like Yin and Yang." To which Dad replied: "You are one twisted barrister."

When I needed privacy during their more boisterous moments, I'd retreat to my bedroom and study. Sometimes, I must confess, it wasn't schoolwork. I'd recently obtained a leftover copy of the previous year's high school yearbook, *The Annual.* My original goal was to check out pretty girls in the upper grades—not just their Picture Day photos, but the "candid" shots because they tended to be more revealing. Before I got that far, however, I grew dismayed. Not by the photographs, but by what I saw in *print.* For example, the freshman class had voted "The Doors" as "Best New Band." *New?* God help that sorry bunch, especially the yearbook editor! After that, I stumbled upon a senior quote from Paul's brother, Chris. His life goal, right there in black and white, was to "drive six times the speed limit at Harper's Bend." In other words, hit *60 mph* at a notorious hairpin turn in town.

I was beginning to understand why adults looked down on our generation.

At school, my circle of friends began to expand. Dave introduced me to a friend of his named Barry Weisberg who went to his synagogue. I had seen Barry around but didn't know him personally. He was supposedly one of the smartest kids in our grade. His other claim to fame was that he'd been an extra in the movie *Jaws*. He was one of the 2,000 beachgoers who raced in from the water, screaming their heads off about the killer shark.

"They gave me $25 and a free lunch to spend the day at the beach," he boasted.

Another interesting thing about Barry was that he kept a "shit list"—literally. It was a little notebook with the names of those who offended him on it. When I asked him how many people were on it, he said "Two." One was a neighbor named Greg who had teased his younger brother, and the other was a boy named Mark who called him a "putz" at summer camp. As for what happens to the people on the list...?

"I'm done with them. Cut them out of my life for good," Barry said with authority.

"Sounds like they're getting the better end of the deal," Dave said.

"Watch it, or you'll be next," Barry warned.

What cracked me up about those two was that they were supposedly best friends, but they were total pricks to each other about 90 percent of the time. In Math, if we were having a quiz and Barry whispered something to Dave, Dave would respond with an exaggerated "What!?" The teacher, Mrs. Monroe, would frown at Barry, not Dave. On the other hand, if Dave was writing away, Barry would slap down on the eraser—sending Dave's pencil catapulting across the quiet room.

"Whose pencil is that?" Mrs. Monroe asked.

Barry would gesture to Dave, who was pencil-less, and then Dave would have to do a quick walk of shame to the middle of the classroom to retrieve it. It was no surprise that Mrs. Monroe separated them from that moment on.

This didn't stop their petty jousting, of course. They'd just find different locations, like the cafeteria, to carry on with the back and forth.

"What are you eating?" Dave inquired one afternoon.

"Tuna fish sandwich," Barry said.

"Why do you say, 'Tuna *fish*?'" Dave asked in frustration.

"Do you want me to say Chicken Salad?"

"No, my point is that your answer is redundant. Tuna *is* fish."

"You think I care what you think?"

"Just say 'tuna sandwich.'

"It's kinda like saying 'added bonus,'" I said, adding my two cents.

"Yeah, well, it would be an 'added bonus' for me if you two would shut up and let me eat in peace," Barry said.

The high school library soon became our hang-out spot. It's probably not something most kids would admit, but that's the way it was. We invited Ernie Fitts, who was now out of his cast, to join us at a long table. He in turn invited a Japanese student named Goskey Yamamoto. Goskey had lots of charisma and could carry a tune, but he had trouble with the lyrics to so many songs. Instead of singing the chorus of The Eagles' "Life in the Fastlane," he'd belt out "Pipes in the Vaseline!" (To be fair, I would struggle singing nursery rhymes in Japanese).

One morning I noticed a fellow freshman who was reading at a nearby table by himself. I recognized him from my French class. His name was Rollie, and he was one of three dozen or so students who took the bus in from Boston as part of the METCO program. My heart went out to him for a couple of reasons. First, because I knew what it was like to attend a new school, and second, because of ongoing racial tensions that seemed to be everywhere. Naturally, I thought back to the bus incident I saw with my family in downtown Boston, but I was also aware some students and parents weren't keen on inner-city students attending local schools. These people flat-out said—to friends, neighbors, and even reporters—that the METCO students brought a "certain element" to the community. Using the word "element" didn't disguise what they meant.

"It's Rollie, right?" I asked as I approached.

Rollie looked up slightly guarded, until he recognized me.

"Yeah. What's up, man?"

"Jay," I said. I stuck out my hand and he shook it. "Are you working on your French?"

"Nah, just a book on the history of cars," he replied.

"Wanna join us?" I said, nodding to a table with Dave, Barry, Ernie, and Goskey.

"All right," he said.

Later in the week, we were joined by Albert Morrison, one of the boys who had had a tough Freshman initiation. Realizing he needed redemption, good ol' Albert began dropping coins in lockers of students who sat on the "Ramp."

"Did the 'Tooth Fairy' visit you last night?" the "Rampers" would ask each other. They compared amounts received and guessed who the mysterious benefactor was. Some suggested it was a teacher, doing some kind of social experiment. Others believed it was Rory Bacon whose father was a high-profile attorney and lived on an estate on the edge of town. Rory was notoriously private and thrifty, according to those who knew him, so these rumors were soon put to rest.

Mrs. Chambers, a veteran Home Economics teacher, eventually caught Albert in the act after hearing what she described as a "slot machine" noise outside her room. I suspected that Albert, like most serial offenders, wanted to get caught. After a brief sit-down with our principal, Mrs. Weber, and a phone call to his parents, Albert vowed he'd make no more "donations." By that time, however, he'd become a school celebrity and was invited up on the "Ramp." The only problem was that his new "pals" were still expecting handouts. Even though he claimed he was no longer allowed to bring cash to school, they still turned him upside down and tried to shake something out of him.

After we took in Albert, we needed another table to accommodate our growing numbers. We didn't care how people looked or acted—as long as they weren't assholes. We prided ourselves on that—being regular guys, flying under the radar.

One morning a popular sophomore named Suzanne Van Fleet entered the library and slowly approached our table. She was one of the pretty girls who eventually caught my eye in the old yearbook. It was rare for someone of her stature to enter the library, much less speak to guys like us.

All conversations stopped as she headed my way. I held my breath.

"Are you Jay? The boy on Moss Hill who went out with Kelly DeSantos?" she asked.

I shook myself out of my daze and nodded.

"Yeah, for a little while," I said.

"We used to go to summer camp together," Suzanne said. "Anyhow, I got a postcard from her. She wanted me to tell you that she and Kenny said 'hello' from Chicago."

My eyes went wide in surprise.

"Tell them both I say 'hi,'" I said.

"Yeah, if I write back, I will," she said, turning away.

"Hey, Suzanne," I said.

She glanced back.

"You like 'The Doors?'" I asked.

"Of course," she said. "Everyone does."

"Right," I agreed. "Last question…"

"What?" She asked, folding her arms.

"How'd you know who I was?" I asked.

Suzanne rolled her eyes. "I had to ask a bunch of people. It wasn't easy."

As she pranced off, my friends chuckled. Rollie clamped a hand on my shoulder.

"I think you just got burned big-time, brother, but don't feel bad. You're still my hero."

At least somebody thought so.

58

As sweet as my mother was, she could also be blunt. She looked at me with alarm in her eyes at dinner one night, as if I had an insect on my face.

"What?" I asked, touching my cheek.

"When did your hair get so 'moppy?'" she asked.

"What's '*moppy*?'" I asked.

"Long and unkempt," she replied. "Like the Beatles."

"Well, that's kind of cool," I said.

"Maybe if you lived in the 1960s. We need to get you to Gerry, ASAP," Mom said to me.

"Hold on," Dad said. "Why take him to Gerry when Richard at the barbershop is half the price?"

"Well, Gerry's been doing it for ages. He knows his head," Mom argued.

"Richard can know his head, too. Richard—head. Head—Richard. Problem solved."

I began to say something, but Mom touched my arm. Her look told me there were battles worth fighting, and this wasn't one of them.

After school the next day, Mom dropped me off at "Rich's Barber Shop" before heading off to do a quick errand in the shopping center. Inside there was a painted plaque above the wall-to-wall mirror: *Better 'Rich' than Poor*. As I settled into one of the leather swivel chairs, I couldn't help but notice a slick-looking guy next to me looking at an issue of *Playboy* while getting his sideburns trimmed. I'll admit I tried to steal a glance. Old habits die hard.

Richard, the proprietor, was a stocky guy with a white goatee.

"You want a magazine to look at?" he asked.

"No, thanks," I replied.

"So, you're Joel's son," he said.

"Yessir," I said.

"He's a funny guy. Always asks who cuts the barber's hair?"

"That sounds like him," I said.

"So, what are we doin' here?" He held the sides of my head and looked at me in the mirror.

"Ah, just, you know…cut it shorter," I said with a shrug.

"Good. 'Cuz usually when we cut, it doesn't get longer," he deadpanned.

The guy with the *Playboy* and his barber let out amused snorts.

Thankfully, Mom returned at that point and Richard asked her what to do with my hair. Mom responded with all these directions, throwing out words like "shape" and "layer." In the mirror, I caught Richard glimpsing at his fellow barber as if to say, *'You believe this lady?'*

When it was all over, I was miserable. My neck was itching and somehow Richard had nicked my ear lobe with the trimmer. When I got home that night Justine's pupils swelled to the size of golf balls.

"What happened? You look like you got in a fight with a lawnmower," she said.

This was only the beginning of my hair disaster. The next morning, I overslept, and as I looked at the clock, I remembered it was Picture Day at school. I grabbed clean clothes and ran into the bathroom. Glancing in the mirror, I was mortified. Not only was my hair short and uneven, but it was greasy. I debated taking a shower, but Dad knocked on the door, shouting that Justine needed the bathroom, and besides, I had to get moving or I'd miss the bus.

After dressing, I rushed downstairs and explained my predicament to Mom. She said that cornstarch was a supposed remedy for oily hair and instructed me to sit on the kitchen stool. She grabbed a box of "Argo" from the cupboard and worked the powder into my scalp. I looked at the clock once again and realized there was no way I'd catch the bus. Thankfully, she dropped me off at school on her way to work.

The minute I took a seat at my usual table in the library, my pals asked how I managed to get dandruff overnight. I told them the whole story and for the rest of the day Barry called me "Corny." No major surprise. Barry was notorious in our circle for giving people nicknames. He called one heavyset junior with a fondness for yellow shirts "Big Bus." A cousin of Dave's with a severe overbite was dubbed "Buck-Tooth-Cousin" or "BTC" for short. The worst of all was reserved for a boy named Travis who often seemed uneasy (constantly crossing and uncrossing his arms, for example). For whatever reason, Barry labeled him with the not-so-catchy moniker "Doesn't-Know-Where-to-Put His Arms."

"How is that a nickname?" I asked. "It's like ten times longer than his real name."

Later in the day, after my photo was taken, I happened to run into my old neighbor Brett. Prepared for the worst, I started to turn away…

"Duuuuude…"

"I know, go ahead. Let me have it," I said, ready for a slew of jokes and put-downs.

"No, BB. I can't even go there. Here, take this," he said, generously handing me his Sox cap.

"Thanks," I said.

"Hey, you still got those Playboy pics?" he asked.

"Nah, my Dad found my stash," I said.

"Sheesh," he said with that familiar grin. "Life kinda sucks for you now, huh?"

As the weeks rolled by, my hair grew out and the temperatures dropped. I noted the change of seasons once again by the chores I had to do. One Sunday morning I was raking leaves in our front yard when Mr. Carney pulled his big

Lincoln into our driveway. His window was partly down, and I could hear the strains of "You Should Be Dancing" by the Bee Gees.

I set aside the rake and waved.

"Look at you, making an honest buck," Mr. Carney said, stepping out of the car. He nubbed out his cigarette in his side door ashtray and closed the door.

"Yeah," I said. "I *might* get that if I'm lucky. So, you like disco?"

Mr. Carney smiled. "Yeah, I gotta admit some of the stuff is kinda catchy. Don't let it get around, all right?"

"I won't. How are things coming along? You know, with the case?" I asked. I figured if Dad was going to be all hush-hush, I might as well go straight to the source while I could.

"Well, it's a long process, but we're getting there," he said.

Just then the garage door opened from the inside and Dad appeared.

"Hey, stop bothering the help," he said.

"I want to negotiate a raise for him. What, do you think Jay—ten bucks an hour?" Mr. Carney said to me with a wink.

"Sounds good," I said.

"Fat chance," Dad said. "He may get a McDonald's dinner out of it. But only if he passes inspection."

"So, tell me, Jay. What do you wanna do when you get older?" Mr. Carney asked.

"I don't know," I answered. "Something to do with sports. Become a sportswriter or sports announcer...who knows?"

"Like one of those Irish hacks at the Globe...Fitzgerald or McDonough," Dad said.

"Speaking of which, I got a joke," Mr. Carney said, setting his briefcase down. "I'm Irish, so I can tell this. Have you heard about the gay Irish couple?"

"No," Dad said, playing along. "Haven't heard."

"Too bad. They're perfect together. Know why?" Mr. Carney asked.

Dad nodded to me, as in "Your turn."

"Why?" I asked.

"Because Patrick 'fits-Gerald' and Gerald 'fits-Patrick.'"

Dad heaved a laugh and both men looked at me. I forced a chuckle.

"Don't forget the leaves in the gutter," Dad reminded me.

As he escorted Mr. Carney through the garage, I concluded that leaves weren't the only thing in the gutter.

59

The holidays rolled around in no time that year. Dad had informed us, well in advance, that it was going to be a "lean" Christmas. I had heard songs about a "White Christmas" and a "Merry Christmas" but never about a lean one. Mom explained it was Dad's way of minimizing expectations, given our financial situation.

I wondered what kind of child my parents thought they had raised. All I ever wanted was quality time with family and friends, and to see the Red Sox win the World Series. Only the last item on that list seemed unreasonable. Besides, I still had Farrah (and Daisy) from the year before.

On Christmas day, when everyone was in the kitchen, I noticed a card on the living room mantle. It was the one Mom had given to Dad after all the presents had been opened. I opened it and read the message:

"We'll get through this. Brighter days are ahead. I just know it! XOXO!"

It turns out Mother Nature had different ideas in the weeks that followed. In early February, the skies clouded up and then it snowed so hard you couldn't see anything but white. Motorists had to abandon their cars on the Mass Pike, and the highway soon resembled a frozen apocalypse. Where the motorists went was anybody's guess. If no one could drive, who could get to them?

Mysteries aside, the "Blizzard of 78" was *the* snowstorm of the 20th century. The drifts were so high they covered our doors from top to bottom. Dad had me climb out through the second-floor window of our guest room to sweep away several feet of the enormous drift blocking our side door. It still took all of us, working in unison, to wedge open the storm door in the mudroom so a body could fit through.

There was so much snow that Dad couldn't even ski down Moss Hill. It would have been up to his waist. And much to our relief, Dad acknowledged that a job of that size went well beyond the scope of his family's abilities. When Dallas and Brett came around later with their snow blowers and offered to clear all our snow away, he readily accepted the offer.

60

When the skies cleared and the snow finally started to melt, Mr. Carney resumed his visits. I wasn't sure how much my parents were paying him (if they'd paid him anything at all at that point), but it seemed they did all they could to express their gratitude, from an open bar to frequent dinner invitations.

I asked Dad if Mr. Carney had a family and he said he *believed* he did, but then he changed the subject. Dad could talk about world affairs, sports, stocks--- anything that was available for public consumption. He wasn't your guy, however, if you wanted to know about what went on behind closed doors.

I didn't bother to explain to Dad why I was asking about Mr. Carney, but I was starting to wonder if there was more to the picture. Why did he always come to our house? Didn't all lawyers have offices? Why couldn't they go there or to Mr. Carney's house? If he had kids, couldn't they come with him, at least once, on a visit to our house? And if he had a wife, why didn't she ever join us for dinner?

One Friday in early March, Mr. Carney and Dad emerged from Dad's office after another long afternoon of strategizing, phone calls, and drinking. Mom asked "Jack if he'd like to stay for dinner and, to no one's surprise (at least not mine), he readily accepted.

After some light table banter about school, sports, and music, Mr. Carney fixed his eyes on Mom.

"Louise, I gotta tell ya, Julia Child's got nothing on you. This meal is sensational," he said. "Childs" came out sounding like *Chise*, and "Sensational" was more like *"shenshaysonal."*

Justine and I exchanged looks.

"Thank you. We're always happy to have you," Mom replied modestly.

"We used to say 'hip, hip hooray' when Mom made a great meal," Justine offered.

"Well, Justine, I hear that hip, hip, hooray, and I'm gonna double it," Mr. Carney said, raising his empty beer glass.

"Emphasis on the 'hips,' I might add," Dad said with a wink at Mom. Mom tilted her head and frowned at Dad.

"Manners, good sir," Mr. Carney said.

Since things were getting silly, I gave Justine a subtle nod. We hurried through our few remaining bites and excused ourselves from the table. As we brought our plates to the sink, Mom instructed Justine to take a laundry basket with clean clothes upstairs. She then asked me if I would take Daisy for a walk. I said I would. Anything to get some fresh air.

Daisy did her business outside and I let her lead the way. Even though I brought her leash with me, she was so well-trained I didn't even need it. As I breathed in the cool night air, I glanced across the street and noticed a Ford pick-up parked near Monetti's garage. I'd seen it a few times recently and wondered if it belonged to Matt's uncle. Maybe there was some truth to the rumored romance involving Mrs. M. and her brother-in-law?

After sniffing around for another minute, Daisy trotted around to our backyard. Rather than try to steer her back to the front, we entered the darkened porch through the screen door. With Daisy on my heels, I started toward the door to the family room.

As I placed my hand on the handle, I glanced through a glass pane and saw Mom in the kitchen, rinsing a plate. Mr. Carney approached and slowly reached around her waist to place a glass in the sink. His chin was in her hair, and he seemed to take in her scent. My eyes grew wide in horror, and suddenly, he kissed the side of her neck.

While I stood frozen in disbelief, Mom spun around and slapped Mr. Carney. He recoiled and grabbed his cheek, appearing incredulous.

"*Shit*," I whispered, shocked. Daisy whimpered beside me.

Mr. Carney muttered something to Mom and retreated to the family room. Mom glared at him, shook her head, and exited the kitchen.

I stumbled back to a porch chair, processing what I'd seen. Daisy sat next to me and pawed at my leg. The night was silent until a car door opened and shut. Mr. Carney's Lincoln started up and the headlights swept through the woods as he reversed it into the street. The coast was clear, but I still didn't want to move.

I knew I would never forget what I had seen, but I told myself there was no point dwelling on it. And I could never say a word to anyone, not even Justine. This was for Mom to work out—and Dad, *if* she was ever inclined to tell him what had happened.

One thing I knew for certain: the amount of respect I lost for Mr. Carney was equal to the amount of respect I'd gained for my mother.

Despite recent events at home, I managed to get surprisingly good grades for the quarter. I'd kept up with my studies while keeping an eye on Mom and Dad. There didn't appear to be any friction—they were still sleeping in the same bed and calling each other "honey." Mom's energy level was surprisingly high. In addition to doing all the usual housework, she was studying for her real estate license.

Some random news as winter turned to spring: we received a postcard from Jeremiah in Hollywood ("To the Shirley Temple Gang…"), Grandma Marjorie turned 80 years old, the Burkes had to put Hunter down (not too many tears shed), Paul's brother Tony married his high-school sweetheart (they eloped to avoid family drama) and Justine got her ears pierced.

With all these changes going on, I still had my old reliable Raleigh Chopper. I didn't want to get rid of it, but I had outgrown it. I needed to upgrade to a ten-speed, Dave and Barry were nuts about bicycling and had invited me to ride with them now that the weather was more accommodating. I didn't expect my parents to buy me a new bike so I asked Mom how I could get my money back.

"What money is that?" she asked.

"The money I'd saved up from my chores," I said. "You guys told me to deposit it all into First Bank. Remember?"

She suddenly looked like she'd eaten a bad oyster.

"What is it?" I asked, realizing I sounded like Grandma Marjorie.

Mom sighed and told me that Dad had to use all our family's money after the Silverberg debacle to make ends meet. That included my $600, too. When I asked why Dad didn't say anything to me, she said it most likely had to do with his pride. She assured me he was working hard to replenish all our accounts and asked for my patience and understanding. Again.

I nodded, but like my bank balance, I wasn't so sure there was any left.

I decided to go for a bike ride with Dave and Barry anyway, even if it meant being cramped on my "banana" bike. I needed to blow off some steam. The guys wheeled into my driveway one Saturday, looking as if they'd just completed a leg of the Tour de France. They wore helmets and sunglasses and had water bottles set in fancy-looking holders.

"How far are we going?" I asked, flipping my Sox cap around.

"Not too far," Barry said, nodding at my chopper. "You sure you're gonna be okay on that?

"Yeah, it's fine," I said. "Let's roll."

We glided down Moss Hill and then the roads leveled out. For a while, I was doing fine. We took a left, then a right, and I was right there with them. We talked, we laughed, and I realized my endurance had improved. All that raking and shoveling, maybe? But then, as soon as the thought left my mind, we hit a long hill. Dave and Barry surged ahead. I tried to tell myself that I was the athlete out of the group, that these guys didn't play sports, that they were brainiacs—and yet how did they get so far ahead of me?

It dawned on me that I had never bothered to ask about our destination. That was a slight problem. I pedaled like crazy to catch up, but our distance widened more.

"Dave! Barry! Where are we headed?!" I shouted. My mouth was as dry as paper.

If they answered, I didn't hear it. And just like that, they reached the crest of the hill and descended to the other side.

A cramp flared in my lower back. I tried to ignore it and lifted myself off the seat, jamming down on my pedals as hard as I could. As I neared the top of the hill, another cramp seized the inside of my right calf.

My whole right leg went numb, and my foot slipped off the pedal. I veered onto the shoulder and jumped off as cars sped past. A drink of water would have been good right then, but I'd dropped the ball there, too.

"Asshole," I said to myself. I was upset with Dave and Barry, but I had to accept some blame for my predicament. I did a few calf stretches and pushed my chopper the rest of the way to the top of the hill, hoping to walk off the cramp.

Feeling some relief, I climbed back on and glided down to an unfamiliar intersection. I looked left, center, and right—neither the guys nor their bikes were anywhere in sight. I was alone and I was lost.

One small bit of luck…there was a service station to my right. I rode past the pumps to a pay phone, leaned my chopper against a wall, and headed inside. A red-headed cashier with a name tag that read "Fran" was kind enough to loan me a dime. I hustled back to the phone and called home. Dad answered on the second ring.

"Thank God you're at home," I said.

"What's going on, Kiddo?" he asked.

Although I was irked by the money situation, I calmly explained my predicament.

"Aw, that's unfortunate. Are you sure the guys aren't looking for *you*?"

I surveyed the area again. Still no sign of Dave or Barry.

"I can't count on that, Dad. So, what do you say? Can you pick me up?" I said, swallowing my pride.

"Look, son, I'm smack dab in the middle of something here. Drink some water, walk off the cramp, and head back," he said calmly.

I was starting to lose my cool. I told him I didn't know how to get back because my bike was old and only good for tooling around the neighborhood and that I wanted to buy a new one and if he—

"What's the address, Jay?" he asked.

I scampered inside to get the information from my new friend Fran, the only one who understood my plight. She handed me a business card and I hurried back to the phone to relay the information to Dad. As I was giving the name of the street, an automated voice interrupted and told me I needed to deposit another 25 cents to stay on the call. I tried to talk over the voice, but the call disconnected.

I slammed the receiver down, sat on the curb, and waited. And waited. I drank some more water and waited some more.

After 45 minutes, our Skylark cruised into the parking lot. As it approached, the window rolled down. *Mom.*

"Sorry it took so long, hon," she said. "I was at the office when your father called."

"That's okay," I said. So, Dad called *her.*

"Um, Jay, these are the Wannamakers," Mom said leaning back.

I looked past her and saw a hefty man in the passenger seat, wearing a V-neck sweater. Behind him sat a petite, well-dressed woman.

"Howdy," Mr. Wannamaker said with a slight southern drawl.

I waved, embarrassed.

"Hop on in, sweetie. We don't bite," Mrs. Wannamaker said.

Mom popped the trunk and I put my bike inside. Nine minutes later we were home. *Nine.* I was so disoriented, I thought I was out by Worcester which was in the middle of the state. I thanked Mom for saving the day, retrieved my chopper, and wished the Wannamakers happy hunting in their quest for a new home.

After putting my bike in the garage, I cruised into the house, passing Dad and Justine without a word. Daisy was resting in the front entrance hall, but I wanted a companion, so I clapped, and she followed me up to my bedroom. Always attentive, always available. I don't know why, but I thought about how much had changed throughout history, but dogs never did. You could go back two thousand years, and I'd bet anything our canine friends would be just as loyal.

I kicked off my shoes and sat on my bed. Daisy jumped up beside me. Suddenly, there was a knock on my door.

"Jay?" Justine's voice sounded apprehensive, but it was also welcome.

"Come in," I said.

She did, sat on the foot of my bed, and scratched Daisy's neck.

"Last time I saw you this mad was in Rosemont. You tried to run away. You're not going to do that now, are you?"

"Nah, don't worry," I said. "I'd just end up at another gas station, asking for someone to pick me up."

She giggled and then turned serious.

"Dave and Barry called to say 'sorry.' I told them what they did was lousy and that you *might* call them back."

I smiled, realizing how much she'd grown up. It seemed like yesterday when she was a toddler, watching Dad perform "When the Wind Blows Free" on his guitar. She held up three chubby fingers and screamed "And dat's how old I am!"

"Hello?" she asked.

"Yeah," I said, pulling away from my memory. "I appreciate that."

"Are you going to talk to Dad?" she asked.

"I don't know. I don't want to say something I'd regret."

"Then write him a note," she suggested.

I thought for a second. I could do better than that. And Justine could help.

****

DECLARATION OF *GRIEVANCE*

We, the children of the Zimmerman household, are gathered at 11:20 p.m. on April 27, 1978. We have undertaken this document to share our frustration.

1.   <u>To our father</u>: We are sorry that the sock company ordeal took a lot out of you emotionally and financially. We also understand your present job is demanding, and you are upset you're not making as much money as before. However, I was disappointed you called Mom to pick me up when I was lost. She was working, too. I also feel disrespected because you took my savings without telling me. I would have gladly loaned it to you.

2.   <u>To our mother</u>: We know you suffer from arthritis. It must make it hard to carry on with a new job—especially one as demanding as real estate. We appreciate you and will help as much as we can. However, if you come home day after day, too tired to cook, and in pain, we suggest you do not work so many hours. Your health comes first!

We hope this DECLARATION will unite us again as a family. We would like to see smiles, instead of frowns, and hear a "yes" occasionally instead of the standard "no." We wouldn't stay up so late if this matter wasn't important! We love and respect you both.

Signed: Jay   Signed: Justine

****

PS Mom, this is Justine. If you aren't going to wear those green shoes anymore, could I please have them?

63

The response to our "declaration" was a success—Mom gave Justine her green shoes. Okay, the reality? The reaction was underwhelming. Dad grumbled "Being dramatic doesn't help," and Mom, often our ally in situations like this, simply said, "We *all* need to do better."

Maybe I went too far. My parents were both Midwesterners and, as a rule, they didn't take well to "showy." The thing was, I couldn't do a heart-to-heart talk with Dad yet because he could talk circles around me.

A couple of days later, I apologized to Mom for being brash. She said it wasn't necessary and even confided that she had asked Dad to attend a counseling session. Well, that suggestion was shot down pronto. They had tried couples therapy many years ago, and Dad said he wasn't going to have "some shrink poke around again in our family business."

Right around this time, Dad's travel schedule filled up with sales meetings, conferences, and trade shows. He returned from Minneapolis on Tuesday, only to head off to St. Louis from Thursday through the following Monday. That window gave Mom a chance to do something she'd been wanting to do for a *long* time.

Early that Sunday morning she picked out "nice" clothes for Justine and me, and once we were downstairs, whipped up some toast and oatmeal. As she finished her coffee, she gave us a no-nonsense stare.

"We're going to have a little family outing today," she said. "There will be no debate or complaints. You kids have five minutes to brush your hair and your teeth."

Mom drove through town with a look that could be best described as a "game face." It was the way a pitcher locked at a batter when he had two strikes in the count.

"Can I ask if we're almost there?" Justine asked.

"No," Mom said.

Two minutes later we parked in the lot of the First Methodist Church. Again, with the "first," I thought, just like my old bank.

"Church?" Justine asked.

"Why did you think you couldn't tell us?" I asked.

"Because I didn't want either one of you to talk me out of it," she said, grabbing her purse and checking her look one more time in the mirror. "Let's go."

A well-dressed gentleman greeted us with a pleasant smile at the entrance and handed Mom a program. At least, I think that's what it was called. It was like the line-up card a manager would give the umpire before a baseball game, so the ump knew the proper batting order.

I was hoping Mom would sit in the back, but she chose a pew way up front. She wanted the full impact—probably because she'd been away so long, it was her way to make amends.

An organ blared and the parishioners rose as the service began. Mom tapped each of us, and Justine and I sprang to our feet.

"Stand straight," she whispered to me. "Don't slouch."

I didn't know I was, but I thrust my shoulders back like a runway model. Just then two well-dressed women came onto the stage and started singing. Mom looked at the paper and started singing right along with a beautiful voice. She showed me the words and I mouthed along.

"No faking," she whispered. "*Sing*."

I did and my voice sounded hoarse and off-key. Mom gave me an exasperated look and held the paper in front of Justine. She was no better.

Things moved along once the minister came out and started his sermon. It wasn't all fiery, but it still made me uncomfortable because he seemed to be making eye contact with me every so often. I wondered if that was by design, to make sure everyone was paying attention like a good teacher would do.

I gazed around the church and realized it could be worse: we could be Catholic. The symbolism of communion, the body and blood of Christ, and all that gave me the heebie-jeebies. And then the crucifix on full display? You wouldn't see something that gruesome on network TV first thing on a Sunday morning.

The other thing that didn't make sense to me was that if God was supposed to be all-powerful, why did he only have *one* son? He shouldn't have any physical limitations. I couldn't picture him saying "Eh, I'm too old to have another." And there shouldn't be any financial concerns. If God was The Almighty Creator, he could whip up a bunch of gold. Some poor families had a dozen kids and they managed to get by. I mean, unless God was concerned about having a large age gap between the two. Maybe he thought his sons wouldn't have a lot in common. But really, if you were going to have a big brother, who better than Jesus?

These were the questions that would get me in hot water, no doubt if I asked them out loud. I started to feel I might be cursing myself just by *thinking* about them, but I couldn't help it. Sometimes things just popped into my mind.

And at least my daydreaming helped me pass the time that morning.

64

As I began contemplating my mortality (thanks, First Methodist), I was reminded that I'd already had two brushes with death in my young life. Once, when I was an infant, I swallowed a bunch of vitamins and was rushed to the ER to have my stomach pumped. How I was able to get my hands on a bottle of adult vitamins is still a matter of debate. Based on the scatter pattern of the pills, however, the prevailing theory was that the bottle was somehow launched like a projectile. Who would do such a thing?

The second time I almost bit the big one was at a swimming hole in Connecticut when I was six years old. Even though I couldn't swim (problem #1), I was curious to see how far out I could walk. If I was as special as I thought I was—maybe all the way. I casually tiptoed right past a sign on a buoy that read, *"No wading beyond this point!"* Well, as you might have guessed, I couldn't read either (problem #2).

Even though the water was up to my nose, no one noticed (or they thought I had it under control, based on my purposeful manner). Well, wouldn't you know it, but there was a sudden drop-off, and I sank like a box of bricks. Fortunately, my babysitter, a 19-year-old German gal named Gabby, saw my head bobbing up and down from shore and swam out to retrieve me. To this day, my parents are indebted to Ms. Gabby and send her a Christmas card every year.

Taking this episode into account, and given my aversion to swimming, you might wonder why I would accept an invitation to go to a lake on Labor Day weekend. Well, that was easy: I would get to spend three full days with Paul. Terri had invited our entire family to join them in Maine at a cabin she had rented for the summer.

After a hearty pancake breakfast, while the adults were enjoying another round of Bloody Marys, Paul, Justine, and I headed down to the dock.

"Make sure you have life jackets!" Terri hollered.

"In the boat!" Paul replied.

Justine and I settled into the bow and middle of the eight-footer, respectively, while Paul untied the lines. It looked like he had grown since the last time I'd seen him—not just taller, but he had also filled out. Paul moved to the back of the boat and started the engine with a hearty tug. As he steered us away from the dock and out of the cove, Justine glanced ahead at the open lake.

"Why does the water look so dark?" Justine asked.

"Because the sun is behind the clouds," Paul answered.

As the wind picked up, so did the current.

"Have you two ever been to a rodeo?" Paul shouted over the engine as we picked up speed.

"Can't say that I have!" I called back.

"Well, hold on!" Paul yelled as his eyes widened.

Justine and I gripped the sides of the boat and Paul turned head-on into the choppy wake—each bump creating sprays and thrills for us. Our screams of joy turned to fear as we hit the wake of another, larger boat—

My stomach rose to my throat as the boat went airborne. When the boat slammed down, and I landed back on the metal seat, the impact jarred my spine.

"That was a blast!" Justine screamed, wiping spray from her face.

"Are you guys, okay?" Paul asked.

"Yeah, I'll live," I said, massaging my back.

Just then a flash of lightning zigged across the sky.

"Whoa, you see that?" Justine asked.

I nodded. If there's one thing about New England weather, it can change in the blink of an eye.

"Storms-a-coming!" Paul hollered.

"Should we go back?" Justine asked, checking her life vest. It dawned on me that I wasn't wearing a vest. As raindrops began to fall, I extended my foot to nudge two life jackets on the floor closer to me in the bow.

"One more run?" Paul said.

"All right," I said. "One more."

"Hold on!" he shouted.

Before I could pick up the vests, Paul twisted the throttle and the boat zoomed straight at a series of white-capped waves. Water and wind lashed my face as we bounced over the swells with a rhythm. The drizzle had turned into a steady rain.

I was exhilarated and terrified as we went airborne again. We landed in a trough with another THUD. The three of us tilted to the port side, grasping for something to hold. Paul's hand slipped off the tiller, and the boat stalled.

"Hold on! I gotta restart— "

Just then an enormous wave sideswiped us, lake water flooding the boat. I looked down and my sneakers were submerged.

"Shit. Help me scoop the water out!" Paul shouted, picking up a plastic bucket.

Instead of grabbing one of the two floating vests nearby, I tried to bail out water with a plastic drinking cup. Wrong choice. Just then, another wave plowed over the side of the boat.

"What do we do?!" Justine screamed. "It's almost up to my knees!"

"Forget it! Jump!" Paul hollered, tightening his life vest,

I reflexively grabbed the two life jackets and leaped into the ice-cold lake close to Justine.

"Jay! Your life jackets!" Justine hollered at me. "You didn't put them on!"

"Is *that* where they're supposed to go?" I joked. There was a method to my madness—trying to keep my little sister from panicking.

"Jay!" Paul yelled, swimming over. "One hand at a time. Loop your hand through the opening."

"No, I'm not letting go," I said, treading water furiously but trying to give the appearance of calm.

I wished I hadn't worn long pants, a sweatshirt, and my favorite pair of shoes. I wished I hadn't put my wallet in my long pants. Most of all, I wished I had paid more attention to Donna during swim lessons, especially when she taught us how to turn our clothes into flotation devices.

"Come on, man. You're not gonna last like that," Paul said.

"More optimism, please," I urged, noticing my knuckles were turning white as I clutched the vests.

"Hopefully someone will see us!" Justine shouted.

I wasn't so sure. A thick layer of mist had appeared over the water. As the dark gray sky rumbled with thunder, I squeezed my two life jackets as if my life depended on it—because it did. Meanwhile, our boat had capsized and was being carried farther away.

"How far to shore?" I asked.

"About a half-mile," Paul answered. "You think you can make it?"

"Well, if we're being totally honest…*No*," I replied, keeping my head just barely afloat. "You guys can try it, though."

"No, I'm not leaving you!" Justine cried.

"Me neither," Paul said. "We stick together."

I wasn't sure I deserved such loyalty, but I was grateful for it.

We agreed to conserve our energy by not speaking but, at the same time, tried to stay in a tight triangle formation. I had no concept of distance or time as I furiously treaded water with heavy legs. One thing I could do to help my situation was to part with my shoes. I managed to kick them both off. My feet were instantly numb, but I felt a little lighter. Anything to stay afloat. It seemed like an eternity, wrists and fingers throbbing until Paul perked up.

"You hear that?" he said.

It was the welcome buzz of an approaching craft. Moments later, the boat appeared out of the fog. A middle-aged man with a skipper's cap and a large yellow poncho was behind the wheel. As he drew closer, I could see he was accompanied by a young man in his late teens.

"Ahoy!" the older man shouted.

A mariner who shouts "ahoy" I thought, in my delusional state. How cliché.

"Are we happy to see you," Paul said.

"Take him first," Justine said, nodding at me.

From what I can remember, they did. Several sets of hands pulled me onto the deck like the day's catch. I know my teeth were chattering and somebody said, "He may be in shock." The next thing I knew was that there was a warm blanket over me, and patches of light blue were visible in the sky once again.

Our rescuers dropped us off at the dock but declined to come up to the house for any kind of refreshments or reward. We thanked them profusely and started up the long embankment towards the cabin. When Mom and Dad looked up from their lawn chairs, they began to laugh.

"It's not funny!" Justine screamed. "Jay almost drowned!

The thing about *almost* dying is that it usually makes a good story, and you get to tell it unless you're incapacitated. If things don't turn out well and you go to the big clambake in the sky, then somebody else will tell it but probably not as well as you would have (unless you were fortunate like Uncle Sam and had a colorful group of friends).

I didn't have to wait long to share my latest near-death experience with the masses. I wrote a personal narrative about the boating misadventure for my sophomore English class and received an "A." My teacher, Mrs. Mims, had given us the following prompt: "*Summer High or Summer Low?* Describe in detail."

Not to go all existential here, but the tricky thing was deciding if my adventure was a "high" or "low." I finally opined that it was too early to tell, as my ultimate destiny had yet to be decided. Sure, I was alive but what would my future hold? I could end up a humanitarian. Having my life spared would be beneficial for me, naturally—and for society. But if I turned out to be a thief or some other kind of degenerate, well, then what? Deep thoughts, indeed.

When Dave and Barry heard about my episode at the lake, they were so sympathetic, so sentimental, so—*not* themselves—that I couldn't stand it. I asked them if they were being sincere, and Barry said I didn't understand Jewish guilt. They were still beating themselves up (or more likely blaming the other) for abandoning me on the bike ride.

I finally blurted out that all was forgiven, just so things could go back to normal. Dave patted me on the back so hard I thought it would leave a mark. Barry vowed that if I pissed him off someday, he wouldn't add me to his shit list, no matter how serious the infraction was. For him that was a major concession.

The holiday season was different that year, but in a good way. We didn't hear the word "lean" except when Mom asked Dad to pick up lean meat at the market for our traditional fondue dinner. The big news was that Mr. Carney helped Dad settle the case with Mr. Silverberg. We were going to get some, but not all, of our money back. Dad paid off the balance for legal representation and that was all she wrote. As for the money he owed me, I kept quiet. It was good enough that we wouldn't have to hear the names Silverberg or Carney again.

Dave needed a break from his extended family's visit, one afternoon, so I invited him over. He brought a Swiss chocolate bar as a gift for all of us to share. It might not sound like all that much, but the thing was the size of a dinner plate. Mom was gracious and asked Dave if he wanted to see our Christmas tree. The problem was that when she turned on the lights, she saw things she didn't like.

"Oh, no, that's not going to work," she said, scrunching her face.

"What's wrong?" I asked.

"Too *bunchy*," Mom said.

I was convinced Mom made up words on the spot sometimes. *Moppy. Bunchy.* But I knew what she meant. There were too many lights and some of the ornaments were too close together. Before long, she was directing Dave and me to move things around from front to back and high to low. At one point, Dave was behind the tree on his back with his hands working the tree like Michelangelo painting the Sistine Chapel.

"Dave, I know you're not a Christian. I hope you won't get into any trouble for this with your parents," Mom joked.

"Probably not, but I better conceal the evidence," he said, wiping off needles from his shirt.

"Just tell them it was the new air freshener in our car," I said.

On Christmas day, I received a few interesting gifts: including a tennis racket, the latest edition of The Guinness Book of World Records, and a heavy punching bag—the hanging kind that boxers used for training. It wasn't something I had asked for but since we already had a weight set in our basement, it went with the territory.

At night I read the Guinness book, and I was riveted. The more I read, the more I was inspired. Not to read, but to break a world record. What kind? I didn't know because there were millions of them. I just needed to find one that was attainable for a 15-year-old New Englander. Growing the world's longest beard was out. I wasn't in the mood to spend 50 years on something like that. And what if I came in second? Same thing with fingernails. Besides, I could never put on a baseball glove if I did that.

After hours of tearing through pages, I found it. A skill that I could master with a reasonable amount of practice…*coin snatching*. The record was 60 by a man named Francis-something, or something-Francis. He lived in England. Or Ireland. It didn't matter. I was too excited. What mattered was the number. *Sixty*. I could do it.

A quick tutorial: to properly coin snatch, you must bend one of your arms back as if you're scratching your shoulder, and stack coins in one column on the flat part of the elbow. Then, in one fell swoop, you whip that arm down and snatch (catch) *all* the coins.

Of course, I needed a substantial number of coins, so I began asking Mom and Dad if I could have their spare change every time they came home. I felt like a panhandler, and they began to feel sorry for me,

"I can start giving you an allowance again," Dad said.

"No, thanks. I could just use some coins," I replied.

"Are you starting a collection?" Mom asked.

"Yeah," I said. "Kinda like that."

For the next several weeks, I practiced in my room every day with the door closed. I was not only committed to the skill but the secrecy of it.

It took a while, but I got the hang of it. I wasn't so sure what kind of coin was needed, so I went with dimes. They were lighter and smaller. I gradually increased the amount from 20 to 30 to 40 to 45 to 55, and then, if you can believe it, 60, to tie the record.

"Holy shit," I exclaimed to myself. I needed a witness. I flung open my door and called out to Justine.

"What's wrong?" she shouted.

"Nothing!" I said excitedly. "Get in here."

She hurried in and I brought her up to speed on my conquest. She was skeptical, but once she saw me replicate my triumph, her face lit up.

"Oh, my God!"

"Now, ladies and gentlemen, the world record attempt…"

I took a long, slow breath and added one more dime to the stack. I was still like a statue. Justine crossed her fingers.

In a flash, I swiped down and *caught them all!*

"TaaDaa!" I boasted.

"You're gonna be famous, Jay!" she hollered, jumping up and down.

At dinner, Justine and I shared the news of my record-shattering achievement. Whether they were exhausted from work, or plain skeptical, my parents were rather blasé about the whole thing.

"I was there! He broke the record!" Justine, my forever ally, exclaimed.

The next day, Dad indulged me and made a telephone call to Guinness. Someone in the "Amazing Feats" department told him they were no longer flying people out to witness record-breaking attempts. The best thing would be for me to write a letter and send a recording of the event.

Since Dad had to sell his camera when we needed money, I turned to Plan B. The next afternoon Matt bounded upstairs and met me in my bedroom. While he set up his new Panasonic video camera on a tripod, I arranged my dimes carefully in stacks of ten. Although I only needed 61, I counted out 70, the big dreamer that I was. I had cleaned each one, so they'd stack better and shine on film.

As for me, personally, I couldn't look like a slouch. If my video was going to be spread around the world, I needed to dazzle. Not like Elvis or Liberace, but I needed to look calm, cool, and collected. I slicked back my hair with some of Dad's Vitalis and put on some slacks to go with a stylish short-sleeved shirt.

When Matt was ready, he pointed his index finger at me. I took a deep breath and went into the drop as I had done before in front of Justine. I caught most but not all. Four random dimes fell to the floor.

"Cut!" Matt yelled.

"*Cut?* What are you, Alfred Hitchcock?" I asked.

"Am I supposed to keep rolling while you're picking them up?" he asked.

"Just, I don't know…keep it rolling. That way it doesn't look like it's edited."

"You're the boss," he said.

I sighed and restacked all the coins.

"Okay," I said.

"Rolling," Matt said and then pointed.

Once again I swiped downward and—

CLANKETY-CLANG! About half the stack scattered off my dresser and onto the bedroom carpet. Matt lowered the camera and scowled.

"Are you sure you've done this before?"

"Yes," I said with frustration.

"Maybe some of that grease in your hair got on your fingers?" Matt wondered.

I looked down at my hands. There was no oil, but I noticed I had a blister on my middle finger. How long had *that* been there?

"I have a blister. That wasn't there the other day," I said.

"Ahh, the ol' blister," Matt said. "Spending too much time with *Rosy Palm*, eh?"

I rolled my eyes. "How about you try to support me here?"

"Okay, here's a suggestion: use your *other* hand," Matt said.

"I can't. I trained with my left hand," I explained.

"Is 'training' the proper word?" he asked.

I showed him my blistered "middle finger" and then tried another swipe with the same woeful results.

"Sorry I wasted your time," I said to Matt as he packed up his equipment.

"Oh, it wasn't a waste. I've got some comedy gold right here," he said with a wry grin.

66

My world record aspirations made me realize I was searching. For what—I didn't know. Acceptance? Attention? Admiration? And why did all those words begin with the letter "A?" This was what testosterone did to the mind and body of a young man, It made you overthink. It made you restless.

Realizing I needed a place to channel my energy that spring, I turned to track and field. You'd think with my arm the javelin would be an obvious choice, right? But here's how it worked, at least in the competition: you sit on your rear end for long stretches, only to rise for maybe ten seconds to hurl an iron bar. No thanks.

I wanted something that could get my competitive juices flowing. Thinking back to my streaking and "Kick the Can" days, I realized I could turn on the jets when I had to. I could "fly"—wasn't that the term Brett or Dallas used?

On the first day, after an introductory meeting and a light jog around the school, I decided my focus would be the mile run. I informed the coach, Mr. McGuinn, a former marathon runner from Ireland. He shared my enthusiasm.

"Awright, Laddy. You're built like a gazelle. Maybe this is your calling."

I was almost six feet tall and had long legs (Mom reminded me of this all the time because I'd leave the passenger seat too far back in her car). The problem was I ended up getting the flu that week, so I missed the next four days of school.

When I returned the following Monday, I was primed to get on with practice after classes were over. My athletic bag was packed with new running shorts, two tank tops, and a pair of Adidas Gazelle sneakers. But lo and behold, another wrench was thrown into my plans.

Like all sophomores, I was enrolled in a PE program called "Outdoor Pursuits." The goal was to promote team building and foster an appreciation for the great outdoors.

The lesson plan that Monday afternoon called for students to gather in the woods to the south of the baseball fields. Our PE instructor had us orient ourselves and then blindfolded us. The goal was to meet up at a rendezvous point within 20 minutes. After ten minutes we could remove our blindfolds for course correction, but that was it. Only the instructor and each team's leader (not me) could speak during the jaunt. The rest of us were supposed to listen to directions and use all our other senses to find our way to the meeting spot.

When the whistle blew, we set off. I took small steps with my hands out. I imagined to anyone driving past in the distance we looked like hostages who were partaking in some sort of sick game to amuse our captors. It wouldn't have been a surprise if someone called the cops.

I heard shuffling leaves, a few giggles, and then someone yelled out, "Water!" Was that my leader? Did it matter? Water was water. I listened for more details. Where was the water? How deep? And why couldn't I speak? Who made up these rules, anyway?

I froze. If I didn't move, I couldn't get wet. I could just wait for the ten-minute break and see where I was—although I had a feeling I wasn't too far from my starting point. I shuffled forward, inch by inch.

"Ahem!" I grunted, hoping someone would take the hint.

No reply. I heard voices but they were farther away. Maybe standing out in the woods alone wasn't the best idea. Were there bears in these parts? I could envision the newspaper headlines…*Disoriented High School Student Mauled by Black Bear!*

And of course, everyone would think I was high or drunk.

Shuffling was getting me nowhere, so I started taking small steps. At that point, it must have looked comical, like something out of Monty Python's "Ministry of Silly Walks." Foot up high, foot stretched out, foot slowly down. Despite feeling and hearing crunches beneath my feet, I was making progress. But then my right foot didn't come down, until—

Splash! It landed in something wet and cold. My ankle turned and I lost my balance. I put my arms out and skidded down what felt like an embankment. I grabbed my lower leg with one arm and ripped off my blindfold with the other. As my eyes adjusted, I could see I had fallen into a ravine. If I wasn't so scraped up, I would have thought it was funny. It felt as if I had tumbled 4,000 feet but it was only about nine inches.

"You okay, Jay?" A familiar voice.

I turned to find Rollie, who wasn't wearing his blindfold. He held out his hand and helped me up.

"Yeah, thanks, Rollie," I said, wiping the mud off my pants. "Where is everyone?"

"Shit, they're already at the rendezvous," he said.

"What? *How?*" I said, stunned.

"You mean, you didn't sneak a peek?" Rollie asked. "After a few minutes, everyone figured out a way to see through it. Or they just pulled it down. The teacher got all bent out of shape and called us in. Game over."

"I didn't hear any of that," I said.

"You were kinda…far back," Rollie said, trying to hold back a grin.

I thought about what Matt had said not long ago. "Everyone cheats."

I shook my head.

"I feel like an idiot," I said.

"Hey, Jay, nah. Respect to you. You're like the only honest soldier. I'd take you on my team any day."

An hour later I had changed out of my dirty clothes and was ready for my first track practice in a week. Even though I had tweaked my ankle, I didn't want to fall any further behind on the depth chart.

Coach McGuinn had set up some trials. He directed all the "lads and lasses" to line up for the mile run. Right away, my ankle gave me trouble, but I tried not to show it. The good news is that I was able to finish. The bad news is that I came in last and was nearly lapped by a freshman. When I took a seat on the bleachers, Coach McGuinn approached.

"You okay, Laddy?" he asked.

"Yeah, fine, Coach," I said.

"Good. I just got to be wonderin' if ya have interest in any other sports, by chance?" he asked.

67

My pride was wounded, but at least my ankle wasn't broken. It was just sprained, according to the X-rays. I ended up with a wrap, not a cast, but I was still going to be on the shelf for a while. While the injury may have prevented me from running, I wasn't going to allow it to keep me from driving.

I completed my first lesson with Dad in the sprawling and mostly empty parking lot of Shopper's World one Sunday morning. Although I never exceeded 15 mph, I learned to park forward and backward…*and* complete a three-point turn. Not bad for a day's work. Dad had me turn off the car and switch seats with him.

"That was fun," I said, settling back into the passenger seat.

"I'm glad you enjoyed it, but it's not supposed to be *fun*. Remember, if not handled properly, this thing can be a killing machine."

Buzzkill, I thought, before wondering why Dad wasn't starting the car.

"So, before we roll out of here, I wanted to have a little talk," Dad said.

A *talk*. The last time we had one of those I ended up taking a round-trip on a chairlift.

"About…?" I asked.

"About your future," he replied.

Dad gazed at the mall through the front windshield.

"The other day I was walking past some shops here and I saw a recruiting station. It got me thinking about the armed forces for you," Dad explained.

"For *me*," I confirmed.

"You're the only other person in this car," he said.

"Like the Army? Or Marines?"

"Or the Navy," he said.

"Dad, you know I'm a terrible swimmer," I said, hoping to shift the tone with some humor.

"Be serious for a minute," Dad said. "I know things have been a little off with us lately, so to help clear the air, it might help to know where your head is at."

I shrugged. "Honestly? I haven't thought too much about my future. I take things day to day. You know I like sports. I like writing."

"Well, okay, but that sounds more like where your heart is. It's nice to dream about pro sports, Jay—we've all done it—but it's a million-to-one shot. And writing? No one gets rich doing that."

"Right," I said, wondering again where everyone's optimism had gone.

"I can't remember if I told you but in high school, I joined the ROTC and was Air Force-bound. I could glide in skiing, but ultimately I wanted to fly," Dad said, his expression turning dreamy.

"You didn't tell me. Then what happened?"

"I lost control on some ice out in Vail, needed spinal fusion, and my dreams of flying went up in smoke."

"Sorry to hear that," I said, and it was the truth.

"I'm sharing all this because I truly believe there's no greater honor than serving your country. I felt that way back then and I still feel it today."

"Dad, look, I'm not a *rah-rah-shoot 'em up* kind of guy," I said.

Dad shook his head. "I guess that's the McGovern effect. You know who he was?"

"Yeah, he ran for President a few years ago," I said. "Lost to Nixon."

"Right. Big liberal. No fan of the armed forces. And let's be clear. He got his ass handed to him by Nixon. The only state he won was—"

"Massachusetts," I said, pleased that I'd retained at least *some* knowledge from my U.S. History class.

"Correct," Dad confirmed. "And so maybe some of it has rubbed off on you. The news, the views...I don't know, your friends, maybe?"

"It's not my friends, Dad," I insisted. "It's me, trying to live in the moment. My biggest concern until this morning was parallel parking."

"Understood," Dad agreed, before giving my leg a tap. "I just want you to keep an open mind when it comes to your future. You never know when the opportunity will knock. Will you do that?"

"Yes, I will," I said, doubting my words as soon as they left my mouth.

Whether it was Dad's "talk" or just feeling more exasperated with each passing day, I transitioned from restless to rebellious. Not like James Dean, smoking and riding motorcycles at 120 miles per hour, However, if there was an opportunity to get out of the house, I took it. Most of the time I hung out with Dave and Barry at the bowling alley playing Space Invaders or at Dave's house shooting pool.

I don't exactly remember when, but Barry started hosting a weekly poker game at his house which included some combination of Dave, Goskey, Ernie, and me.

For the inaugural game, I wanted to buy in with all the dimes I'd saved from my Guinness world record pursuit.

"What the hell? Do I look like a meter maid?" Barry asked.

"Money is money," I replied.

"If I win, I'm not taking all this. You can give me an IOU," he said.

"Don't be a schmuck, Barry," Dave said confidently. "And you're not gonna win. I will."

Dave's confidence was misplaced. I ended up winning that day—and many others. "Beginners luck," Barry grumbled, but I felt like I had a knack for it. It wasn't so much having terrific hands as it was being able to read expressions and body language. We'd usually play five-card draw or seven-card stud, but occasionally, we'd play a game called "Guts" where the pot would get huge.

By the end of the summer, I had made as much money playing cards as I'd lost during the Silverberg fiasco. And for the record, I was keeping my cash hidden in my bedroom this time around.

In our constant search for entertainment during those sizzling summer days, the guys and I devised an idea to put on "theme concerts." Dave's house again was the prime venue. Aside from his parents having the best (loudest) stereo system, we had on-site access to props. His older brother had an electric guitar in his closet, and his sister stored a box in the attic which had wigs and costumes from her high school drama days. With both siblings off at college and Dave's folks scheduling Saturday as their "date night," the stage was literally and figuratively set for showtime. For a few hours, we could transform ourselves into legends Jagger, Dylan, Hendrix, or newer artists like Tom Petty and Elvis Costello.

The boy who once emulated baseball stars was now pretending to be a rockstar. Times had changed.

I had been thinking about Andrea a lot since the guys and I started putting on our rock (or should I say 'mock?') shows. We had all the bells and whistles, but we were missing an audience. More to the point, we were missing screaming female fans. I thought of all the girls I knew and Andrea was at the top of the list. Honestly, she *was* the list.

It was quite a stroke of luck, then, when Dad came home one Saturday morning, and mentioned he'd run into Andrea's father, Stan, at the hardware store.

"Small world," I said. "Did he say how Andrea's doing?" I asked.

"Well, you can find out for yourself," he replied. "I invited them over for dinner next weekend."

I tried to act low-key, but a charge ran through my body. On the day of the dinner party, the following Saturday, I cut the lawn and even helped clean the inside of the house. Mom and Justine, meanwhile, prepared the meal (chicken, wild rice, carrots, cranberries, and French bread). The house smelled like it did during the holidays. After showering and putting on a nice outfit, I joined my family in the kitchen.

Dad handed me a small glass that was half full of what appeared to be white grape juice.

"What's this?" I asked.

"Chardonnay. A little token of appreciation for your help today."

"Thanks," I said, taking a whiff.

"I'm not going to say 'anytime,' but you're welcome. Take it slow," cautioned.

I took a small sip and raised my eyebrows. It wasn't my first rodeo, but I pretended it was.

"Whoa, interesting," I said.

"Glad to hear that," Dad said with a grin.

As Dad reached for the cup, I pulled it back and downed the rest of it.

"Don't wanna waste it, but people actually enjoy that?" I asked, wiping my mouth. Our guests soon arrived, and the showy greetings once again made me want to puke. It was the sight of Andrea, in a green dress, that kept me centered. As always, she seemed more attractive than I remembered her.

The seven of us ate in our dining room, where we often spent Thanksgiving dinner with Grandma Marjorie. The parents dominated the conversation which centered on foreign affairs, stocks, and of course, politics. None of them hid their disdain for the governor who was rumored to be a Democratic candidate for President.

"You can't say his name with a straight face," Stan said.

"Sounds like something two-year-olds would say when their diapers are removed," Dad chimed in.

The adults roared, while Andrea, Justine, and I traded bewildered looks.

After dinner, with the kids handling most of the cleanup, the families retreated to the living room, drinks in hand. After some more small talk and another refill of beverages, Dad put the soundtrack for *Grease* on the stereo. The parents started tapping their fingers and feet to the beat. I pulled up a chair next to Andrea.

"It's about to get interesting," she said.

"It already has been," I said.

"You mean, all that crazy talk about politics?" Andrea asked.

"Yeah, well, that, and my dad offered me wine earlier," I said.

"No way. He's cooler than my dad," she said.

"He has his moments, I guess."

"How was the wine?"

"It had a nice bouquet," I said, trying to imitate a connoisseur "You want to try some?"

"I'm game," she said, arching her eyebrows.

We went to the kitchen and Andrea served as the lookout. Despite our best efforts at cleaning up earlier, the kitchen counter still looked like something you'd see at a fraternity party. Bottles of gin, vodka, rum, club soda, Coke, and 7-Up littered one side, while chardonnay and cabernet were uncorked on another.

Classy guy that I was, I poured two Dixie cups of Cabernet and handed one to Andrea.

"To reunions," I said.

"Third time, if I'm not mistaken," she said.

"And thus, the charm," I said, now in full cornball mode.

We drank and each made curious faces.

"Interesting," she said. "So, listen, I met your friend, Paul. He came into Nelson's. I work there part-time."

"The restaurant here in town?" I asked. "I've never seen you there."

"No, over in Marlborough," she replied.

"Ah, okay. So, tell me, what did Paul have to say?" I asked.

"He said you were a good guy."

"You sure about that?" I said with a wink. Holy moly, when was the last time I winked?

"Am I sure he said it? Or am I sure you're a good guy?" Andrea asked.

"Both," I replied.

"I'm pretty sure the answer is 'yes,' and 'yes,'" she said with a smile.

I grinned and held up my cup again. We toasted to whatever it was we were feeling. Warmth? Joy? We had crossed a bridge in our connection. As we passed a mirror on the way back to the living room, I noticed my face was flushed. I was pretty sure it wasn't the wine.

We reclaimed our seats and watched our parents dance. The moment "You're the One that I Want" came on, Andrea leaped to her feet and held one hand to

Justine and one to me. The three of us danced in a circle and soon the whole room was grooving like we were on *American Bandstand*.

At the end of the evening, as Mr. Hayes went to retrieve his family's jackets, Andrea dabbed my face with a cocktail napkin.

"You have a little dessert on your face," she said.

"Oh, great. How long's that been there?" I asked.

"A few hours," she said with a mischievous grin and then leaned closer. "By the way, you might want to keep that napkin."

When the coast was clear a few minutes later, I raced up to the bathroom, locked the door, and unfolded the napkin. Andrea had written her telephone number inside.

70

The summer after my sophomore year was a blur. Our family rarely took vacations, but we stayed at a posh hotel in Hyannis (near the Kennedy compound). I tried lobster for the first time and didn't like it, much to Dad's relief. I also spent more time in, on, and around the water which, given my history, was surprising. Justine and I collected sand dollars at Sandy Neck Beach, and Dad shot some amazing film of a humpback whale when we were out on a whale-watching expedition.

Good times, but I missed Andrea. I felt something physical being away from her, just the way I felt something physical when I was near her. And I don't mean in the *loins* as a medieval writer would say. It was somewhere between the heart and the head. I guess that's what a crush was. Aside from sending her Cape Cod postcards, I found myself doing sappy things like doodling her name in the sand with my foot. Justine called me a "hopeless toe-mantic." It was a Dad joke, but it made me laugh.

The night we returned home, I staked out a comfortable spot in Dad's office and once everyone was asleep, I called Andrea as I'd promised in my last note. She already had my return date committed to memory and informed her folks I might call past her normal bedtime. We spoke into the early hours of the morning and then talked at least once every day after for I don't know how long. The cat was out of the bag—we were an item--and it became a collective effort to set up times for us to get together. Our folks not only agreed, but even offered to drive us to tennis dates, the movies, and so on.

The only thing that stopped our momentum was school. It was the last thing we wanted, but the parents drew a proverbial line in the sand (and not the "toe-mantic" kind). Education trumps blossoming romance, Mom said. Although Andrea and I were enrolled at different schools, we had comparable items on our "to-do" list. Junior year was crucial.

One prerequisite was the PSAT or Preliminary Scholastic Aptitude Test. It was a trial run for the dreaded SAT, which most colleges prioritized when evaluating applicants. Maybe because I just saw it as practice, it was a walk in the park for me. The proctors gave us two hours, but I was in and out of the session in less than one.

Another key requirement was Driver's Education. The instructors for these courses were often maligned and at our school, it was no different. Reginald Ramsey had a reputation for being "touchy-feely." It didn't matter if you were male or female—the word was that his one-hour sessions gave a whole new meaning to the phrase 'hands-on' experience. There were never any credible reports of Ramsey crossing the line, but the countless rumors and Mr. Ramsey's appearance (hunched posture, large darting eyes) were enough to make even the most emboldened students feel uncomfortable around "Handsy-Ramsey."

Dave, Barry, and I worked out a schedule so we could go with each other during our lessons. To tell you the truth, I didn't mind Ramsey or the lessons. The only thing that threw me was the rotaries—or roundabouts as they're known in other parts of the country. I didn't get the concept. It was the equivalent of funneling cars from all directions into a giant lawn mower and seeing how the blade shot them out.

I managed to get through the full set of lessons with minimal input from Ramsey. Dave was a different story. Ramsey had to offer constant reminders and stomp on his brakes one time when Dave was about to run a stop sign. Another time Ramsey made Dave redo a parallel parking job three times, the last of which almost resulted in a concussion.

"You can do it, David. Use your mirror and look for oncoming traffic," Ramsey said, touching Dave's right arm.

Dave, flustered, spun in his seat to check traffic, and—*BAM*—his forehead smashed glass. Dave being, well, *Dave*, had failed to realize his window was up. Barry and I laughed so hard in the back we fell to the floor. Poor Dave had a bruise on his noggin for days after that incident.

The other thing the three of us did was land programs on our school's new FM radio station, WYUJ. All we needed to do was turn in a written program description to the office and, once approved, complete an application for the FCC. Once the FCC signed off on the application, they'd mail our official broadcasting licenses. Unlike a driver's license, no photographs were needed—just a signature.

The day our documents arrived, the guys and I were on cloud nine. Who would have thought we'd be legal on the airwaves before the streets? The only directive was that we had to refrain from using any of the "seven dirty words" that landed George Carlin in a heap of trouble.

Dave named his show "Into the Mystic"—an hour of light folk and rock music named after the Van Morrison song. Barry's program was called "Boss Tunes" and featured Bruce Springsteen songs, including those he wrote for others. My program was entitled "Rock 'n Roll Greats of the '50s, '60s, and '70s." Barry gave me a hard time about the title being too long and I dismissed him by asking "Aren't you the guy who created the 'Doesn't-Know-Where-to-Put-his-Arms' nickname?"

If you thought being known as "on-air personalities" would give us a certain prestige amongst our schoolmates, think again. Other than our family members and a few of our friends, we didn't have much of a listener base. It didn't matter because we were doing our shows for the experience, not the ratings. Of course, to keep things interesting, we'd occasionally make up stories about girls with sexy-sounding names like "Heather" requesting songs.

My PSAT scores arrived, and they weren't too shabby. In English, I had a 56, and in Math, I scored a 63. When my counselor, Mrs. Steiner, saw my scores, she invited me into her office for a chat. She wanted to know if I had reached out to any colleges for applications. I told her I hadn't and asked for suggestions. She mentioned Williams or Amherst, if I wanted to stay in-state, as well as Dartmouth, Bates, Bowdoin, and Colby.

When I relayed the details of my conversation to Mom and Dad that evening they were pleased. At the same time, they seemed preoccupied.

"You're not going to tell me we're moving, are you?" I said, looking around to see if anything had been stowed away.

"No. What I want to share relates to this and the discussion we had in the car not long ago," Dad said.

Oh, *that* discussion, I thought as my body tensed. Dad went on to tell me how he had met a Three-Star Army General while getting a haircut at Richard's. They got to chatting and the General, a man named Fallbrook, suggested I apply to one of our nation's fine service academies.

"Dad…" I began to protest.

"You don't recall our conversation about opportunity knocking?" he asked. "I mean, Jay, this is pretty serendipitous."

"It is *something*," I acknowledged.

"Here's the thing," Dad said. "It's like starting an inning on second base. You'd bypass being a grunt and graduate as an officer."

I looked at Mom. She opened her palms. "It's just a chat, Jay."

"Roger that," I said.

At 7:15 p.m. the next day, General Dale Fallbrook knocked on our front door. That's right, *our* door. Dad was so good at sales that he even got the General to make a house call.

Since General Fallbrook was retired, there was no obligation for him to wear his uniform. He looked the part—square jaw, short hair, and spine straighter than a goal post—yet he was surprisingly warm and engaging.

The three of us spoke in Dad's study where all the important discussions took place. The general wasn't like Mr. Carney—he didn't drink—so Dad served him a club soda in a glass with lime. Dad abstained from booze during this meeting which told me he wanted to make a good impression. He also gathered my last quarter's report card, FCC license, and PSAT results to present to the General.

General Fallbrook seemed impressed and asked me about work and sports.

"I plan on applying for jobs after Christmas when I expect to have my driver's license. I'm also going to try out for either the tennis or baseball team this year."

The General looked up from my documents and shared his belief that I had a good foundation in place—not only with my school achievements but with having a solid home life.

Dad beamed like a holiday light when he heard that and then asked about "next steps." General Fallbrook outlined the progression. Each applicant had to complete a physical fitness test and secure a nomination from one of our state's senators or a local congressional representative. It was a lengthy process, but well worth it if I was accepted into the academy. I also needed to complete a physical fitness evaluation.

As Dad finished scribbling notes on a legal pad, General Fallbrook asked if he could have a few minutes alone with me. Dad readily agreed and exited the office.

"Your father's excitement certainly is apparent," he said. "Is yours at the same level?"

"To tell you the truth, sir, no. Not at this moment," I admitted.

"Well, I commend you on your honesty," General Fallbrook said.

I was glad I had been straightforward. You can't con a con and you can't generalize with a general—or something like that.

"Thank you, Mist—um, *General* Fallbrook," I said.

"Here's what I'm going to tell you, Jay," he said, leaning forward. "You're a fine young man. I can see that. But if you allow someone else to choose your path for you, you may end up lost. Trust your instincts."

"I appreciate that, sir," I said, reflecting on my wayward Outdoor Pursuits experience.

"The admissions office is going to make a call on applicants. They know what they're doing, and they pick the best candidates. If you feel more inspired in the coming days, go ahead and apply. Give it your best shot. I'd be happy to write a referral letter. But if I were you, I'd also apply to other schools to c-y-a."

"I'm sorry, General—" I said, not understanding.

"Cover Your Ass," the General said.

I smiled. "Thank you, sir."

71

I called Barry the next day and told him I was going to miss our weekly poker game because I needed to work on nomination letters for my academy application.

"You're actually going through with this army thing?" Barry asked.

"My dad started the process. I'm going to see it through," I replied.

"No offense, but I can't picture you in a uniform. Unless we're talking about McDonald's," he said.

"Good one. Speaking of which," I said. "Have you started looking for a job yet?"

"No. I've thought about being a male escort, but you need to be 18," he said.

"Yeah, okay, let me know how that turns out," I said and hung up.

I sat for a moment with the phone in my hand, recalling that Andrea had mentioned that the Nelson's restaurant in my town was hiring.

I called her to express my interest and she was thrilled.

"I'll make the call right now. When can you interview?" she asked.

"Next week," I said. "Any day after school."

She told me she'd call me right back and less than five minutes later the phone rang. I scooped it up on the first ring.

"Five o'clock. Thursday," she said.

"You're the best," I said and thanked her.

I told my folks, and they were thrilled. Dad even offered to drive me (this was no fool's errand). He cleared his schedule for Thursday afternoon and dropped me at the front door of Nelson's Creamery at 4:58.

"Remember," he said. "Eye contact, strong voice, and let them know why they need you."

"Got it," I said.

Once inside, I asked a middle-aged woman in a white shirt for the manager. She told me to take a seat on a stool near the grill in the back before disappearing through a set of swinging doors. A minute later the manager appeared through the same doors. He was a short Middle Eastern man with deep brown eyes and a thick mustache.

"Hey, guy," he said with a smile. "I'm Abdul. Come on back."

I had never been called "guy" before, but it didn't bother me. Maybe it was a term of endearment in his culture, like "buddy." Or maybe it was just an Abdul thing. I followed him back into the kitchen and then we made a sharp turn into a tiny, cramped office.

"Sit down, guy," he said. "You make me feel like a midget."

I squeezed into the chair by the door.

"So, you know Andrea from the other store?" he asked.

"Yes, sir," I said.

"You sure?" he asked.

"Yes," I said, caught off guard. "We used to go to school together. And our parents are friends."

"The thing is," he said. "She said she doesn't know you."

He held up his hands and my jaw dropped.

"Andrea *Hayes*?" I asked.

Abdul shook his head, but a second later, he burst out laughing.

"Ima just kidding' with you, guy," he clapped his hands. "We used to work together. One of my favorite people ever."

"Oh, thank God," I said, relieved.

"If Andrea says you're good, we're good. When can you start?"

And like that, I had a job. Before it could even sink in, I was going over my availability and receiving a new, plastic-wrapped uniform—polyester blue pants and a checkered blue and white shirt.

My very first shift was the next evening. Per my request, Abdul put me on the schedule for Friday nights, Saturday nights, and Sunday afternoons, since those were the only days that I had transportation. As you'd expect, I started as the low "guy" (pun intended) on the totem pole—busing tables, cleaning up spills, and washing dishes. However, it wasn't long before my responsibilities expanded. Soon I was restocking items in the various bays and helping with inventory, which meant counting items in the stockroom, the "Chiller" (walk-in refrigerator), and the "Big Freeze" (sub-zero freezer). Doing a "Big Freeze" inventory—counting frozen patties, packages of French fries, and so on—was the worst. You needed an Arctic-style hat, jacket, and gloves if you planned to be in there for more than 30 seconds.

Within a month, I was promoted to cashier. This meant that I rang up checks from diners and took some of the simpler walk-in orders, like coffee and sodas. On a side note, these beverages were always on the house for police officers and firefighters. I became friendly after a while with a guy on the local PD named Kevin. He was a big sports fan and he'd give me the latest news and scores he'd picked up on his radio.

It was Officer Kevin who broke the stunning news about the 1980 U.S. Men's Hockey Team upsetting the USSR at the Lake Placid Olympics. A few customers overheard and soon the entire restaurant was standing and singing "The Star-Spangled Banner." Nelson's wasn't a bar, so these weren't drunk patrons—they were proud Americans. I admit I got goosebumps and felt more patriotic that evening than I did during our country's bicentennial.

It wasn't long before Abdul trained me on scooping cones (there was an art to it) and making milkshakes so I could help with the to-go orders. Most customers didn't realize how difficult this was, especially in the middle of a rush when we had to replace the flavors with a new container from the big freezer. It was like trying to scoop cement. No kidding, within a month, I noticed my right forearm looking larger than my left. I hoped it would help in sports somewhere down the road.

Abdul complimented me on my interaction with customers and soon had me waiting tables, too. The tips were great, but when one of our cooks quit, I was on the move again. The story of my life.

Next, he trained me on the grill over the course of a week. I started with morning shifts, making eggs, pancakes, French toast, bacon, and sausage. Once I had the hang of that, I learned the lunch and dinner menus. I became skilled at cooking burgers (the secret was in the touch) and even frying clam strips—a Massachusetts specialty.

Even though I sometimes ended up with burns on my hands and came home smelling like burnt cooking oil, it was a valuable experience because I could apply the skills at home. I even gave Justine a few lessons.

On Mom's 45th birthday, we surprised her by serving her breakfast in bed with a platter full of pancakes, scrambled eggs, bacon, and fresh strawberries.

I didn't think it was any big deal, but she was almost moved to tears by the gesture.

And then she asked, "Did you wash the strawberries, honey?"

72

In early March, I was notified that the physical fitness part of my West Point application had been officially scheduled for the following Sunday morning. Things were in motion, and I started to get an uneasy feeling. Meanwhile, wonder of all wonders, Dave was the first out of our group to get his driver's license. He drove Barry to Nelson's one Saturday night after my shift ended and we sat in a corner booth discussing my news.

"Just call in sick," Barry suggested.

"My dad would make me go anyway. There's too much riding on it," I said.

Dave gave me a tap with his knuckles. "There's something I heard that Springsteen did to get out of being drafted."

He went ahead to share a story about how "the Boss," as he was known, intentionally stayed out late, and partied before his medical exam during the height of the Vietnam War. The draft board ended up rejecting him.

"What do you think? Worth a try?" Dave asked.

I held up my hands. "What's good for the 'Boss' is good for the…"

"Ice cream scooper," Barry said.

The following Saturday Dave picked us up after dinner and drove to the parking lot of their temple, or synagogue. We parked under the cover of a crooked pine tree, near a large dumpster—in case we needed to toss any evidence. It all seemed nefarious, and sacrilegious, too, but if they didn't mind, I didn't mind. In our bag-of-tricks, we had a 12-pack of Schlitz Beer, three joints, and a half-dozen containers of nitrous oxide (also known as laughing gas) which Barry had scored from a cousin who worked at a party store in the mall.

The point of it all was to compromise my performance at the fitness test and sabotage my chances of getting accepted by the academy.

We started by passing around a joint inside the car. I was a little preoccupied, so I stayed quiet while Dave and Barry discussed things like which of us had the best radio show introduction, and who had the best posture. I should have been feeling relaxed, but I was getting annoyed with the inane chatter going on around me.

"How about some music?" I suggested.

Dave popped a cassette into the car's tape player and "Wild World" by Cat Stevens emanated from the speakers.

"How many good songs does an album need before you buy it?" Barry asked.

"Two," Dave said.

"Three," said Barry.

Here we go again, I thought, feeling a headache coming on.

"Sometimes one—if the song is that great. 'Don't Fear the Reaper' is a perfect example," Dave said.

"No, for one you just buy the 45," Barry argued.

"Okay, *enough*," I said.

"Whoa, what's your deal?" Barry asked.

"Do you guys even realize what's missing from your concerts?" I asked, popping open a beer.

"A smoke machine?" Dave guessed.

"Girls," I shot back.

Dave and Barry traded looks.

"Never occurred to me," Dave said.

"Obviously. Don't get me wrong, guys—we've got a great group of friends—but we're almost seniors. Why am I the only one who has a girlfriend?"

"Well, what's that saying about a blind squirrel?" Dave asked.

"You're a riot," I said and then flicked his ear.

"Somebody's a little edgy," Barry said. "Are you ready for the good stuff?"

The 'good stuff' was nitrous oxide. We'd learned this was the ingredient in the bottom of whipped cream containers that caused the topping to shoot out. I'd seen Rene, our new dishwasher at Nelson's, do it one time and he ended up with a face full of milky drool. The way to bypass the sticky dairy part was to use the actual gas canisters.

Barry inserted the tip of a pen into the canister and filled a purple balloon with gas. Once it was the size of a softball, he squeezed the neck of the balloon and held it out in front of me.

"You're the guest of honor," he said. "You go first."

"Are you sure about this?" I asked.

"Yeah, trust me. You'll feel like you're at the dentist but in a good way."

I took the balloon and inhaled the contents. Or I should say that I tried to. For some reason, I had trouble taking in the gas.

"Come on, you gotta breathe in," Barry said.

I tried again, but the balloon didn't deflate. I even tried swallowing, but then I burped.

"I don't know, maybe I'm too full," I said, handing it back to him.

"Too full?" Barry asked. "Dave, show him how it's done."

I handed the balloon to Dave. He wiped off the tip, put his lips over the opening, and tried to suck in the gas. He shook his head right away.

"Nah, something's not right."

He set down the balloon, grabbed the cardboard packaging, and examined it under his car's dome light.

"Hey, dumb shit," Dave said. "This isn't Nitrous Oxide—it's *Carbon Dioxide*."

"What?" Barry said. "No way."

He ripped the packaging from Dave's hands and read the label.

"Oops," he said. "My bad."

"My *bad*? You ass!" I hollered. "I could have brain damage!"

Barry jumped out of the car, and I chased after him. He may have been a faster cyclist, but he was no match for me on foot. I wrestled him to the grass by the dumpster and pinned him down with my knees. Since he didn't put up a fight, I wasn't sure what to do next. At last, I reached into his front pocket.

"What are you doing?!"

Ah-*hah*. I felt it. His tiny, spiral notebook.

"No!" Barry hollered in protest.

I opened the book and confirmed I had what I was looking for: Barry's Shit List (it even read *'Barry's Shit List'* on the inside flap).

Barry grew serious—then irate—flailing at me to snatch it back. I jumped to my feet, ripped the booklet in half, and tossed it into the dumpster.

"No more shit list, Barry. And no more being a shithead," I said.

He began to climb into the dumpster when we were engulfed by a flashing blue and red light.

Two police officers stepped out of the car. One had a hand on a flashlight and the other had a hand resting on his service revolver.

"Oh shit," I heard Dave say inside the car.

The officers heard it, too.

"You in the car, step outside. Put your hands up where I can see them," instructed the officer with the gun.

Dave did as he was told.

"What's going on here, gentlemen?" the officer with the flashlight asked.

"Just messing around," Barry said.

"We can see that. Why are you messing around *here*?" he asked, shining his light on each of our faces.

"My friends and I were coming back from a movie," Barry said. "And then I realized I needed to return some books to the temple for my parents."

It was bullshit, but it was better than anything I had.

The cop with the flashlight stepped toward me. He tilted it up to get a better look at my face. I wondered if he had noticed my bloodshot eyes or smelled marijuana on my clothes. I instinctively took a step back.

"Don't you work at Nelson's?" he asked.

"Yes, sir," I said, realizing the voice sounded familiar.

"It's Jay, right?"

I adjusted my eyes and saw that it was Officer Kevin.

"Yeah," I said. "How are you, Kevin? Er, Officer Kevin."

Kevin nodded to his partner, who removed his hand from his revolver.

"Okay, boys," Officer Kevin said. "If you did your errand, and whatever else, then it seems like it might be a good idea to wrap things up and head home."

We couldn't have agreed more.

73

Despite the "misadventures" of the night before, I managed to get up at 5:30 in the morning when my clock radio alarm blasted like a diving submarine. I dressed as I would for PE at school, with gray sweatpants and a sweatshirt over a tee shirt and shorts.

I made my way downstairs and found Dad leaning against the counter, drinking a cup of coffee. He'd set out buttered toast and grapefruit wedges for me.

"Thanks," I said.

"Big performance today. I can feel it," he said, pumping a fist.

The only thing I felt was a headache, but I was fairly sure it was from fatigue, not neurological damage. I raised my fist as well.

The test was at an Air Force base about 20 miles away. The ride over was quiet and I was thankful Dad didn't ask me about my evening. He didn't say much of anything until he dropped me off in front of the brick building's entrance. Then it was a quick confirmation on where he'd wait for me after the test, followed by a hasty "good luck."

After an ID check and the completion of some paperwork in the lobby, I was directed to the gymnasium where about two dozen other high school hopefuls were seated. Most of them looked like confident army types. Only a few looked like me—the regular guys who didn't have their hearts in it.

The gymnasium doors closed, and two men rose from the front row of the bleachers. One was a typical Sergeant type in uniform who was there to fire us up about "country and flag." He drove home the point that strength and agility were assets that could make the difference between life and death in a pitched battle— not just for us as soldiers, but for our unit.

The next guy up was the director of the day's operations. He wasn't in uniform, so I couldn't tell his rank, but he had a whistle hanging around his neck. He gave us a rundown of our drills and told us what to expect. We would all be assigned to cadets who would log our results. All candidates were expected to show respect to the cadets, who weren't much older than us, and to each other.

The cadets split us up into groups of six. Each group would go through four rotations or activities. These included pull-ups, push-ups, as well as an agility run and a basketball throw. It was a lot like my 7th-grade fitness test.

I started well, doing 18 pull-ups, which was the second-best in our group. The guy who did the most wore a "Mean Machine" sweatshirt with the sleeves cut off to show off his biceps. When we moved on to the push-ups, I was told my back needed to be straighter and they would only count the ones with proper form. This meant that instead of the 50 I counted, I was credited with 31. Not bad, but two other guys did better, including Mean Machine. When I stepped up to do my agility run, I noticed Mean Machine pointing at my shoes and whispering in amusement to another candidate. I looked down and realized that in my morning fog, I had put on two different shoes. One was a track shoe; one was for basketball.

"Hey, what are you? A two-sport star?" he said, nudging his new buddy.

I ignored him, took my place at the starting line, and listened for the signal from the cadet holding a stopwatch beside me.

The second he blew his whistle I knew I was doomed. One shoe had too little grip while the other had too much. I ended up slowing down to play it safe--doing more of a trot so I wouldn't pull a hamstring or roll an ankle. I finished in last place.

After that, it was on to the finale: the basketball toss. The deal with this was that you had to kneel on a mat. There was no running start, so it boiled down to my arm and upper body strength,

I was penciled in last for this drill, with "Mean Machine" throwing right before me. He grunted like an Olympic shot-putter and sent the ball sailing. A cadet on the other side of the gym had to back up to avoid being struck. As the ball landed, he marked the spot with chalk,

"You're up, 'Two-sport,'" he said with a wink.

"All right, knock it off," the cadet watching the line said. He picked up the ball the other cadet had rolled back and handed it to me.

"Remember, knees behind the line," he said.

I nodded, kneeled, and wiped any residual sweat off the ball. With Mean Machine's words lingering in my brain, I reared back and let the ball fly. When it landed, it was a good three feet past the muscle head's spot, I stood and gave him a nod.

"Just *one*, 'Sport,'" I said with obvious satisfaction.

74

From that day forward, I had a newfound confidence.

I tried out for the Varsity baseball team, chewing bubblegum and nodding to all the Rampers who looked at me sideways. I may not have set foot on their precious ramp, but they looked at me as if I had crossed a line by walking onto their field. Well, I had come from the field of hard knocks—they just didn't know it yet.

Most of them were dipshits (except Rollie) but I had to give credit where credit was due: they could play ball. The team was coached by Mr. Ackerman, who used to be my PE teacher in middle school (the one who told me I had a "cannon" for an arm). He didn't remember me, but I couldn't blame him. I had grown six inches at least and put on a few pounds.

After the first day of tryouts, Coach Ackerman called me into his office. He saw potential but was blunt with my options. I could ride the bench with varsity or play on the junior varsity squad to get "seasoned" for the following year. It was a no-brainer—I chose playing time with JV, even if it meant I'd have to put up with some barbs from the varsity players.

I could claim one small victory around that time. I passed my driver's license test. Dave and Barry were psyched to make all sorts of plans for Boston/Beaches/Barbecues (the killer "B's" they said), but I told them I needed to lay low for a while. Of course, they asked why, and I told them I was trying to clean up my act—no poker, no beer, no pot.

"No concerts?" Dave asked.

"Not unless it's Donny Osmond," I said.

With my job, radio show, and baseball, my schedule was packed as it was. And of course, I still needed to make time to see Andrea.

One evening Andrea and I were sitting at my porch table eating popsicles and comparing our driver's licenses.

"Your middle name is Alan?" she asked.

"Hold on, is that what it says?" I joked.

She playfully slapped my hand. "Do you know what that means?"

"That it's not my first or last name?" I shrugged.

"It means your initials are J-A-Z…*Jaz*. How about "Jaz" as a nickname? And then you could change your radio show format to jazz?"

"Maybe not," I said.

"Oh, don't be such a grump," she said.

"You can call me 'Jaz.' But I'm not changing a thing about my radio show. 'Rock and Roll Greats' is here to stay."

We teased each other like that all the time and no one's feathers got ruffled. When strangers would ask how we met, Andrea would say "he knocked me off my feet." The curious folks would try to correct her and say, "You mean he *swept* you off your feet?" And, of course, she would go on to explain the whole dodgeball incident which probably left them wondering why she was with me.

The following week an envelope arrived in the mail for me. The return address was from our representative in Congress. I had written to the honorable congressman, along with our two U.S. Senators, respectfully asking them to nominate me to the U.S. Military Academy. To my amazement, the congressman replied that after "careful consideration" he would be pleased to nominate me.

While I had mixed emotions (part shock, part fear), I knew I couldn't hide the letter from my parents. Of course, Dad was ecstatic. He asked if he could borrow the letter the next day so he could make copies at work. He wanted to send one to Aunt Patricia and Mom wanted a copy to mail to Jeremiah.

What's more, my folks took Justine, Andrea, and me out to dinner at Anthony's Pier 4, a legendary and pricey seafood restaurant in Boston by the waterfront. Although I still disliked lobster, I must have eaten three dozen steamers. The evening was undoubtedly a celebration for me, and I was incredibly grateful, but I also had the sense that Dad also saw it as some sort of validation for him. And that was okay because, for the first time in a long time, he looked at me like he was proud.

75

In August of 1980, I was 17, driving, dating, and about to embark on my final year of high school. Aside from the US Hockey team winning the Gold Medal at the Lake Placid Olympics, the world wasn't taking too kindly to the new decade. Mount St. Helens had erupted and the conflict between Iraq and Iran seemed poised to blow up. It also appeared more likely that the U.S. would have a new leader in the coming months.

And yet as far as the Zimmerman family was concerned, we had found stability. It had been six years without a move—a record. I was going to be a senior and Justine would be a freshman. We'd be attending the same school for the first time since Winnicott Elementary.

Meanwhile, a new family moved into Burke's house across the street. Justine took an interest in their son, Chase, who was a freshman lacrosse player. He was a nice enough kid, but I was protective of my little sister. I'd also heard from Matt that Chase had scooped up a few of my old lawn-mowing gigs.

"Just be careful, sis. You know how guys are," I cautioned.

"Um, like you were when Kelly lived there?" she suggested.

"No comment," I said.

"I think you're just bummed that he's taking over your old jobs. And he makes more than you did," she said.

"Ouch," I said. "How much does he charge?"

"About 15 bucks for a yard, sometimes more," she answered.

I furrowed my brow. "Holy crap. Now I *really* don't like him."

The *bigger* news was that Paul had transferred to our High School. His parents didn't agree on much, but they set aside their differences on this matter because of the quality of education. While Coach Ackerman and a certain segment of the "Rampers" were excited that his enrollment would help our baseball team, I was glad to have my old friend back in my life.

On the first day of school, Paul waited for me at the front entrance. We gave each other skin and caught up on all "the haps." Some things he knew from Chris, like the fact that Brett was going to a community college in Worcester, and Dallas was working full-time as a mechanic at a local repair shop. I told him about Andrea, and he remembered her.

"The mixed doubles babe, right? Works at that ice cream shop?" he asked.

"That's the one," I said.

"But is she *the* one?" Paul asked, sounding like a prying mother.

"Time will tell, my friend," I said in jest.

Paul then asked if Maura was still seeing Ricky Catano, which I thought was interesting. I told him I hadn't seen much of Catano, and life was better that way.

When the first bell rang, we entered through the main doors near the Administration Office. My instincts had me leaning right, toward the library.

"Where are you headed?" he asked.

"Um, library," I said.

"Okay. I'm gonna get something to eat in the cafeteria. Wanna come?"

"No, thanks," I said. "I already had breakfast and I've got some overdue books to return."

I realized it was the same excuse that Barry had given Officer Kevin, Except in my case, it wasn't a lie. Paul nodded and said he'd catch up with me later.

In the library, there were familiar faces at our tables and some new ones as well. Brian "Sully" Sullivan, whom I'd played with on the JV team was now in our ranks. So, too, was Henry Witherspoon, of all people.

"Henry?" I said, puzzled.

"How's it going, Jay?" Henry asked.

"You better not let Catano see you sitting here," I cautioned.

"Screw him," Henry said. "He stole my lab, Kody, for a weekend—just because his dog was in heat, and he wanted a litter to sell."

"Kind of a *bitch* move if you ask me," Barry cracked, before Henry and I shot him looks which made him clam up.

At lunch, I sat with Dave, Barry, and Sully. My eyes scanned the cafeteria, searching for Paul. I finally spotted him on the Ramp, sitting at a table with Scottie Gartner of all people. We made eye contact, and he gave me a low-key nod. I nodded back.

"Who are you looking at?" Sully asked.

"My friend, Paul," I said.

"The new kid?" Barry asked.

"He's not new," I said.

"Hey, isn't that your sister up there, too?" Dave asked.

I followed his gaze to another area of the Ramp. Justine and our new neighbor, Chase, were sitting next to each other at a table.

"Yup," I said.

"Wow. She's already cooler than you'll ever be," Barry said.

"Eh, who needs cool?" I asked. "I've got you guys."

76

While it felt like things were headed in the right direction with college on the horizon, I still had a few boxes to check off—like completing the SAT. I needed the scores for my application to West Point.

Of all the possible locations for the SAT to be given, the powers that be decided on our school's cafeteria. The Ramp had been roped off, so it was odd (and enjoyable) to see Scottie and all his cohorts forced to sit at regular tables on the lower level. They looked completely ill at ease among the "common folk." Heck, no one looked comfortable—it was the most stressful day of any high school student's life.

I tried to tell myself I had kicked butt on the PSAT, but it didn't help much. I caught a glimpse of Dave, but he was far away and didn't see me. Same for Rollie. There was no sign of Paul, Barry, or anyone else I knew. They had been scheduled for the following weekend.

I picked up my #2 pencil and doodled as the proctor-in-chief, a woman I didn't recognize, welcomed us and started in on the instructions. The first half-hour was just making sure we had the correct answer sheet, the proper test, the right number of pages, and the necessary supplemental materials. Then she went into the guidelines about what we needed to do if we had a question or needed to use the bathroom. After that came the typical assessment warnings about talking and using forbidden items like compasses, protractors, and calculators.

By the time I opened my exam booklet, my brain was already in a fog. The first section was math, and the questions were far more difficult than those on the PSAT. The second part, Language Arts, was where I hit the wall. The comprehension passages were long, and I became lost in them—as in daydream lost. Someone's chair moved and I snapped out of it. A student on the other side of the table was leaving. I looked over at where Dave was sitting, and his chair was empty. Many others were, too. The cafeteria was only about one-third full.

"Okay, everyone, another reminder…ten minutes remaining," the monitor said.

Another reminder? When was the first one? And *ten* minutes?

I snatched up my pencil (still sharp) and answer book and furiously began bubbling in the multiple-choice sections. A, C, B, D, D, A, B…hmm…haven't had a C for a while. C-C-C. As I finished the last question, a monitor arrived to collect my answer sheet and test.

I had been riding some highs for a while, and naturally, that meant I could expect some lows. That was life. Ups and downs.

I shook off my performance because I had to work at Nelson's late that afternoon. As I was about to clock in, Abdul pulled me aside and told me he was promoting me to the position of Assistant Shift Supervisor.

"What this means is you're officially an A.S.S., guy," he said, with his inimitable laugh.

I took no offense and laughed right along with Abdul. Aside from a significant raise, I'd get to wear a far more comfortable, white cotton shirt. Life was grand for those 15 seconds, but then the other shoe dropped.

"By the way," Abdul said, turning serious. "I hear you know a guy named Ricky Catano."

"Why?" I asked, narrowing my eyes. "What did he do?"

"Nothing. He applied for a job as a dishwasher. He said he knows you."

"*Knows* me?" I asked, feeling my stomach clench into a knot. "No, not even close. Abdul, he's"

"Listen, guy. We're desperate. Rene left. He has experience from the Steakhouse down the street."

I sighed, defeated because it wasn't my call.

Abdul was the manager. I was just an A.S.S.

My performance on the SAT and Catano's hiring had me down in the dumps that December, but there was one more blow to come that month. Dad and I stayed up late to watch the Patriots on Monday Night Football when Howard Cosell shared the tragic news with the viewing audience that legendary musician and former Beatle, John Lennon, had been shot to death outside his New York City home. Dad and I reeled back in our seats as if blasted by the wind.

The players on TV kept playing. How could they? Didn't they know? The outcome of a football game suddenly seemed trivial. Dad must have felt the same way because he turned off the TV.

"So senseless. What's this world coming to?" Dad said, clearing his throat.

I shook my head, trying to fight off the tears. Dad gave me a pat on the shoulder and left the room. All alone, I let it all out. Soon crying turned to cursing and then questioning…*why*? I wasn't sure who I was asking. God? The universe?

In silence, I heard Dad's office door close.

I was about to go upstairs to tell Mom and Justine the news but then thought better of it. Why disturb their sleep to share a story about evil once again rearing its ugly head? As I stood in our foyer, I heard Dad's voice. I thought he had called someone on the phone, but as I stepped closer to his office, I realized he was *praying*:

"For they cannot die anymore, because they are equal to angels and are sons of God, being sons of the resurrection…"

My eyes grew wide in surprise. Dad may have left religion, but it had never left him.

For my next "Rock and Roll Greats" show, I played "American Pie" by Don MacLean, and then only songs by The Beatles and John Lennon after that. I felt as if I should do more, like a moment of silence, but I realized silence on the radio wasn't such a great idea. At the end of my hour, I dedicated "All You Need is Love" to Andrea. She'd told me she listened to my show when she could. I hoped the song would reach her.

When I got home that night Mom told me Andrea called and asked that I call her back before nine. I looked at my watch, walked to Dad's vacant office, and dialed her. Andrea picked up her phone on the second ring.

"How'd you know that was my favorite Beatles song?" she said as her greeting.

"I didn't," I said. It was the truth.

We spoke for at least an hour and arranged to meet up for Christmas shopping at the mall that Friday night. There were not only things to buy for our family members but also a holiday work party Abdul was hosting the next night. He had asked all guests to bring a cheap (but funny) item for a gag gift exchange. We stopped by a party store and Andrea bought a package of fake dog poop, while I went with a coffee mug that was crafted like a miniature toilet. Like minds.

We loaded our bags in the trunk of Mom's car, and I started the engine to remove some frost that had accumulated on the windshield. As we slid into the car, Andrea noticed an apple in the console.

"Is this your apple, 'Jaz?'" she asked.

"It's my mom's," I replied. "That nickname's kinda growin' on me."

Andrea smiled. She picked up the apple and examined the stem.

"You know the saying, 'He likes me, he likes me not?'" she asked.

"I thought it was *love*, not like," I said.

"Well, whatever it is," she continued. "You can do that with an apple."

Andrea turned the stem in a clockwise motion while reciting "He likes me, he likes me not…"

"Don't I get a turn?" I asked.

"Only if you have your own apple," she said softly.

I threw up my hands in exaggerated despair. Andrea grinned and continued to twist the stem while alternating the phrases. At last, it broke free on 'he likes me.'

"I knew it!" Andrea exclaimed.

"Wait a minute…you pulled it off!" I shouted.

I reached for the apple, and she intercepted my hand with one of hers.

Our fingers locked, and then our eyes did as well. Energy seemed to pass between us, and I leaned forward to kiss her. As always, her lips were soft and moist. I put my hand up to her face and then caressed the back of her neck. She took hold of my wrist and gently pulled my arm away.

"That was so incredible. You know me, I just want to go slow," she explained.

I sat back. I felt a little bit like Daisy when Dad gave her a nudge to stop her from climbing up onto the chair. Rebuffed.

"You're upset, aren't you?" She asked.

"No," I said. "I'm just…"

"What?" she asked, still holding my hand.

"The apple didn't lie. I'm crazy about you. In every way," I finally admitted.

"Welcome to my world," she said, looking me in the eyes again. "I don't expect you to understand, but if you can be patient with me, things are going to get even better. Keep that faith."

"Faith," I said, taking her hand. "The more I hear about it, the less I know."

79

Less than 24 hours later Andrea and I pulled up to Abdul's house for our employee Christmas party. We hadn't spoken about anything serious on the drive over and it was better that way. Snow flurries drifted through the air which added to the aura of the season. As we exited the car with our wrapped gag gifts I could hear "Holly, Jolly Christmas," by Burl Ives wafting out of the house.

Andrea and I made our way up the walk to the open front door, stomped the snow off our feet, and peeked inside. The party was in full swing, packed with revelers. Abdul spotted us and his face lit up—almost as much as the flashing wreath he wore around his neck.

"Look at you two!" he said, ambling over to hug us both. "Better stay away from the mistletoe."

A tall, fair-skinned woman wearing a hat with reindeer antlers appeared at his side. She was almost my height—meaning she dwarfed Abdul, too.

"Hi, I'm Patty—Abdul's wife," she said. "Welcome. "

We exchanged greetings and handed Patty our gifts. Abdul pulled me aside and whispered in my ear.

"I'm like you, guy. I like American women."

He gave me a playful nudge and I gave him a thumbs-up. Patty told us to help ourselves to refreshments and food. Andrea and I started for a plate of cookies but never made it because we were intercepted by some of our coworkers. Just then, Abdul stepped onto his coffee table and tapped his beer bottle with a spoon.

"Listen up, my friends! For anyone here who happens to be underage, I don't want you drinking any beer—which happens to be outside by the grill in a blue bucket filled with ice! *Blue bucket. Ice!* We have plenty of blow-up mattresses. If you need to spend the night, our casa is your casa!"

"That last part didn't sound like Arabic!" I shouted.

Abdul pointed at me, hooted, and jumped off the table to mingle.

Over the next hour, Andrea and I snacked and drank a modest amount. Andrea even got me to dance to a song or two. After that, we sat around the living room and opened the gag gifts which were randomly distributed.

I had a good laugh when I unwrapped a tiny dancing Santa Clause that showed a butt crack. There seemed to be a common theme with all the gifts.

Just then one of our shift supervisors, Beth—the woman who greeted me on the day of my interview—looked closely at Andrea.

"Sweetheart, is one of your eyelashes coming off?"

Andrea touched her lash and quickly rose to her feet.

"Oh, thank you," she said before excusing herself to look for an available bathroom.

"Hope I didn't upset her," Beth said. "We women just try to look out for each other."

I smiled and waited for Andrea to return. When she didn't come back after five minutes, I grew concerned and went to look for her. I found her at the top of the stairs, appearing from a hallway restroom.

"Are you all right?" I asked.

"Yeah. Can we maybe go outside?" she asked, dabbing an eye with a tissue.

A minute later we were standing by the garage in the bitter cold.

"Andrea, what's going on?" I asked.

"I'm not sure how to say this, Jaz…" Andrea began until she was distracted by the slamming of a car door.

A familiar voice suddenly crooned "Breaking up is harrrrrrrd to do…"

I turned to find Ricky Catano strolling up the driveway, holding a gift bag.

"Aw, what's the matter? Trouble in paradise?" he sneered.

"Can you ever give it a rest?" I asked, turning to face him.

"Aw, you're a tough talker when you have a lady by your side," Catano said.

"Just go enjoy the party, Ricky," Andrea said.

Catano snickered. "I'll go in when I want to go in. That okay with you, Andrea? And by the way, Jay, consider this a compliment: she's tougher than that bitch Paul you hang out with."

I looked at Andrea. "Maybe you should go back inside…"

"Jay, no," she pleaded. "He's not worth it."

"Wanna do this, Jay?" Catano said, placing his bag on a snowbank.

I moved towards him and set my feet the way I did when I was about to slug my heavy bag, Catano went into a boxer's stance as well.

"Hey, you two are crazy to be out here without these!" Abdul hollered.

He meandered down the walk with our jackets and almost slipped. I doubt he would have passed a breathalyzer, but he still knew what was happening in his yard. Abdul handed the jackets to Andrea and narrowed his eyes.

"Everything all right, here?"

"Sure thing, Boss," Catano said. "Just exchanging season's greetings."

"Yeah, Abdul," I said. "It's all good. But we need to run. Tell Patty thanks."

"All right. We'll catch up later," he said, giving me a knowing look.

I took Andrea's hand and led her toward our car. Catano picked up his bag, shook his head at us, and walked with Abdul to the house.

I started the car and turned on the heater but not the radio. It was obvious neither one of us felt jolly. I was working my jaw the way Dad did sometimes when he was behind the wheel. Andrea, meanwhile, looked out the window, deep in her thoughts. After three blocks I pulled over.

"So, Andrea, something just kind of dawned on me," I said.

"What's that, Jaz?" she asked.

"When we were back at Abdul's, you knew Ricky's name. And he knew yours. But as far as I can tell, you two haven't worked together yet. You don't go to school together, so…"

Andrea looked out the window and spoke softly.

"If I say I've been holding back telling you this, you'll get the wrong idea. It's complicated, but I don't want you thinking the worst…"

"I don't even know what I'm thinking," I said. "Just curious."

"My mom's been married three times. Her second marriage was to Ricky's father. They lived with us for about a year, but it didn't work out. So, he was my step-brother, for a while…"

Wow. I took a breath as I took in all the new information.

"I know it doesn't excuse his behavior, but life kind of took a bad turn for Ricky after that. He's resented my mother and me ever since."

"And about 99 percent of the world's population," I added.

"True. And it's pretty obvious you're not in the lucky one percent either," she said. "Look, Jay, as far as he and I are concerned, it's all history. But if you want to know anything about that situation, it's okay to ask."

"No, that's not necessary. I'd rather look forward than back. So, then what about Stan? He's husband number three?" I asked.

"Yes. We like Stan and we hope Stan sticks around," Andrea said, taking my hands into hers. "I'm sorry, Jay. I feel like I'm putting you through the wringer here."

"You don't need to apologize, Andrea."

"Well, maybe not for Ricky. But there's something else. That's why I wanted to talk to you back there before the interruption. To explain…"

"Explain what?" I asked.

"Why I've been emotional. Pulling back, going slow…" she said.

"Hey, it's okay," I said.

"I guess I'm a bit like my mother. Trust issues. But if I can't trust you, who can I trust in this world?" Andrea asked and then reached up to remove her beanie.

"What are you doing?" I asked.

She looked at me without a response, except to remove one of her barrettes. To my surprise, there was hair attached. She placed the barrette on the dashboard, then took off another attachment, and another…until the sets were lined up in a row.

Andrea kept her gaze on me, her scalp revealing several bald patches.

"That hair on the dash is fake. But this is the real me."

I felt like I had been punched in the heart. Tears swelled in my eyes.

"Oh Andrea," I whispered. "You have cancer?"

"No, you sweet man," she said, touching my face. "It's called Alopecia. It's not a disease—more of a condition—that creates hair loss."

"So, you're not…*dying*?" I asked.

"Well, only on the inside as the saying goes," she said, forcing a smile.

Saying sorry didn't sound right. It would suggest I viewed her situation with pity. My hunch was that she didn't want sympathy—only understanding.

"Thank you for sharing this with me. You're beautiful," I said. She wrapped her arms around me and held on tightly.

80

WYUJ had grown in popularity and expanded its format, thanks to the vision of Principal Weber and an alum named Nick Dorschu. In addition to being an on-site counselor, Nick volunteered to be the station's "General Manager." Some slots were filled by teachers for things like poetry readings, others were reserved for live performances by the school band. Nick had even allowed Barry to play some excerpts from "clean" comedy albums, like Steve Martin, during his show.

Next on the agenda was a live broadcast of a school sporting event. Nick approached me in the studio after my shift one evening and asked if I'd like to be the play-by-play announcer for an upcoming varsity basketball game. I jumped at his offer and suggested the broadcast might be more authentic if I had a color commentator by my side. Nick gave me a thumbs up and I ended up choosing Dave.

Granted, Dave wasn't an athlete—at least not in the four-sport variety. On the flip side, he had radio experience, he was funny, and we had a good rapport. When I asked him to join me to provide color for the game, he agreed but only if he could "plug" his radio show.

"Deal," I said.

The game was scheduled on a Thursday night and both teams were mediocre, at best. There wasn't much at stake and there wasn't going to be any big promotion for it. Once the microphones were set up, Nick placed a copy of each team's roster and a scoresheet at our broadcast table. I figured I'd have to do the scorekeeping, as well, which was no biggie given my Strat-O-Matic experience.

Once the game tipped off, I did my best to describe the action, trying to recall how Johnny Most had done it all those years ago when I'd sat near him in the "Garden." Dave couldn't add much in terms of analysis, so he talked about a certain player on the other team who resembled a sitcom star.

"Dave, we're on the radio," I offered as a reminder. "It may be hard for our listeners to appreciate that."

"Yeah, well, they'll have to take my word for it," he said. "It's uncanny. And by the way, when can I let our listeners know about my show, 'Into the Mystic?'"

"Maybe during our next break in the action. We've got Boucher up at the free throw line, trying to put the good guys up by two," I answered.

After Paul sank the second free throw, the horn beside us beeped for the game's first substitution. Dave just about went airborne.

"*Yeesh!* What the heck was *that?*" he cried out.

"That's our first substitution, Dave."

"Why's it so loud?"

"Well, if we had a packed auditorium, it might be necessary," I said.

"I'm gonna get some chips from the snack bar. Do you want anything?" Dave asked, confusing a substitution with a quarter break.

"Listeners, a reminder, we're live on WYUJ, still in the first quarter," I said, hoping Dave would get the hint. "The home team is ahead, 8-6, in a defensive duel."

"I'll take that as a 'no' on food," Dave said, pushing away from the table and starting to rise—

I whipped off my mic and hopped to my feet, catching myself as I was about to utter the most offensive of all the seven dirty words—

"*Fuc*—ryin' out loud, man. You're not going anywhere," I warned Dave, grabbing him by the shoulder.

"Hey, sit down!" a spectator shouted at me with his hands up. "You're tall man!"

Dave ignored me and turned back to the fan, completely unfazed.

"No, *I'm* Talman…he's Zimmerman!"

The following week, Mrs. Steiner, my counselor, summoned me to her office. I had been preoccupied with things and hadn't checked my student mailbox in a few days. She closed the door and encouraged me to take a seat. I noticed she had a printout in her hand.

"I suppose you know what I have here?" she said.

"No, ma'am. I don't, but it looks official," I replied.

"Your SAT scores," she said with a dour expression.

She handed me the printout and I looked it over. Unlike my PSAT results, which had pretty much rocked, the SAT scores left a lot to be desired. To put it in Boston slang, they were "wicked" bad.

"Yikes," I said. "I'm not surprised. I had a little trouble finishing the Language Arts section."

Mrs. Steiner stared at me. I tried to hand the document back to her, but she waved it away as if I had transmitted a virus to it.

"Well, that's unfortunate," she said.

"Is it possible to take the test again?" I asked.

"You may. But these scores won't be voided. So, can you refresh me on your college plans?"

"Well, I've applied to West Point," I said, taking on an upbeat tone. "And I received a nomination."

Her expression was unchanged. She was one tough nut.

"I presume you know your fellow student, Mr. Gartner?"

"Yes. But I don't call him 'Mr. Gartner,'" I said.

"Of course. Well, he applied to West Point as well. And I feel compelled to say this—don't get your hopes up. The academies rarely take two applicants from the same school."

"I'll keep that in mind," I said.

"Okay, so other options," she said, trying to move me along.

"Well, when we spoke earlier in the year you mentioned Amherst?"

"UMass? That's possible."

"No, Amherst. And Williams. As I recall, those were your suggestions."

Mrs. Steiner stifled a laugh.

"Well, I'm sorry, dear, but that was before...*those*." She pointed again at the offending document in my hand. "You'll need to reassess your options."

After the meeting, I felt like I needed to reassess a lot of things. I still hadn't heard from West Point, but after what Mrs. Steiner had said, the odds weren't exactly in my favor. I could deal with no military academy, but no college at all would be a genuine problem. I didn't want to be working at Nelson's forever.

That spring I tried out for varsity baseball again. I wasn't delusional—I knew a baseball scholarship wasn't in the cards like it was for Paul. But it was my last shot at relevance in the sport I loved.

On the first day of open tryouts, I lined up behind the mound with a handful of other pitching hopefuls, including Sully. Why not go with my strength? After loosening up with a few light tosses to the second-string catcher, Coach Ackerman told Scottie Gartner to grab a bat.

"You bet, Coach!" Scottie replied as if he'd been offered a brand-new Mercedes.

He put on a helmet and stared out at me triumphantly as he dug in beside the plate.

"Hey, Jay! I got my acceptance letter from the academy. You?"

I shook my head, more out of disdain than as a reply.

"Let's go, gentlemen!" Coach Ackerman yelled.

I exhaled and went into a full windup, putting everything I had into a fastball. Scottie swung and missed. The catcher couldn't raise his mitt in time and–THWACK—the ball lodged into the fence behind him.

The onlookers were stunned, including Paul and Rollie, who were taking grounders in the adjacent field. They nodded and pointed at me.

"Holy shit," Scottie said under his breath. He looked at the ball, and then back at me—as if verifying that I was the one who had thrown it.

"Jay, my man!" Coach Ackerman called out enthusiastically. "I remember you now. You're the one with the 'cannon.'"

That evening Paul gave me a lift home after tryouts. I was still pumped when I walked through the door. But when I saw Mom and Dad sitting alone at the kitchen table, I pumped the brakes. There was an envelope between them. As I kneeled to pet Daisy, I saw a blue paper bag on the floor by the leg of Dad's chair. There was a fancy bottle inside.

"Hey, slugger," Dad said with a smile.

"Hey," I replied, standing up. "What's happening?"

"You've got some mail here," Mom said.

"Looks like the one we've been waiting for," Dad said.

The moment had finally come. I walked over to the table and picked up the envelope. It had a red West Point, NY postmark.

"I'd rather not sit down," I said.

"Suit yourself," Dad said.

I carefully opened the envelope and began to feel butterflies swarming in my gut. My future was going to take a turn, one way or the other.

I glanced at the letter. The salutation was to "Candidate Zimmerman." I read the contents quietly, and then reread it.

After absorbing the news for another moment, I dropped the envelope and letter on the counter and exited the room.

"Jay?" Mom asked.

"You won't need to make a copy of that one!" I shouted from the bottom of the stairs. "And, Dad, I appreciate your optimism, but maybe you should give that champagne to someone else!"

I took refuge in my room for the next few hours. Until it was dark. Until it was quiet. After everyone had gone to bed, I went down to Dad's office and called Paul. I knew he was at his mom's place, but I needed someone to talk to. He picked up, but he sounded groggy.

"Sounds like I woke you up?" I asked.

"It's all right," he said. "What's going on?"

"They didn't take me," I said. "The academy."

"Sorry, man. But, I honestly think you dodged a bullet. No pun intended," Paul said.

"Me, too," I replied. "But why do I feel guilty?"

"Probably because part of you feels like you let your dad down."

"Yeah, it could be that," I sighed.

"He'll get over it," Paul said. "Wait until baseball season starts. Then he'll be right back in your corner."

"Right. Except there's no guarantee I'll make the team—"

"Stop," Paul said. "I've never seen Coach so impressed as he was when you fired that laser."

"You're not just saying that to cheer me up?" I asked.

"I'm saying it because it's a fact," he replied.

83

Paul was right. The sting of my West Point rejection letter was soon offset by my inclusion on the varsity baseball roster.

As it turned out, though, the only thing my newly chiseled right arm was doing for most of the year was lifting a water bottle to my mouth on the bench. When the games started to count, Coach Ackerman stuck with his guys, namely Todd Henderson, and Sully. Sure, I practiced with the team and dressed for all the games, but it was difficult for me and some of the other fresh faces to crack the lineup. We were favored to win our league with most of our starters returning, including Rollie, who manned third base. The addition of a versatile talent like Paul also helped our league title prospects.

In the fifth game of the year, we were leading something like 12 to 1, and Coach Ackerman finally put me in…as a *right fielder*. During the seventh and final inning, I dropped a pop fly that would have ended the game. We still won, but my miscue had given the other team life and they pushed across a few more runs. Not the kind of debut that would make headlines.

In the locker room, Rollie gave me a supportive tap on the shoulder as he passed by, but most of my other teammates either ignored me or imitated me misplaying the ball. From somewhere I heard Paul tell the guys to shut up and the whole room went silent.

A second later he came around the corner of the locker and sat on the bench next to me.

"What happened on that play?"

"I just lost sight of it," I mumbled.

That weekend I had a rare Saturday off from work. Dave and Barry asked if I wanted to head up to Crane's Beach with them and I declined. Meanwhile, Andrea invited me to join her for lunch with her cousin in Chestnut Hill and I even turned her down.

The reason was that Paul wanted to schedule practice together in our old field. He hit some fly balls to me. I caught some and misjudged others.

After our practice, we retrieved Matt and watched a Celtics playoff game at my house against Philly. The three of us hadn't been able to hang out much, especially since Matt had enrolled in a vocational school, but it was just like old times.

The spring of 1981 was much like the summer of 1975. But this time the buzz in Boston was about basketball. The Celtics were contenders for the NBA title and featured a budding superstar in Larry Bird.

At some point in the first quarter, Paul went to the kitchen and asked me for the score. I leaned forward and relayed the score—as I saw it.

"Not even close," Matt said.

"What?" I asked. "What are you talking about?"

"You need glasses, buddy boy. This is why you're having trouble tracking the ball," Paul said.

Mystery solved. At least it wasn't my coordination.

"Will you guys still like me if I have four eyes?" I asked.

"We don't like you with two eyes," Matt joked.

"I missed all this," I said. "Hanging with the boys."

"Just like you missed all those fly balls," Paul said.

"Hey, I've got some news, too," Matt said. "Speaking of 'misses'... Guess who's gonna have a baby?"

Paul and I stared at each other in disbelief.

"You got someone pregnant?" I asked. "I didn't know you had a—"

"No, you dickwad. My mom's having a baby. I'm gonna have a little white brother."

"Matt, that's fantastic," Paul said, giving him a pat on the shoulder.

"Yeah, congrats, buddy," I said, shaking his hand.

"Thanks, fellas," Matt said.

"So, what did you mean about the 'missus,'" Paul asked.

"I said 'misses.' Looks like the little frisbee didn't do its job after all," he said, giving me a knowing look.

Paul stared at us, lost.

"Birth control," Matt said.

"Long story," I added.

I crossed my arms and looked at Mom with mock frustration.

"All those times you were doing *smell* checks," I said. "You could have been doing *eye* checks."

We were sitting in the waiting room of Dr. Gottler, a local optometrist.

"Okay, give it a rest," Mom said.

"Whose side of the family has bad eyes?" I asked.

"Probably your father's. Mine is heart disease," she said.

"Oh great. So, first I go blind, then I'll have a heart attack," I mused.

"All this drama. You sound like Dustin Hoffman."

A door swung open and a man in a white coat with a gray beard looked in our direction "Jayson Zimmerman?"

Ten minutes later, the vision test confirmed what we all suspected: I was nearsighted. Dr. Gottler asked if I'd ever had concerns about my vision previously. I answered that it would have been hard for me to know because I thought I was seeing exactly what everyone else was seeing.

"And you've been driving my car all around town," Mom said.

"Hey, no accidents," I said, holding up my hands.

"Don't jinx it, kiddo," Mom replied.

"Maybe this is why I messed up on the SAT," I said.

"Hmm, I don't think so, unless the questions were posted on signs 100 feet away," Dr. Gottler said with a wry smile.

There were far worse things in the world than having eye problems, but I was already wondering how many questions I'd answered incorrectly because I couldn't see the board. How many pitches had I swung at and missed? How many girls had winked at me and—

"Young friend," Dr. Gottler said, steering my attention back to him. "You have three choices: contacts, eyeglasses, or both."

I grimaced. The idea of inserting tiny plastic discs onto my eyeballs freaked me out. It was on my list of things I never, ever wanted to do--somewhere between skydiving and eating raw fish.

"Glasses," I said.

When I showed up for my next shift at Nelson's, Andrea was there—having been called over to our location by Abdul because we were short-staffed on servers. She complimented my new eyewear and whispered that it gave me a scholarly, yet sexy, look. As challenging as it was, we tried to keep our PDA and personal conversations to a minimum, especially with Abdul and Catano on the premises.

Although Catano pointed and did a silent guffaw when he saw my glasses, he was unusually reserved. He stayed in the back and worked diligently on cleaning the dishes from the dinner rush.

"Maybe he's maturing?" she asked with fingers crossed.

"Well, the night's still young," I said.

About a half hour later, while Andrea was taking an order at a corner booth, Catano came out from the back to retrieve a bus pan beside her. As he stood up, he reached out toward her face.

"Hold on, 'Sis,' I think you have something up here," he said, before tugging off a handful of her hair extensions.

Andrea flinched and immediately ducked for cover below the counter as she covered her scalp. An elderly couple in the booth looked on with their mouths agape.

"Oops, my bad," Catano said, dropping the extensions into the bus pan. He shot me a look before scurrying through the swinging doors into the kitchen.

I pocketed my glasses and bolted from the cash register towards the back of the restaurant. Out of the corner of my eye, I thought I saw two other female servers comforting Andrea. I kicked open the swinging doors, and Catano was waiting with his hands up—

"Aww, here comes the hero…"

CRACK! I hit him with a left jab above the right eye. He staggered back towards the kitchen sink. As good as that felt, I knew it wasn't enough. I threw a right cross that grazed the top of his head as he caught his bearings.

"Guys, stop!" Abdul yelled from somewhere.

I did, Catano didn't. He lunged and put me in a headlock. We grappled and he drove me against the large dishwasher. I used one hand to loosen his grip and the other to keep my balance. Somehow my left hand ended up inside the open dishwasher. Catano noted this, grabbed the door lever, and slammed it down like a guillotine.

I screamed in agony as pain shot up my left arm, My eyes closed and for a second I thought I might pass out. When I opened them again, seconds later at the most, I was somehow free from Catano's hold. Abdul and several customers, including Nick, the arm wrestler, had him wrapped up and were pulling him away.

"Fuck you, Jay!" he screamed. "Fuck you all!"

I glanced at my left hand and saw that it was swollen and oozing blood. Someone, I don't even know who gave me a bag of ice wrapped in a towel. But I wasn't thinking about my hand.

"How's Andrea?" I asked.

86

The fallout from that evening was serious but not surprising. Catano was fired and I was suspended indefinitely. Abdul had no choice because the incident was reported to Nelson's home office, and being an A.S.S., I was technically Catano's superior. Despite the violent nature of the confrontation at Nelson's, no charges were filed. The last thing Catano wanted was to have the police investigating him, or his home, and I was more than happy to move on from anything having to do with him.

On the medical front, I ended up with a cast on my left hand after X-rays showed I had a broken fourth metacarpal bone. Andrea borrowed her mother's car and met me in the emergency room of the hospital around 1 a.m. She had gotten her hair clips back but was wearing a Red Sox cap.

"I'm sorry," I said. "I know you didn't want me to stoop to his level."

"Please, You were so gallant, like my knight in shining armor," she said, touching my right hand.

"That's funny," I said. "There was a comic in *Highlights* magazine called 'Goofus and Gallant' and for a while, I was a far cry from Gallant."

"I loved that one," she said. "But I don't mind when you're a little bit of a Goofus, too," she said.

One interesting development was that I was allowed to keep my spot on the baseball team. Coach Ackerman lobbied Principal Weber and emphasized two key points: 1) the incident did not occur at school, and 2) even though I had a cast, it would be good for team morale to have me around. Unlike my last altercation in seventh grade, I came out of this one looking pretty good. I was the guy who defended "a cancer patient" from a bully (after a while I stopped clarifying—why let facts get in the way?).

By the end of the baseball season, our team was 17-1 and tournament-bound. We won those three games and made it to the Division finals against Townsend High School. Even though we were playing at a neutral site (a minor league stadium, in fact) we were the home team based on our record.

Things went well for our squad early but then the wheels started to fall off late in the game. Paul, who had a double and a triple to drive in all of our runs, messed up his ankle after a collision at home plate and had to leave the game. Also, our pitching staff was running on fumes. My old Braves teammate, Todd Henderson, was heroic but he could only take us so far. By the end of the eighth inning, his arm was dead. And unlike all the other games, the championship was scheduled for nine innings—or more. That meant "Sully," our other starter, needed to hold onto a 4-2 lead in the ninth. Only three outs were needed to seal the deal for us.

I hadn't moved from my spot on the end of the bench and, superstitious as ever, didn't plan to. I glanced around the ballpark and found familiar faces:

Andrea, Mom, Justine, Matt, Mrs. M., and Terri (Paul's mom). There was no sign of Dad. He told me he might be late because of an afternoon conference call.

Paul limped over and sat beside me. I took off my glasses and put them in my pants pocket.

"How's the ankle?" I asked.

"I'll live," he said. "Listen, you might want to get ready."

"Yeah, right," I said.

"I'm serious," he said. "I heard the coaches talking about needing a fresh arm. Sully pitched two days ago."

Whether it was fatigue or nerves, Sully had to battle from the start. The leadoff batter kept fouling off pitches and drew a walk. The runner then stole second, so Coach called for Sully to intentionally walk the next batter. The hope was that a ground ball would improve our chances for a double play. Unfortunately, the next batter beat out an infield single to load the bases. Coach Ackerman shouted to me from the other side of the dugout.

"Zimmerman, need you to warm up!"

I was stunned. "Coach, I got a cast on my arm!"

"Not on your throwing arm!" he hollered back.

Paul yanked me up by the sleeve. "Let's go, buddy."

He grabbed a catcher's glove and limped out to a spot beside the dugout where we could toss the ball. As he lowered himself into a catcher's stance, I ramped up the velocity.

When play resumed, the Townsend side raised hell, trying to distract Sully. It worked. His next pitch drilled the batter in the shoulder. The runner on third scooted home, clapping his hands. The score was now 4-3. The bases were still loaded and there were still no outs.

"Time!" Coach Ackerman yelled to the ump and then waved at me. I looked at Paul and he grinned.

"Go get 'em, *Ace*…"

I trotted out to the mound fully aware that one side of the ballpark was hooting and hollering, while the other was apprehensive and quiet. Coach Ackerman, Sully, and Scottie Gartner waited near the rubber. None of them touched it—another superstition. Sully handed over the baseball without even looking at me.

"My bad, Jay. I put you in a crappy spot," he mumbled.

"Cut it out," Coach said. "You just didn't want to make this save too easy for Jay."

Sully nodded and trotted back to the dugout. The first one to greet him was Paul who gave him a big pat on the back.

"Let's go, boys!" Paul bellowed to our teammates. His leadership was undeniable, and the intensity was infectious.

"You got it, Jay!" Rollie shouted from third.

Soon both benches and cheering sections were raucous.

"Coach, are you sure about this?" Scottie asked.

Coach turned to him with a glare that could make wood catch fire. Scottie shut his mouth and put his mask back on.

"Fire up that cannon, Jay," Coach said. "It's your time."

He hustled back to the dugout and Scottie returned to his spot behind the plate. Suddenly, Townsend's coach bolted from his dugout.

"Hey ump, he has a cast on his arm!" the coach said.

"Contrary to what you think, I'm not blind," the home plate umpire said. "You want to file a protest?"

At that moment I realized I'd forgotten something. I took my glasses out of my pocket and wedged them underneath the bill of my cap. I must have looked like a sorry sight because the Townsend players and their supporters began laughing and pointing.

"Nah, never mind," the coach said with a quick shake of his head.

Mind over matter, I thought, recalling a nugget of advice from Dad. I don't mind and they don't matter. I put my glove on my left elbow, since it wouldn't fit over my cast, and tossed a few light warm-up pitches to Scottie. I wasn't going to give anything away.

"Okay, batter up!" yelled the ump behind the plate.

I stepped on the rubber and the throngs began cheering once again. Scottie put down some fingers, the typical signs, but he and I both knew it was for show. A fastball was the only pitch in my repertoire. As the batter dug in, I reared back and let it fly. Right down the middle—the ball popped in Scottie's mitt like a firecracker.

"STEERIKE!" Screamed the ump.

Mumbles in the stands. Players on both teams perked up.

Scottie gave me an encouraging nod and tossed the ball back.

I took a breath, wound up, and threw again. This time the batter swung—and missed. Another pop in the glove.

"STEERIKE TWOOOO!"

"One more like that!" Scottie said, throwing the ball back with force.

I stared down at the batter, the plate, and Scottie's glove. I tuned out everything else and went into my delivery again.

Another swing, another miss. *THWAPP* as leather met leather.

"STEEERIKE THREEEE!"

The fans on our side roared. Paul let out a "whoop" from the dugout.

I kicked some dirt off my cleats and rubbed the ball. Could I do it again—two more times? I took slow, steady breaths trying to keep my heart from racing.

The next batter was a lefty. I began to wonder if I had ever faced a lefty but steered myself back to the moment. Screw it. The plate and the target were still the same.

I reared back and fired another heater. The batter closed his eyes and somehow made contact. The ball sailed high into the air. Not far, but high. On an infield pop-up, the pitcher is supposed to get out of the way, so I scampered into foul territory. As I did, my glasses dropped to the ground.

"Somebody!" Coach Ackerman yelled, pointing to the ball.

I felt a crunch under my feet as the ball landed in Rollie's glove. The third base umpire held up a fist and hollered "Out!"

Two down—but I was also down a pair of glasses. I reached down to pick up the frame and what was left of the fractured lenses.

"Hold up!" The third base umpire shouted and waved at our dugout. "Coach?"

Coach Ackerman jogged to the mound once again. He'd worn down a path in the grass from all his visits.

"What's going on, Jay?"

"My glasses," I said. "They're busted."

I showed him the remnants of my eyewear. He glanced over at Townsend's on-deck circle. Their mammoth slugger, who'd already hit two solo homers, eyed us like a hungry lion.

"Jay, we could walk Brutus over there and face the next batter…then just take our chances in extra innings."

"No," I said, shaking my head. "I can do this."

Just then I noticed something shimmering on the grass right in front of me. It was a pull tab from a soda can. I picked it up and handed it to Scottie.

"Why are you giving me trash?" he asked.

"Just trust me. Hang it from your mask," I said.

Coach shrugged and Scottie did as I asked, attaching the tab to the bottom wire of his catcher's mask.

"Let's play ball!" The home plate ump barked.

Coach tucked my frames and cracked lenses into his windbreaker pocket and sprinted back to the dugout. Scottie lowered his mask, tab, and all, and crouched behind the plate.

I stepped back on the rubber and detected the glint of the tab in the late afternoon sun. That's what I focused on. After Scottie put down another phony signal, I went into the windup and threw…

The pitch was *just* high.

"BALL ONE!" There were immediate boos from our supporters.

My next pitch was a bit lower… "STEERIKE!"

The count was now even…one ball, one strike. The slugger gave a reassuring thumbs up to his bench.

I wound up—my third pitch—*WHOOSH*. Swing and miss.

Slugger cursed and shot daggers with his eyes.

"Try that again," Brutus said, stomping the ground with his cleats.

"Let's go, Jay. *Eliminate* him!" Scottie said.

I grinned at the callback to one of my favorite nicknames. As I stepped on the rubber, everyone in attendance rose. I kicked up my front leg and let the pitch fly for all the marbles—

CRACK! The ball sailed high and far down the left-field line. It was like Carlton Fisk's epic Game 6 liner from 1975. "If it stayed fair…"

"Foul ball!" the third base ump shouted as the baseball hooked just left of the foul pole.

I could hear the collective sighs from our fans. As the ball bounced around in the parking lot, a man picked it up. Without my glasses, I couldn't make out his face, but I recognized the posture and the walk. *Dad.*

He pretended to wipe his brow and then lowered his hands… "Take it easy."

I grinned and took another deep breath to relax. Easy for Dad to say. But that made me wonder. *Take it easy.* What if he was telling me to ease up on my velocity? The last pitch was as hard as I could throw, and the behemoth with cat-like reflexes still drilled it. If he could hit that, he could hit anything.

I gestured to Scottie, asking him to go through our signs again. He put down his index finger for a fastball and I shook my head. He did it again and again, and I shook him off twice. He cocked his head, puzzled, and put down two fingers for a curve—the upside-down peace sign. I shook again, starting to feel like a wet dog with all my head shaking. He finally put down three fingers for a change-up and I nodded. He did it one more time to confirm and I nodded. For two guys who had hardly spoken since elementary school, it was incredible how the game of baseball allowed us to communicate without words.

As the chants reached a crescendo, I gripped the seams of the ball and focused again on the tab hanging from Scottie's mask like a silver goatee. I reared back but at the last second, took something off the pitch. Brutus was out ahead but he still managed to connect.

CRACK! The baseball caromed off the corner of the third base bag. And suddenly everything slowed down. The ball popped back towards the infield as the runner on third headed for home. I was closest and dove—

With my right hand, I grabbed it out of mid-air and tossed it off-balance to Scottie. He stretched toward me, keeping his foot on the plate for the force—the ball arriving in his glove a split-second *before* the Townsend runner's slide.

"OUT!" cried the home plate umpire, punching the air. "BALL GAME!"

The muscle-bound slugger looked on from first base in disbelief and slammed his helmet into the dirt as reality set in. There was an explosion of cheers from our side of the stands and before I knew it, I was mobbed by Paul, Sully, Rollie—and all the rest of my teammates.

I tried searching for Mom, Justine, and Andrea in the raucous crowd, but I was already engulfed in a mass of jubilant faces. Within seconds, I was hoisted and carried away on a mountain range of shoulders.

It's not often in life that your longest day is your best day. This one was and I didn't want it to end. The trophy presentation, hugs, speeches, and interviews felt surreal. I had been a part of a championship team before (who could forget '76?) but these moments had an impact that·was hard to explain. There were tears of joy followed by tears of sadness. Many of us had played our last game, and in just a few weeks we'd be saying goodbye to high school for the last time.

Late that night I sat on our screened porch alone, enjoying the quiet. Everyone had gone to bed, but I wasn't sleepy. Just then Dad came out of the house in pajama bottoms and a tee shirt.

"What do you say, 'Champ?'"

"Not much," I said. "What are you still doing up?"

"In all that excitement, I forgot to tell you more mail came today for you."

I nodded. There had been a stack of admission envelopes that I'd been setting aside. I hadn't bothered opening them because my mind had been on the big game.

"Thanks. I'll get to it," I said.

"Look, I also wanted to tell you I'm proud as hell of you."

"Thanks, Dad, but you don't have to—"

"Yeah, I do. I was pushing for the academy because I thought it would make you a man. The thing is you already had those qualities—discipline, courage, and commitment. You showed this at school and work. Whether you struck that guy out today or he hit a grand slam didn't matter. You already rose to the occasion, my boy."

Instead of trying to find fault with his words as I often did, I took them to heart. I waited for the lump in my throat to go down before responding. But it wasn't going to go away. Besides, who needed words? I looked my father in the eyes and hugged him tightly.

"Love you, son," he said.

"Love you, Dad," I said back.

The following Monday I showed up late to school because I had to get my glasses replaced. With classes in session during the first block, things seemed unnaturally quiet. I made my way down the empty corridor toward the library and felt a pang of nostalgia. On the wall to my right, someone had written graffiti over graffiti. The title of the Fleetwood Mac hit "You Make Loving Fun" had been changed to "You Make Loveing Funny."

If anyone thought there'd be a hero's welcome for me as I entered the library, they'd be mistaken. When I approached our regular table with the guys who had a free period, no one said a word. No one even looked up. All eyes were on Dave and Barry as they debated which Stephen King novel was better, *The Shining* or *The Stand*.

Barry finally acknowledged me.

"Where the hell were you on Friday? I tried calling you," he said.

"I was at my ballgame."

"Which ballgame?" Dave asked.

"The playoff game, You guys didn't—"

I cut short my reply when I noticed Henry, Goskey, and Ernie holding back laughter.

"You guys are bullshitting me," I said, finally catching on.

"We were there," Dave said. "Way back in the nickel seats."

"I didn't get what was happening," Barry admitted. "But I'm pretty sure the right team won."

At lunch Scottie Gartner found me exiting the line with my food tray. He shot a disapproving look at Dave and Barry and pulled me aside.

"Hey, no offense, buddy, but you're sitting with us today. Champions' table," he said.

"Seriously?" I asked.

"Hell yeah. I'm beyond serious," he replied, wrapping an arm around my shoulder.

Barry and Dave were perplexed as they watched the interaction play out.

"I'll catch up with you guys in a while," I said with a shrug.

"*Seriously?*" Barry asked, imitating my response from seconds earlier.

"Hell yeah," I replied with a shrug. I then nodded to Scottie. Ready.

Scottie cleared the way and even carried my tray as I followed him up the Ramp. I was at once greeted with pats on the back and high-fives by baseball teammates and other varsity athletes. The popular girls smiled. Justine gave me a thumbs-up from a corner table. I then noticed Paul descending the Ramp's rear exit. I gave him a nod and he nodded in return.

"Take a seat, Jay," he said, pulling out a chair like he was a maître de.

"Hold on," I said, pushing the chair aside. "I just wanna take a look."

I strolled around the Ramp and peered out at the students dining below—as if I was "King of the Hill." Some underclassmen glanced at me and then turned away as if they weren't worthy.

"So, this is what it's like," I said.

"Yeah," Scottie said, holding up my tray. "Come on, let's eat."

I held up a finger on my right hand and cast my eyes on Dave, Barry, Henry, and Goskey sitting about 15 feet away.

"Hey, guys!" I shouted with a wave. "Up here!"

Dave looked around, trying to place my voice. He finally spotted me and tapped the others. They looked up, puzzled.

"What are you doing, Jay?" Scottie asked.

I had recently seen the film *Animal House* so what I was about to do next was not original by any means. But it was going to be so rewarding. I picked up the container of applesauce from the tray Scottie was holding, leaned back, and let it fly at my friends' table. The apple sauce exploded on impact and splattered Barry's shirt.

"What the hell?!" he said. He stood up and threw a milk carton at me. I ducked and it hit Scottie.

In seconds, food and beverages were raining everywhere.

The battle was on.

The discipline was harsh. Aside from spending three hours cleaning the cafeteria that afternoon, I was assigned lunch detention for the final three days of school. The Ramp was officially closed—cordoned off with yellow police like a crime scene.

On the last day of school, Principal Weber summoned me into her office before I had finished my lunch.

"Leave the rest," Mrs. Weber said curtly. "Come with me, please."

I followed her into her office, pulled the door closed, and sat in the empty chair that faced her desk.

"So, Mr. Zimmerman, in addition to your present discipline, I've decided you will not be eligible to attend senior prom. I think that's prudent, given your role in starting the chaos," she said.

"I understand," I said. I had thought about the prom situation, and it wasn't any skin off my back. Even though Andrea's school didn't have a formal prom, they were holding a graduation party for seniors—and their dates.

"You do?" Mrs. Weber asked.

"Yes," I said. "Seems appropriate."

Mrs. Weber looked relieved. "Well, I'm glad we agree. You know, I've been in meetings with the district, parents, and board members the last few days. Ironically, you'll be the first student to know the Ramp closure will be permanent.

I couldn't help myself. I smiled.

"You don't appear disappointed," Mrs. Weber said.

"Let's just say I won't be shedding any tears."

Mrs. Weber adjusted her glasses and leaned forward in her chair.

"Are you hinting that your actions were premeditated?

"I'm not even hinting, ma'am," I said.

Our Class of '81 graduation ceremony was held on our high school's baseball diamond—what better place? I invited Paul to sit with Dave, Barry, and me, and he accepted without hesitation. Parents and guests watched from the bleachers, fanning themselves with programs, as we sat amid the masses on the infield dirt. Diamonds in the proverbial rough, I thought to myself.

The guys had spent time together at the prom so there was no need to break the ice. Paul ended up taking our former neighbor and bus mate, Maura, as his date. Dave and Barry, meanwhile, brought girls they'd met at their temple. What's more, they had even convinced their dates to attend one of their "mocks" concerts the night after.

"So, you've got girlfriends then?" I asked.

"I wouldn't call them girlfriends. More like groupies," Dave confided.

As Mrs. Weber assumed control of the microphone and delivered a rather stoic send-off, I let the guys in on a little secret: Paul had been a co-conspirator in Operation Food Fight. He'd also grown tired of the cliques at our school, and the Ramp as a status symbol.

"You're kidding. Well done, gentlemen," Dave said.

"Give the credit to this guy over here," Paul said. "It was all his idea."

"Damn, he is pretty good at keeping his cards close to the vest," Barry conceded.

"Thanks. And since we're being candid, you've got a pretty good arm, Barry," I said, recalling his milk toss at the food fight.

Everyone chuckled, and Mrs. Weber began reading the names of graduates, in alphabetical order.

"Leslie Aaronson…Joseph Abercrombie…"

I had a while to wait—a very long while—but that was okay. I leaned back in my seat, feeling at peace. At one point in my life, I had wondered if I needed better friends. Not anymore.

I'd finally found them.

Epilogue

After living in Massachusetts for over a half-dozen years, it was time to put down some "new roots" in the late summer of 1981. A new chapter awaited me as I set off for college. In the months that followed, there were some significant developments:

- ❖ The multi-acre plot of land which included our "field" was sold. Word has it the developer hopes to build a new housing tract. I'll miss our misshapen, lumpy diamond.

- ❖ Dave and Barry enrolled at the University of Pennsylvania where they continue debating important topics like who consumes more water in a day.

- ❖ Matt graduated from Summit Vocational School, Class of 1982. He plans to attend Fitchburg State University in the fall and loves being a big brother to little Michael.

- ❖ Paul accepted a baseball scholarship to Boston College and is majoring in Economics. He batted .389 in his freshman year. We talk and write often—and already have tickets for the opening day next year at Fenway.

- ❖ Justine broke up with Chase and says she's focused on her courses and field hockey now. She continues to give me a hard time because she had to find a new place to eat in the cafeteria.

- ❖ Mom continues to thrive in real estate, despite her occasionally achy joints. Justine and I still tease her about having the cleanest trash in town.

- ❖ Dad took on a new position at his company which allows him to work from home on occasion. He enjoys the extra time with Mom, Justine, and Daisy.

- ❖ Andrea attends Dartmouth University, not too far from where I am at the University of New Hampshire. We're both enrolled in creative writing programs. She told me that's all I'm allowed to say because I've shared far too much already.

Acknowledgments

I'd like to thank all my friends, near and far, who have provided me with support and a sense of belonging over the years. Aside from the bonds we forged, our shared experiences have created enduring memories. I'm grateful to my sister, Kristi, for being my first and best audience. Sincere thanks to my pal, Smitty, for helping motivate me when I needed to push this work across the finish line. Much gratitude to Jonathan at iFlow Creative for his editorial assistance. Also, a big thank you to Sophia and her team at Simple Site Launch for designing a website that goes way beyond my pay grade.

Above all, I'm indebted to my late parents, who helped me understand that while cleanliness is indeed next to Godliness, it's through laughter and love that we can overcome anything.

***

For more information and updates, please visit my website:

www.jcwesslenwriter.com

Made in the USA
Las Vegas, NV
15 March 2024

87271295R00116